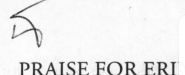

PRAISE FOR ERI

"Sexy and fun!"
—Susan Andersen, *New York Times* bestselling author of
Playing Dirty, on *Anything You Want*

"Erin Nicholas always delivers swoonworthy heroes, heroines that you
root for, laugh-out-loud moments, a colorful cast of family and friends,
and a heartwarming happily ever after."
—Melanie Shawn, *New York Times* bestselling author

"Erin Nicholas always delivers a good time guaranteed! I can't wait to
read more."
—Candis Terry, bestselling author of the Sweet, Texas series

"Heroines I love and heroes I still shamelessly want to steal from them.
Erin Nicholas romances are fantasy fodder."
—Violet Duke, *New York Times* bestselling author

"A brand-new Erin Nicholas book means I won't be sleeping until I'm
finished. Guaranteed."
—Cari Quinn, *USA Today* bestselling author

"Reading an Erin Nicholas book is the next best thing to falling in love."
—Jennifer Bernard, *USA Today* bestselling author

"Nicholas is adept at creating two enthralling characters hampered by
their pasts yet driven by passion, and she infuses her romance with
electrifying sex that will have readers who enjoy the sexually explicit
seeking out more from this author."
—*Library Journal*, starred review of *Hotblooded*

"They say all good things come in threes, so it's safe to say that this is Nicholas's best addition to the Billionaire Bargains series. She has her details of the Big Easy down to a tee, and her latest super-hot novel will have you craving some ice cream and alligator fritters. This is a romance that will be etched in your mind for quite some time. The cuisine and all-too-dirty scenes are enough to satisfy, but the author doesn't stop there. This novel may also give you the inkling to visit the local sex store—incognito of course. It's up to you."

—*Romantic Times Book Reviews* on *All That Matters*, TOP PICK, 4.5 stars

"This smashing debut to the new series dubbed Sapphire Falls is a cozy romance that will have readers believing that they'd stepped into the small Nebraska town and settled in for a while. This well thought out story contains likable characters who grow on you right away, and their tales will make you smile and want to devour the book in one sitting. Four stars."

—*Romantic Times Book Reviews* on *Getting Out of Hand*

"The follow-up to the debut of the hot new series Sapphire Falls will wow readers with its small-town charm and big romance. This story teaches us that everything does happen for a reason and true love can be found even where one least expects it. The characters are strong and animated. It's a complete joy and highly entertaining to watch the plot unfold. Paced perfectly, a few hidden surprises will keep bookworms up past their bedtime finishing this satisfying tale."

—*Romantic Times Book Reviews* on *Getting Worked Up*, 4 stars

"The Sapphire Falls series has quickly become a favorite amongst romance readers because of its small-town charm and big-time chemistry between the lovable characters This installment is extra steamy and the storyline captures the comedic yet sweet tale of country boy who meets city girl. Travis and Lauren's banter is adorable!"

—*Romantic Times Book Reviews* on *Getting Dirty*

"If you are a contemporary romance fan and haven't tried Erin Nicholas, you are really missing out."

—*Romantic Times Book Reviews* on *Getting It All*

"The fourth installment in the Counting on Love series will sweep readers off their feet. It's the perfect friends-to-lovers story with a little humor and a lot of steam. Cody and Olivia make a fantastic couple, and readers will adore their journey. Get your hands on this one ASAP!"

—*Romantic Times Book Reviews* on *Going for Four*, 4 stars

"Nicholas's tendency to give her fans a break from the hot-and-heavy stuff by making them laugh every now and then is genius!"

—*Romantic Times Book Reviews* on *Best of Three*, 4.5 stars

Twisted Up

ALSO BY ERIN NICHOLAS

Twisted Up

ERIN NICHOLAS

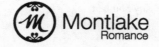

Montlake
Romance

Published by Montlake Romance, Seattle

www.apub.com

Amazon, the Amazon logo, and Montlake Romance are trademarks of Amazon.com, Inc., or its affiliates.

ISBN-13: 9781503936782
ISBN-10: 1503936783

Cover design by Shasti O'Leary Soudant

Printed in the United States of America

Writing dedications is like looking back through old photos. You remember all the people who have been there for the big, important, happy moments—and the ones who have been there for all the moments.

This book is dedicated to Nick, Nikoel, and Derek, who put up with lots of "Just let me get a few more words first," dusty shelves, and Crock-Pot meals, but who also totally get it. This is a team effort, and you guys are my team, always, through it all. I love you!

It's also for my mom and dad. I wouldn't be who or where I am without you, and I'm so happy that I get to share all of this with you. Thank you for . . . everything. I love you!

And for Kim, Lindsey, and Liz. You girls see the good and the bad sides of it all—and you're still here! That means everything.

CHAPTER ONE

Jake Mitchell is back in town.
Jake's back.

Avery felt her heart rate accelerate as the text messages rang in on her phone. That ticked her off. She didn't want her heart to speed up from a couple of text messages about that guy. She'd known the chances of him showing up today were good.

Exactly why she'd put her friends on the lookout.

She could handle seeing him if she knew she was going to see him. It was when he surprised her that she acted like an idiot.

Avery took a deep breath and reached for the mason jar in front of her. They needed to fill only three more for the centerpieces, and the decorating for the alumni dinner would be done. She wrapped the blue ribbon around the mouth of the jar, tied a bow, filled the jar with blue and white glass stones, and set a white votive candle on top. All the while attempting to ignore her phone and slow her heart rate.

He's here.

Now all her friends had checked in.

Her alert system had worked. Now she was ready.

Avery was proud of her steady hands as she lit the votive and placed it in the nest of silver and blue confetti on the center of the table. The metallic-blue streamers running from under the edge of the white tablecloth down to the floor were a bit much, in her opinion, but she was only one person on the decorating committee, and she'd been outvoted.

"Avery, sorry I'm late. We got hung up at the farm this afternoon."

Avery looked up to see Ben McDonald striding toward her. He was wearing ripped jeans and a T-shirt splattered with paint.

"Hey, Ben," Avery said, trying not to frown.

He wasn't just late. He was two hours late. But she knew that the whole town was stirred up with work out on Montgomery Farms, helping prepare for the visit from the family everyone hoped would buy the farm . . . and save the town.

"So you need some lights hung?" Ben asked.

She pointed to the rolls of twinkle lights. "Yes. But we also need the wooden structure put together to hang them from."

Ben looked from the lights to the two-by-fours propped against the wall. He sighed. "Let me get some guys over here."

Avery smiled and nodded. "Thanks."

She didn't feel bad. This was Ben's ten-year class reunion, too.

Besides, this was Chance. If someone called for help, people came to help.

"Avery!" Stacey, her reunion cochair, came rushing up. "I'm so sorry I'm late!"

Avery sighed and wondered how many times she was going to hear that sentence today.

"I was out at the farm."

That was the other sentence that had been uttered at some point by all her crew, reunion-committee members, and just about every other person who lived in Chance.

There were, of course, many other farms around Chance, but she knew Stacey meant Montgomery Farms. A massive 350 acres of the best apple and peach trees, pumpkins, strawberries, and watermelons in the state made Montgomery Farms the largest business and employer in Chance. It was, by all measures, *the* farm in town. Actually, calling the operation a farm was a gross understatement.

"I was helping with the welcome baskets for the Bronsons, and I lost all track of time," Stacey told her.

The Montgomery Farms sale was the biggest thing on anyone's mind. And rightly so. The town of Chance needed Montgomery Farms to be even more impressive than usual.

Gigi Montgomery, the CEO and lifelong Chance resident, was sick and needed to step down. There was no one in the family who would or could take on the position of CEO, so the Montgomery family had finally decided to look for a buyer. Two brothers from Kansas had come forward with interest and would be coming with their families to Chance in two weeks to take their first look at the farm in person. They had been involved in their own family farming operation, but they were fourth and fifth in a line of six siblings and wanted to go out and do something on their own.

It was a big deal. A bigger deal than a class reunion. If the sale didn't go through, Chance was in trouble.

They were really working on putting their best foot forward. That had meant a new coat of paint on buildings, general landscaping and cleanup, and a deep cleaning and refreshing of the farmhouse where the family would stay during their visit.

But it wasn't just the farm that needed to wow them. *Chance* needed to make a great first impression on the Bronsons. It was, after all, where their kids would go to school, where they would go to church, where they would shop and socialize. So the town had been busy with everything from installing new awnings on the businesses on Main, to putting together welcome baskets, to getting playdates arranged for the kids while their parents were in meetings.

"It's fine," Avery assured Stacey. "It will come together."

It always came together. That was one thing she really loved about Chance.

"Okay, I'll head into the kitchen and make sure things are on track."

Avery went back to the centerpieces and had just placed the last one in the middle of the last table and was straightening the streamers when Stacey again came rushing up.

"Avery!"

She looked up and frowned at Stacey's wide eyes and breathlessness. "Everything okay?"

Was there a shortage of salad dressing? Were the potatoes undercooked?

"Jake's here."

Jake.

She sighed.

God, for five minutes she'd forgotten about him.

Or had stopped wondering where he was and what he was doing, anyway. Now he was front and center in her consciousness again. Dammit. It was her fault this was big news. But she'd wanted to be *warned*, not reminded every ten seconds. "The girls told me."

"No. I mean, he's *here*."

Avery straightened quickly. "Here?"

"Here."

Avery felt her heart begin pounding, and she suddenly felt a little breathless herself. She pressed her hand to her chest. Oh, crap. She wasn't ready after all. "Like *here* at the school?"

She pivoted quickly to look around, but she forgot she was holding the streamer. It moved with her, sliding over the tablecloth . . . and tipping over the mason jar and candle in the process. Avery reached to right the jar, but not before the flame touched the tablecloth.

Suddenly the entire middle of the table was on fire.

"Avery!" Stacey exclaimed.

"Dammit!" Avery whipped the cloth to the floor and reached for the water bottle she'd set on the edge of the next table. It was empty. *"Dammit!"*

She was the fire chief. She could *not* be responsible for burning down the school. Avery pivoted to run for the kitchen and the fire extinguisher they kept inside the door.

But she ran right into a solid chest.

Even in that split second and before her mind really engaged, her body recognized it was pressed up against Jake Mitchell. Awareness flooded her system, and she felt like she'd just downed five cups of espresso—jumpy, with more energy than her body could contain.

He was *here*, all right.

She quickly stepped back and opened her mouth, with no idea what to say.

Jake said nothing, either. But he raised the extinguisher he'd been holding at his side.

She couldn't deal with two disasters at once, so she grabbed the extinguisher, pointed it at the tablecloth, and sprayed. A moment later, the fire was out.

She stood staring at the white cloth with the huge black hole in it, the confetti scattered everywhere, the white foam . . . and knew she'd still rather be looking at that, and worrying about clearing the smoke smell from the room before the party started, than turning around and looking at Jake.

But she was going to have to turn around. She knew that he'd stand there—likely smirking—until she did.

"It's not every day that you get to hand an extinguisher to the fire chief to put out a fire that she started."

Of course he'd bring that up. Jake Mitchell was good-looking, charming, sexy, funny, and certainly not a gentleman in any way.

She pasted on a smile and turned. "Hi, Jake."

God, he looked good. He'd dressed up for the reunion. He wore black pants and a deep-blue dress shirt, a few shades darker than the royal blue of their school colors. His tie was a mix of geometric shapes in black, gray, and blue. The blue brought out the deep-sapphire color of his eyes—it sounded cheesy even in her mind.

Avery struggled to maintain her composure. She hadn't seen him in two months. Two months and six days.

She was also ticked she knew that.

For nine years they'd had a no-contact-no-conversation rule. It had been a good rule. During those nine years, she hadn't run into doors because she'd been distracted by looking around for him, she hadn't dreamed about him at night, and she definitely hadn't lit anything on fire.

Nine good years.

Then a year ago—on June 14, to be exact—Chance, Nebraska, had been hit by an EF4-level tornado.

And Avery had been hit by the realization that for nine years, she'd been lying to herself about not caring about or being attracted to Jake . . .

They had both been up at city hall, but they hadn't even seen each other until the warning siren went off and everyone headed to the basement for shelter. It was close quarters, people tightly gathered in the middle hallway—the safest place in any structure, surrounded by load-bearing walls and devoid of windows—when she'd stepped on someone's foot. She'd turned to apologize and found herself face-to-face with Jake.

"Sorry about your foot," she'd said. She'd been breathless and hated that he could make her breathless even in the midst of a natural disaster.

"Definitely not thinking about my foot right now," he'd said.

Avery could distinctly remember the way her entire body seemed to melt at that. The heat she could feel standing so close, the intention in his flirtatious words, the gruffness in his voice, the sexy grin, all made her feel like he was stroking his hands over her body, preparing her for more. Much more.

Then, when the building began to tremble as the tornado roared by, Jake had wrapped his big, strong arms around her. And when the lights flickered and then went off, he'd kissed her.

He'd *kissed* her. She had, naturally, kissed him back. Why wouldn't she? They were trapped together in a scary, potentially life-threatening situation.

And he was a damned good kisser.

The best she'd ever had.

Of course, she'd known that even before his lips had touched hers. He'd been amazing even at age eighteen.

Damn him.

It was the way he took her face in his hands, and how there was just a breath of a moment where she could have said no, and then when he first captured her lips, it was only the lips. It was like he was savoring the moment. Then she'd slid her hands up his chest to his shoulders and sighed, and that was when he groaned the sexiest groan she'd ever heard, tipped her head to the side, and opened his mouth over hers. That, too, had lasted for a bit, building the anticipation, and then his tongue had stroked along hers, slow and sweet and deep.

Even remembering it now, Avery felt need clench hard and deep within her.

A loud clatter jerked her back to the present.

As she stared up at Jake, she was eternally grateful for whoever had dropped whatever they'd dropped.

She'd been staring at him this entire time, reliving that kiss, on the verge of sighing out loud.

"You don't seem surprised to see me." He grinned right on cue.

She pulled her shoulders back and narrowed her eyes. "Someone told me you were in town."

"Three someones, I'm guessing. I made sure to drive by Liza's hair studio, and I waved at Kit and Bree on my way past the square."

She took a deep breath and worked on not blushing. Or gritting her teeth. Jake had a special talent for making her do both. His cockiness knew no bounds. It was amazing how she could be attracted and irritated at the same time. "My friends might have a few other things to do than pay attention to you, you know."

He shrugged. "You'd think. It was weird how they all three reached for their phones and started typing as soon as they saw me."

Subtle, girls. Way to be subtle.

She opened her mouth, but then he held up her phone.

"I'm back."

He'd seen the texts. Of course he had.

"Thank goodness the emergency-management system in this town works better than my personal notification system."

They couldn't have texted her fifteen minutes ago? Had he driven straight over here? If he had, why? It was early for people to be arriving for the party.

"You needed warning I was on my way?" he asked, eyebrow up. He stepped back and looked her over from head to toe.

It took everything she had not to squirm.

At least she was confident she looked good.

Her dress was a pale green and fitted. It had straps that arched over her shoulders and crossed in an *X* in the back. With her deep-red hair, she had fewer color choices than most women, but green was a good one on her. Her hair was curled and pulled up into a twist. She was even wearing earrings. She was the fire chief, and her job didn't have her using a curling iron or putting on dresses and heels very often. As much as she'd hated it, she had known that Jake would be here tonight, and she'd wanted to look amazing. Tonight she felt feminine and beautiful.

But when Jake's eyes were on her, she felt a lot more than that. Like hot and tingly and squirmy. Just to name a few things.

She'd definitely needed warning he was coming. He knew it. And he knew why.

Ever since that tornado last summer, whenever Jake would blow into town, he'd somehow manage to immediately "run into her" and they'd end up making out.

It was appropriate to use storm terminology. Jake was the emergency-management specialist for the city of Kansas City, and when he came home, it was like a hurricane hit without warning. Sure, he always initiated the first kiss, but Avery hadn't once pushed him away. It seemed as soon as Jake put a hand on her, nothing existed except her senses of touch and taste—and nothing could override the urge to do a lot of both. Then he went back to Missouri, leaving a mess of emotions in his wake that it took days for her to sort through, and she'd swear, *again*, that she was done with him.

She'd sworn she was done with him four times now since last June.

"Well, I appreciate all the preparation you put into tonight for me," he said with a grin as his gaze ran over her again.

She felt her entire body flush. He was not talking about the confetti or the candles.

"The only prep I need when you show up is a warning so I can find a great place to hide until you blow over." She crossed her arms, trying to look unaffected.

She tried with everything she had to *not* respond to him, of course. She'd definitely gotten better at hiding her reactions to him. But even now her nerve endings were jumping up and down, like excited puppies that hadn't seen their favorite guy in too long.

Jake! Jake! Jake! Pet me, cuddle me, kiss me!

She was already anticipating the kiss that she was absolutely, positively *not* going to let happen.

Of course, she'd said that every time.

"So it's kind of an emergency when I get back into town?" Jake asked.

She lifted a shoulder. "Something like that."

He grinned. Which made her frown.

"That's the nicest thing you've said to me in a long time. Not *ever*, of course," he added. "There was that one night where you said *very* nice things to me—but it has been a long time."

Avery felt her face heat up. It had been ten years since she'd said *very* nice things to Jake. Those had been along the lines of "Oh, yes," "Oh, please," and "That feels so good."

The thing was, there were a lot of nice things she could say. Like, "Your blog on community action plans was great," or "The donation you made to the Boy Scouts was so generous," or "You looked really good in that photo in *Newsweek*."

So what if she followed his blog and read his articles on emergency management and had tuned in on two—okay, maybe four—of his online webinars? As the fire chief in Chance, it was her professional obligation to follow one of the nation's most respected emergency-management and disaster-relief specialists.

She'd learned a lot from him and admired him. Professionally. From afar.

She barely noticed that he was even better-looking now than he had been in high school.

He was a good guy.

But he was a good guy who believed his own hype. Avery liked to think she was helping keep his ego in check by not letting on that she believed it, too.

But all that did make it harder to resist him.

Still, she would for one very good reason—there was always something more important pulling him away. He'd left after graduation, after every trip home, after every kiss. And he'd leave again at the end of this weekend. She and Chance would never be enough to keep him here for any length of time.

Avery had a hard time forgiving him for that.

Yes, he was a big, important guy who did big, important things. Yes, those big, important things saved lives.

She simply couldn't help being irritated that these things were far away from Chance.

As if to prove her point, Jake's phone *dinged* in his pocket. He pulled it out and frowned at the incoming text. Avery watched as he typed in a response.

Jake had grown up as a part of the perfect family. The Mitchells had always been the core, the backbone, of Chance, and Jake was a fifth-generation Mitchell. But he'd left the family and their legacy for what he considered greener pastures.

Avery would have killed to have a family like his. She would have happily given a kidney or an arm for *his* family. She would have been more than satisfied with his mom's meat loaf on a weekly basis and the chance to take piano lessons on their baby grand—things Jake had *complained* about. Not to mention being a part of a family that belonged, who supported one another and made a lasting, positive impression on the people lucky enough to be around them.

Jake had had it all, and he'd still left for greener pastures.

He was always looking for more and, to a girl who would have given anything for even half of what he had, his attitude seemed ungrateful. She didn't have a lot of patience for ingrates. Even ingrates who had rock-hard abs and shoulders, light-brown sun-streaked hair, and blue eyes that always seemed full of mischief.

Jake turned his attention back on her. "Now, where were we?"

But before she could respond, his phone rang. With an exasperated sigh, he silenced it without looking at the screen.

"I was about to remind you that the night I said those nice things, I'd had a lot of peach schnapps," Avery told him. "If you need your ego stroked, you should go find your grandma. She always has wonderful things to say about you." Fern Mitchell went on and on about Jake every chance she got, in fact.

He grinned. "My grandma isn't going to say the kinds of things I want to hear from you, A."

She gritted her teeth again. He was the only person who called her "A," and he did it in spite of her asking him not to. Worse, she was afraid she'd miss it if he did ever stop. It was intimate. Too much so. It reminded her of the night they'd spent together when the nickname had started.

Thinking about that was not going to help her hide how he affected her.

"All you're going to hear from me is 'Get out of my way,'" Avery said, grabbing the end of the burned tablecloth and crumpling it into a ball.

"Now when you say things like that, I take it as a challenge." Jake took the cloth from her. "Wouldn't want you starting it on fire again," he said.

She frowned. "What?"

"You're looking so hot, you might—"

"Give me a break," she muttered.

Jake chuckled as she knelt and swept the glass stones back into the jar and then set it and the candle back on the table with a *thunk*.

"I'll take this out to the dumpster," Jake said, indicating the cloth he held. "Where are the extra tablecloths and stuff?"

"Tablecloths are in the storeroom, but the streamers and stuff are out in the shed," Avery said. "I'll go."

"I'll go with you."

"No." Okay, that had been firmer than it needed to be. She adjusted her tone. "Thanks anyway."

"You might have to reach for something high," he reasoned. "Can't have you climbing on things in those heels."

Yeah, yeah, he was six-foot-something and full of muscles, and she was five foot five. But she had muscles. She kept in great shape. Firefighting was no cushy job. "I've got it. No problem." She climbed ladders to the tops of buildings, carrying tools and hoses. She could retrieve a box of streamers and confetti.

"Still, I'd feel better going along."

She sighed and looked up at him. She wasn't going to win this battle. No matter how many warnings she put up to guard herself against Jake, he always took her by surprise, and it always resulted in her getting weak in the knees and warm all over—some places more than others—and kissing him back.

Well, if she was going down, at least she could try to hold on to what remained of her senses—and pride—instead of pressing up against him, sinking her fingers into his hair, opening her mouth, and moaning like she usually did.

"Fine. You can come help me," she agreed and started for the door.

Jake was clearly taken aback by her concession, because it took him about five steps to catch up with her. "I'm glad to see you're being reasonable about this."

"Yep, reasonable. That's me."

He snorted.

The butterflies that were rocking out in her gut at the idea of Jake kissing her in the shed were incredibly annoying.

Ignoring the way he made her feel shouldn't be this hard. It wasn't like he was a part of her daily life or regular routine. She didn't daydream about him *every* day.

Besides, in her daydreams he wasn't just charming and hard in all the right places. He was also the guy who had worked next to her when the tornado had hit their hometown. The man who thrilled her with the way he took charge and made everyone feel in control and secure in the aftermath of the destruction . . . and then *stayed*.

Since it was her daydream, she also chose to make him an average guy who lived and worked in Chance and had no frequent-flier miles and no governors, CEOs, or presidents in his phone's address book.

In real life, though, Jake was the guy who had kissed her and then left the next morning without a good-bye. Six times.

It was the constant leaving and the constant Chance-as-an-afterthought thing that had very effectively convinced her that real-life Jake Mitchell was *not* the guy for her.

Avery's job was to prevent fires and disasters in Chance or, when they happened, deal with them quickly and with the least amount of excitement and disruption. Smaller fires, smaller crises, smaller problems—that's what she was all about. Jake, on the other hand, headed straight into the big disasters, the huge problems. He was most alive when he was in the midst of a major catastrophe, and without massive storms and large earthquakes and vast flooding, he would be out of a job.

She'd found out that when Jake had bolted three days after the last tornado, he'd been due in Washington, DC, to meet with Homeland Security officials. She also learned that he'd been behind the immediate response from the state and the National Guard support they'd gotten.

But it remained that *he* had not been there. Chance was too small, too insignificant, for him to get too involved with.

If she thought that was a perfect metaphor for their relationship as well, she would never admit it.

"Hey, Jake!" someone called from behind them just as they reached the outside door.

They both turned. "Hey, Steve." Jake greeted a classmate of theirs who'd shown up to help Ben with the twinkle lights.

"You going out?" Steve asked.

"Just to the shed. For streamers," Jake said.

"Well, grab the storm box, too," Steve said. "We've got a bunch of stuff in here, too, but if you're going out there anyway, we can always use more flashlights."

Avery frowned. "You think we need the boxes?" The weather service had predicted some possible thunderstorms later on, but a thunderstorm hardly called for one—or more—of the emergency-supply boxes. They'd probably drink and dance through the whole thing. If the DJ turned things up loud enough, they might not even know anything happened until they were splashing through puddles on their way home.

"Some stuff's moving in," Steve confirmed with a nod.

"Some stuff." Not a thunderstorm, then. No one in Chance really sweated thunderstorms. It took more than lightning, thunder, and pounding rain to get them worried.

Avery looked around the gymnasium. The reunion committee was busy all over the huge space as well as other areas of the school, like the kitchen and the media room where they were putting the final touches on the video presentation for the night. "Be sure everyone's aware," she told Steve.

He was probably overreacting, but better safe than sorry. All he'd have to say was "Possible storms tonight," and everyone who'd lived in Chance for any period of time would know what to do.

"You got it," Steve agreed.

Avery pushed open the side door to the school's gymnasium. The wind caught the heavy door, slamming it against the side of the brick building.

"Damn."

The wind was whipping around the cars parked on this side of the building, leaves and debris swirling between and over the vehicles.

"Damn," Jake agreed.

Avery didn't like the look of the roiling gunmetal-gray clouds overhead. "Those don't look good."

"You under a watch?" he asked.

Avery knew he was asking about a tornado watch. It was a public-alert term that meant conditions were right for a tornado to develop.

"It's June in Chance, Nebraska," she said. "We're kind of constantly under a watch."

Chance was a lot of things—quirky, quaint, friendly, clean, welcoming, progressive . . . and unlucky.

Chance sat right in Tornado Alley, the section of the country most at risk and most hit by twisters. In fact, her town held the dubious honor of being the hardest-hit town in Nebraska, and one of the most targeted in the whole Alley. They had been hit by numerous storms and tornadoes over the years, but they had specifically been hardest hit by EF4s, one of the strongest and most damaging categories of tornadoes. A town hit by an EF4 got local attention. Being hit two years in a row by an EF4 got statewide media coverage and a couple days of mentions on The Weather Channel and CNN. But when the media found out that last year's twister was the ninth EF4 to hit in one county and the fifth to hit one small town in the course of sixty-one years, Chance had become infamous. That many EF4s in one place was . . . unbelievable. They were a statistical anomaly. The tornadoes and the town they seemed to hate had generated interest from weather authorities, historians, and even supernatural experts from all over the country. Some of the spiritual types had gone so far as to question if Chance were cursed or built on an ancient burial ground or if someone had angered the gods.

Avery knew everyone in town was holding their breaths and watching the sky this year whenever the wind kicked up or a weather front moved in. They knew the warning signs.

Like roiling gunmetal-gray skies.

"Good point. Maybe we should grab more than streamers, after all," Jake said.

"You mean like boxes of flashlights, blankets, battery-powered weather radios, and first-aid supplies?" Avery asked drily.

Jake grinned. "For instance."

There was plenty of all that inside the school, in the shed, and in various locations all over town. It was one of their strategies to be sure that supplies and tools were readily available no matter where you were when the storm hit. If nothing else, Chance, Nebraska, had lots of practice on how to prepare and recover from a tornado. But, as Steve had said, you could never have too many flashlights if the power went out.

"Come on." She put a hand flat on top of her head where the pins were holding her style together and stepped out into the wind, heading for the shed.

Fat raindrops began falling the minute her heels hit the blacktop between the school and the shed.

Great. So much for her hair. Or her dress, for that matter.

At least Jake had seen her before she was a wet mess.

She frowned at that. She *didn't care* what Jake thought.

She inserted the key in the lock on the shed and started to turn it when a huge gust of wind looped around the building, rocking her on the three-inch heels that she was not used to wearing, let alone balancing on.

She felt Jake's hands on her hips, steadying her.

Uh-huh. He was *so* helpful.

She got the key turned, and the door swung inward. They both lunged inside.

The building was huge. Half of it was used for general storage of everything from candy bars for the concession stands to gym mats and an old copy machine. The other half was used as a maintenance shed where Mr. Victor, the school's maintenance man, kept his tools and workbench, even the lawn mower.

The place was secure, and inside they could barely hear the wind howling. Avery took a deep breath and squelched the feeling of déjà vu. They were not going to get stuck out here together in a tornado. They were going to get the supplies and get back inside. And if everyone ended up in the basement, she was staying far away from Jake.

Avery headed for the shelving unit where the storm supplies were kept—across the room from where Jake stood.

She was reaching for the huge plastic tote, grateful now for the extra height from the heels, when the heavy metal door they'd come through slammed shut, throwing the room into complete darkness.

Perfect.

Déjà vu, indeed.

She heard Jake moving in the dark and the sound of a doorknob turning.

A locked doorknob not *quite* turning, actually.

And then the click of the light switch by the door. But nothing happened.

"Light's out," Jake said unnecessarily. "And the door's locked."

No, *now* things were perfect.

"Dammit," she muttered.

"And," he added, not sounding a bit concerned by it all, "my phone's not getting any reception in here."

Of course it wasn't.

"There's a big garage door on the other side of the building where they drive the tractor and Bobcat in and out," she said.

"Without power, that door is probably not going up." Yeah, he didn't sound concerned at all.

"You can't get it up anyway?" she asked.

He chuckled, but to his credit did not make the juvenile comment about getting things up that she'd been expecting. "Unlikely. But I'd check, if I had some light."

Right. First things first. They needed light.

She grabbed for the tote in the general area she'd been reaching. "There have to be flashlights around here somewhere," she muttered. She just needed to hold it together until she found them. As she pulled it from the shelf, it occurred to her, briefly, that it was nowhere near heavy enough to be full of flashlights and radios, but she dropped it to the floor and knelt to open it anyway.

"You okay?" Jake's voice came to her in the dark.

"Of course I'm okay."

But she wasn't okay. The room seemed smaller with the lights out, and she was aware that he was only a few feet away. She heard his shoes scuffing on the cement floor and knew he was coming closer. Her heart rate sped up, and she had to concentrate on her breathing.

Breathing. One of the most automatic functions in the human body. Stupid.

"Well, I hate the dark. You have those flashlights close by?" he asked.

His voice seemed to have gotten deeper in the dark, and a shiver went through her in response.

"Working on it," she muttered, pulling the lid off the plastic bin and praying there was at least one flashlight in there. They needed some light. Light would make her stop thinking that in the dark she might "accidentally" touch something she shouldn't. Of course, she'd have a good excuse then . . .

She rummaged farther in the bin with no luck. She was now elbow deep in a container full of what felt like socks.

Socks. An entire bin of them.

A bluish light came on.

"Here you go."

She looked over her shoulder. Jake had his phone on.

"Flashlight app. Sorry I didn't think of it sooner."

She could see his grin above the glow.

"Thanks." She glanced up. "Why's the electricity not on out here?"

He tipped the phone so the light shone on the empty socket overhead. "No bulb."

"Ah."

They continued looking at each other in the dim light. It felt almost cozy.

Stupid.

After several seconds, Jack shone the light on the bin at her feet. "Socks?"

"Apparently."

Grateful for something to concentrate on besides Jake and how good he smelled, she lifted a sock out. It was white with bright blue letters that spelled WILDCATS down the side.

"I'm guessing we'll find these in the apparel booth at the next football game," she said, tossing the sock back in with its mate. She snapped the lid back on the box. "Until then, these won't do us a lot of good." She grabbed the handles and started to stand, intending to return the box to its spot on the shelf. But as she lifted it, Jake stepped close.

"Let me help." He reached out.

"I've got it." She turned toward the shelves and stepped on his foot. "Ow."

God, this was so much—too much—like last time.

Except this time they were completely alone.

"Well, get out of the way!" She shoved the box onto the shelf, her elbow hitting his arm. "This shed is huge. There are a hundred other places you could stand."

"I'm trying to help."

She gave a short laugh. "You're trying to drive me crazy."

"By supplying a source of light and offering to lift a box for you?"

"By standing so *close*." She put her elbow into his side and pushed at the same time.

Of course, he barely moved.

"I'm being a gentleman." But he sounded like he was smiling.

She didn't dare risk looking at him to confirm it. Because he was still so *close*.

"You haven't been a gentleman toward me a day in your life."

She was still facing the shelves, but she felt him move closer yet.

"I protest that statement," he told her.

He was directing the light at the shelves in front of them. She was grateful that he wasn't trying to see her expression. With the light trained on the shelves, she could see that the bin directly in front of him on the second shelf was labeled STORM SUPPLIES.

But suddenly, getting into those supplies was far less important than the conversation with Jake.

"You protest based on what?" she asked.

"On the fact that I took you to your first and only prom and made sure you had an amazing night."

He had done that. She could still remember everything about that night—her dress, his tux, the way he'd been so attentive and had made her laugh, the way he'd danced with her, holding her close and making her feel safe, the sweet kiss on the lips he'd given her when he'd taken her home. Ten years later and she could conjure up every detail of that fairy-tale night. The night she'd started falling in love with him.

"And on the fact that on the night of our graduation, I was very sweet and made sure you came first," he said.

Avery actually gasped at that. And she wasn't a gasper. But that was so . . . in your face. Even for Jake. Jake teased and flirted and insinuated, but he'd never come right out and talked about them having sex that night.

And at that simple mention, her entire body heated up and seemed to strain toward him, ready to do it all again, just like that.

Damn him.

"Getting me drunk on peach schnapps and out of my panties makes you a gentleman?" She tried to focus on the sarcasm rather than the memory of his hands slipping under her sundress, his big palms sliding over her thighs and up to her panties before tugging them back down her legs and tossing them over his shoulder with a glint of mischief and affection in his eyes.

She had to clear her throat after *that* particular memory reel played through her mind. "I don't think that's the typical definition," she said when she was sure her voice would sound calm. "It's sad that you're still so hung up on that night."

He chuckled, and the sound tickled over her like he was running his fingertips up her arm and down her back.

And she knew that he knew she was full of crap.

He wasn't the one hung up on that night. That was her. That was all her.

But no one had ever affected her like Jake did. And she didn't even *like* him.

Avery immediately took that back. She did like him. She just didn't *want* to like him.

She wanted to be upset and angry at him for leaving. For not even telling her he was leaving. And she was. That had hurt. But she was most angry with herself. She'd looked up into his eyes when he'd asked her to prom and had immediately started thinking that it was the start to the future of her dreams. After prom they'd spent time together after school and on the weekends. He'd never called her his girlfriend or said they were dating, but it felt like dating to her. And she'd been giddy. Jake was an amazing guy—every girl wanted him—and he'd chosen *her*. But more than getting a great guy who treated her like a princess, being with Jake also meant that she would be a part of her dream family. Jake's mom and dad were like second parents to her. She loved Jake's mom with her whole heart. If she and Jake were together forever, she and Heidi and Wes would be together forever, too.

It had seemed so perfect. So right. Like destiny.

And after he left, clearly not head over heels and ready to walk down the aisle with her, she'd been humiliated and hurt. She'd finally confessed all of her mixed-up emotions in a letter. She'd apologized to him for getting wrapped up in the imaginary happily ever after and for assuming things she shouldn't have.

She'd hoped that he would believe that her feelings had been all about his family. She hoped he'd believe that she wasn't in love with him and she was moving on.

She'd hoped that *she* would believe those things, too.

But now, ten years later, she was still definitely hung up on that night.

"Don't feel bad for me, Avery Jane," Jake said. "The memories of that night kept me company for a good long time in basic training." He leaned in closer and dropped his voice. "And because I know you're clinging to that excuse for how *you* acted, I won't point out that you weren't all that drunk."

She worked on breathing. It was so crazy, but even now, the idea that he'd been off with the Army National Guard, alone and homesick and thinking of her, was romantic and got to her.

For the five seconds it took her to remember that he'd left for the Guard mere hours after making love to her without a good-bye or an explanation and that once he was gone, he was really gone.

She turned suddenly, again catching him in the ribs with her elbow, hoping he'd step back and give her some space. "Taking me to prom and buying me a souvenir shot glass does not make up for the fact that a true gentleman would have told me he was leaving the next morning *before* my bra came off. And a true gentleman would refrain from bringing it up and kissing me every time he visits."

Elbow in his ribs or not, Jake was right there, nearly on top of her, when he said gruffly, "Not even the pope could have looked into those big green eyes that night by the river when you told me you'd never been really kissed and not wanted to be the first."

Instantly she was back at that river, the area lit by the moonlight and the glow from the bonfire, the air heavy with humidity and anticipation. They'd camped at the river with most of the senior class. There were sleeping bags and blankets all over the riverbank that night, and very few of them had held only one person.

Jake had been cocky, but funny and sweet. He was full of himself and yet, somehow charming and thoughtful at the same time. There hadn't been even a hint of nerves on his part, but she'd known she could say no at any point. She'd known exactly how much he wanted her, yet she'd felt safe and protected the whole time. The entire night had been better than she could have imagined, and it was all because of Jake. He'd made it amazing, even as a teenage boy with a virgin who was naive enough to not know *exactly* what to do. But she'd been smart enough to know she wanted to do it with him, and she'd figured things out pretty quickly. She'd been willing and eager. He'd done what any guy in his place would have done—he went for it. All the way.

When she'd found herself making out with Jake at the river and he'd asked her to stay all night, she hadn't been worried about a curfew. Her grandmother had always complained that Avery wasn't a typical teenager who went out on the weekends and stayed out past midnight. It hadn't kept Ruth from having male friends over, but it had, apparently, cramped her style a bit.

So that one night she'd been a very typical teenager. She'd gotten drunk, tried smoking, and gotten laid.

The memories were still enough to get her hot and bothered.

Another good reason to stay away from him. He'd only kissed her over the past eleven months, but that was only because she'd been careful not to let him get her somewhere completely private. He'd pulled her behind the cotton-candy booth at the fair, kissed her behind the Christmas tree in the town square, and behind the bleachers at a football game.

Not that she was keeping track or anything.

Had they been somewhere more private, perhaps with a door and not much light . . .

"I know you want to kiss me now," she said.

"Of course I do. Kissing you is one of my favorite things about visiting Chance."

That should have stopped her. That reminder that he was only visiting, that this wouldn't be enough to get him to stay.

But it didn't.

"Then get it over with." She grabbed the front of his shirt and pulled him in, putting her lips to his.

Every time. Every damned time.

Jake couldn't believe it.

Every time he kissed this woman, his world went up in flames. Ironic.

He knew he shouldn't keep doing it, but he couldn't help it. And now *she'd* kissed *him*.

Holy hell.

Kissing Avery Sparks was the best kissing in the world. Being kissed *by* Avery Sparks was the best *thing* in the world.

At least until she let him get her naked.

She was still holding him close with her hand gripping the front of his shirt. But he wasn't going anywhere.

He ran one hand up her back, cupping her head, while bringing her hips closer with the other. She moaned and wrapped both arms around his neck.

He stroked his tongue along her lower lip, and she gave a soft whimper as she opened for him. Lust exploded in his gut, and the hand on her hip flexed, bunching the material of her dress.

With her heels, she was five eight to his six three. Still not quite tall enough to line her parts up just right with his parts.

But there was a workbench about ten steps to his left.

Kissing her deeply, he began walking them toward the bench. Avery was either too caught up or had the same idea, because she went along easily.

When they bumped into the worktop, their mouths disconnected long enough to suck in some air. They stared at each other in the dim light for a moment, breathing hard.

"A." That was all he could manage.

She paused for a heartbeat. Then she whispered, "Yes."

He knew somehow that it wasn't an acknowledgment of the nickname. It was an agreement to do exactly what he wanted to do.

He set his phone to the side, the soft light giving them at least a little illumination for what was about to happen, and put both hands on her waist and lifted her up onto the table. He was impressed. The thing didn't even wobble. It was nice and solid. Perfect.

Stepping between her knees, he ran his hand up her back again and urged her forward into another kiss.

"Damn you, Jake," she muttered against his lips, her hand sliding over his chest and her knees tightening around his waist.

He chuckled. She didn't like reacting to him, but she couldn't help it. He loved that. More than he should.

He never should have kissed her in the basement at city hall. Up until then, he'd been fine. He hadn't thought of her more than every single time he came home to Chance before that kiss. But since then . . . well, it wasn't quite *every* day. More like 362 days a year.

But it wasn't like he sat around Kansas City pining for her. He wasn't pathetic. He dated, he had sex—he had *lots* of sex—with other women. He didn't have a picture of Avery, he didn't know if she had any allergies, and he didn't know what kind of pizza she preferred. He wasn't *stalking* her.

He did know that she wore vanilla-flavored lip gloss, that her skin was the softest he'd ever felt, and that one deep sigh from her could make him harder than the best dirty talk from any other woman. But he wasn't obsessed or anything.

He did, however, like the idea that whenever she walked through the town square—which was every day—she'd think of him and the time he'd kissed her there. Or that every time she went by the high school football field—again, every day—she'd think of him and the time he'd kissed her there.

Yes, it was all about his damned ego. The thing had a way of getting him into trouble. But it absolutely would not let him continue to ignore the one and only woman to ever dump him.

Jake felt his tie loosen, then slide free from his collar. He grinned. He knew what she was going to think about when she walked by this storage shed from now on.

He ran his hand up and down her back, kissing her softly as she undid the buttons of his shirt. He hadn't kissed her sweetly like that since their first kiss all those years ago. Now when he surprised her in Chance, it was always a nice, hot, deep, wet one to keep her nerves humming for a while after he was gone.

The sweet kissing was nice.

She pushed his shirt off his shoulders, and he had to move his hands to let it fall to the floor. It occurred to him briefly to worry about it getting dirty on the shed's floor, but Avery's hands went to his fly, and he suddenly didn't give a damn about anything but getting her hands on more of him. And getting his hands on more of her.

As the zipper of his pants went down, so did the zipper on the side of her dress.

The silky green material parted, and he had to pause to stroke his hand over the smooth skin of her back.

He immediately noticed the lack of a bra in his way. And was very thankful for that unencumbered path.

"God, A. You feel so damned good."

Her hand slid into the front of his pants, along the length of his erection. "Ditto," she muttered. She increased her pressure. "Dammit."

She didn't want to want him. That was no surprise. That she couldn't fight her desire was . . . awesome.

He slid the straps of her dress off her shoulders and down her arms. She pulled her arms free to let the straps fall. Whether she liked it or not, she was all in.

Without a bra in the way, she was naked from the waist up in only a few seconds. He cussed the lack of full lighting. But he had plenty of other senses left.

His hand explored every detail of one bare breast as he leaned in, kissing her again, much less sweetly this time.

Her fingers sunk into his hair as she kissed him back, arching into his hand. He dragged his thumb over her stiff nipple, and she made a delicious sound in the back of her throat.

Her hands dropped between them, cupping his erection with both hands this time, stroking firmly up and down, the friction of his underwear heightening the sensations zipping along his nerve endings. He pressed into her touch, making some noise of his own.

Then she went skin to skin, and Jake forgot how to breathe for a moment.

She pulled her mouth from his but kept her hands against his steel-hard length. "I can't believe I'm doing this with you."

He held her head with one hand, looking into her eyes. Even in the barely-there light from his phone, he could see they were wide. "But you are. You're here with me. You want me."

She didn't say anything.

He leaned in and kissed her, stroking deep, tongue to tongue, rolling her nipple between his thumb and finger and pressing the proof of his own desire firmly against her hands.

He leaned back, both of them breathing heavily. "You want me," he repeated. "Don't you, Avery? You want *me*."

She pulled her bottom lip between her teeth and closed her eyes.

"Oh, no, you don't." He let go of her delectable breast to take her face in both his hands. "Open your eyes. Look at me."

She did, clearly reluctant.

"You know who you're with," he said. "You know who's kissing you, who's touching you, who's about to make you beg."

Her eyes widened again at that, and she opened her mouth to reply. No doubt with an argument.

"There will be no pretending this didn't happen or that you were caught up in the moment or that I took advantage of you. You and I are both here, and we both want this, and we're both doing this."

She didn't move. She didn't speak. He didn't think she even blinked. Seconds ticked by.

He didn't care. He'd stand there all night to hear her admission that she wanted him. She was half-naked in his arms, her lips swollen from his kisses, and he'd bet very good money that she was hot and wet for him. But he wasn't going to do one damned thing until he heard her admit that she wanted this—*him*—as much as he wanted her.

"You'd better enjoy this," she finally said. "It's a once-in-a-decade thing."

The huskiness in her voice belied the flippant words, and Jake felt his grin all the way to his toes.

"Oh, Avery Jane, there's no way in hell I'm not going to enjoy this."

"Then let's get on with it."

"You've been waiting for this for a long time." Ten years, if she was anything like him. God, he hoped she was.

Had he known how far under his skin this little redhead would get, he would have said "Hell, no" to his mother's suggestion he take Avery to their senior prom. He'd been avoiding any romantic entanglements with girls since the summer before, knowing he was leaving the morning after they got their diplomas. And then, the one girl he thought he'd be safe with, whom he could in no way fall for, had been the one to steal his heart in one night.

And he *definitely* would have left her at his mom's house on graduation night and gone to the river party all alone. Putting Avery in his pickup that night had been the start of . . . something. Something he couldn't believe was still making him itch.

"What do you need here to get moving?" she asked. "A little 'Oh, God, Jake, I've never gotten over you'? Or how about 'Oh, Jake, I've been dreaming about this moment for ten years'?"

Something like that would be great, actually. He frowned. "My favorite of your lines—and there were many—was 'That was amazing.'"

She snorted. "I was a virgin. What did I know?"

A virgin. Right. That had been a big deal to him. It still was. Avery had been an eighteen-year-old virgin. She'd been beautiful, though in a quiet, almost accidental way. Still, he was sure there had been guys willing to help her with that whole virginity thing long before he looked down into those green eyes and thought, *How did I miss her?* But she was smart. Very smart. There was a reason she'd held off on having sex in high school and then suddenly given it all to him.

The whole thing had still made him feel stupidly special at the time. Actually, it still did.

"Put a condom on already."

He was jerked out of the past by the bossy, restless, bare-breasted woman in front of him.

Jesus. She was here. Right *here*. Ready and willing. What the hell was he doing reminiscing about the last time he'd gotten her bra off? She wasn't even wearing one tonight.

He was an idiot.

"You don't have one?" he asked, running a hand up the outside of her thigh.

She tensed. Then groaned. "Are you flipping kidding me? Jake 'the Wonder Stud' Mitchell doesn't have a *condom*?"

He felt his eyebrows rise. "Wonder Stud?"

"Sounds better than *manwhore*, doesn't it?"

"What makes you think I'm a manwhore?"

"Oh, for God's sake." She pushed him back and slid from the workbench to the floor. "I have condoms in my purse. In the *school*. But you should know, the chances of my coming back out here are about fifty-fifty."

He caught her arm before she could take a step. "We're locked in."

She blew out a frustrated breath, as if she'd forgotten. He liked that he could make her forget everything going on around her. "Well, I guess there's always the next time we're both in Chance and there's a sudden need for streamers," she said flippantly.

"Avery."

She sighed. "This is probably a sign that we shouldn't be—"

"Take off your panties."

She froze. The sound of the condom wrapper ripping open, however, seemed to catch her attention, and she turned.

"You're such an ass sometimes."

He nodded and took her hand, pulling her back to him. "I know."

He could only hope that was enough to hide how much he wanted this woman, and how much he wanted to matter to her.

Jake couldn't believe how hot it was pushing his pants to the floor and sliding on the condom as Avery watched. It was still damned dark, but he knew she saw enough.

She kicked off her shoes and reached under her skirt. After a little wiggling, she tossed a tiny thong onto the floor on top of her heels.

She took the one step that separated them without a word. He cupped her head first, kissing her fully. But her hands wrapped around his cock, stroking him firmly, and he lost every intention of doing anything but thrusting deep.

With a growl, he grabbed her ass, lifted her, and deposited her back on the workbench. He stepped between her knees, and she had to pull up her skirt, bunching it at her waist, so she could spread her legs.

Perfect.

He kissed her, palming one breast, while his other hand cupped her wet heat.

She moaned, and he slid his middle finger into the slick sheath. Her legs parted farther, and he felt her fingernails digging into his shoulders.

With her tight around his finger, he so wanted to taste her, to feel her grip his hair as he licked and sucked her to orgasm. There were a lot of things he'd learned since they'd last been together. If he hadn't rocked her world before, he sure as hell would now.

But there was an overriding need to get inside her, to drive deep and hard until all she could do was hold on and scream his name.

Yeah, that sounded pretty damned good.

He dipped his head, licking, then sucking her pebbled nipple, content with only that taste for now. He did, however, lift his hand from between her legs and take a long lick of the sweetness coating his finger.

"God, Jake. Please."

And there was the begging. "All you needed to say."

He pulled her to the edge of the table and positioned himself, then thrust.

They gasped together. Sensations raced through him, and he paused, fully embedded, his body throbbing yet relieved at the same time.

After a moment, he slowly pulled out, then thrust forward again.

Avery dug her heels into his butt, her fingers gripping his shoulder, and let her head fall back.

It seemed that she was at his mercy, and a surge of hunger hit him so hard that his rhythm picked up without conscious thought. He went with it. No question. Especially when she was gasping and moaning and saying things like, "Yes, Jake, yes."

All too soon, he felt her body tightening, and he had no ability to slow down and pull back at that point. His hands grasping her ass hard, he thrust deep and fast, spiraling them both toward their climaxes. The sound of Avery calling his name as she came was the hottest thing he'd heard—in about ten years.

CHAPTER TWO

Ten years had done nothing but good for Jake in the sex-'em-up department.

Avery's entire body felt like Jell-O, and though she knew getting as far from him as she could was the right idea, she couldn't seem to move.

Her ass was permanently a part of Mr. Victor's workbench.

That was going to be hard to explain Monday morning.

Jake was leaning into her, his hands braced on the table on either side of her, still breathing hard. "Holy crap," he said gruffly.

She liked that.

God knew she was going to have to think back on the fact that he'd been as wild as she had been when she was feeling horrified later that she'd let it go this far with him.

She shifted. That caused much of her body to rub against much of Jake's—again. She sucked in a quick breath and pushed him back.

"Maybe for our twenty-year reunion we could find a bed. That might be a nice change."

He leaned back and grinned. "Anywhere, anytime."

Avery pushed her hair back from her face and closed her legs.

Knees together. That would be a good rule to put in place when Jake was around.

She slid to the floor and straightened her skirt, searching the area in the dim light for her shoes and panties.

Shoes in particular, she supposed. Missing those would be most noticeable, but she'd really like her panties back. If she walked around without them all night, she'd be thinking about Jake constantly.

She laughed to herself. As if she wasn't going to be thinking about him anyway.

Locating both shoes, she bent to put them on. When she straightened, she saw her thong dangling from Jake's finger. She grabbed it without a word—because what was she going to say—and started to put it on.

However, she discovered quickly that thong before heels was another good rule to put in place.

He moved in behind her and steadied her with his big hands on her hips.

Again.

She was throwing all her heels away as soon as she got home.

Because it would have been ridiculous to take off her shoes again, she let him hold her up as she lifted first one foot, then the other, before shimmying the thong into place.

Her cheeks were burning when she turned to face him again. The lighting was dim, and she hoped he couldn't see the flush on her skin. When she'd first stripped off his shirt and run her fingers over the muscles of his chest, shoulders, and abs, she'd been cursing the lack of light. Now it seemed a blessing.

"Okay, so . . ."

That seemed an appropriate thing to say at the moment. With that she grabbed his phone and headed for the shelving units, determined this time to find the right box and then either pound on the door until someone heard them or knock the damned thing down before she lost any articles of clothing.

How had no one come to find them already?

"A, wait."

She grabbed the tote with the supplies and started for the door. "Come on, tough guy. Knock the door down. Or take it off its hinges or something. I know you can get us out of here."

"Avery. Stop. Wait." Jake's hand grasped her upper arm.

She started to pull free when he said, "Listen."

"To what?"

"Outside."

She paused and focused on the fact that there was a world outside the shed for the first time in a good half hour.

She heard what he heard immediately.

There was a low rumbling outside. The heavy steel of the building muted it, but it was there. A growling, a groaning—however it was described, it meant the same thing.

Tornado.

Her chest got tight and cold, like a fist of ice was squeezing her heart. She couldn't move. She felt tears well up.

This couldn't be happening. Not again. Not now. It had only been a year. They'd *just* come through this. The town was getting ready to show off for the family from Kansas. They'd worked so hard. They were so proud of everything they had to offer.

And now this. Another twisting, swirling monster was coming after them.

Avery turned to face Jake. "No," she whispered.

He didn't answer. He didn't need to. His face said it all—worry, combined with grimness and a bit of resignation.

Now that she was listening, she could hear the sirens. The sirens were all too common a sound in Chance. They were the signal that a tornado had been sighted and everyone in hearing distance needed to take cover. Right now.

Jake took the box from her hands, dropped it to the floor, and tore off the lid. He handed her two flashlights while he grabbed two more. Shining the bright light into the box, he found a radio and turned it on.

"The counties of Hall, Hamilton, Adams, and Clay, you are under a tornado watch until ten p.m.," the broadcaster said.

"No mention of a touchdown?" Avery frowned and knelt next to Jake, reaching for another radio.

"That doesn't mean there isn't one." Jake started turning the tuning dial for another station.

"I need my phone." She had to be in touch with her crew and the storm watchers and the mayor. *Dammit.*

"It's inside?"

"With my condoms," she said drily.

Condoms. She'd needed *condoms* in the shed behind the school at her high school class reunion. Avery shook her head.

"Do you seriously carry condoms around in your purse?" He sounded irritated.

She did not have any condoms in her purse. If she'd gone into that school building, she would *not* have come back out.

And she would have missed some of the best sex of her life.

Dammit.

Workbench or not, Jake Mitchell knew what he was doing.

She frowned at him. "What?"

"You often find yourself in situations like this where you might need one without warning?" He sounded pissed.

What did he have to be pissed about? Like he cared about her condom use when he wasn't around. It was so like Jake to think he was the only guy she might need a condom for.

Of course, she hadn't needed a condom, or any other birth control, for almost two years now.

She stood swiftly. "My condoms are none of your business."

She turned toward the door and started banging on it with a closed fist. "Hey! Anybody! We're in here!"

Jake grabbed her from behind with an arm around her waist, lifting her off her feet. He turned and set her down so that he was between her and the door. "Stop it. We can't go out there, and you know no one else is out there, either. They'd better all be under cover."

"We have to get out of here!" She felt the panic crawling over her like ants scuttling over her skin, making her jumpy and irritable. She was stuck in here while the rest of the town was out there hunkering down. Did everyone have shelter? Had they found the emergency boxes in the school? Was everyone aware of the approaching storm? She couldn't just sit in here and wait and wonder. Why couldn't she have brought her phone out here? At least then she could reach out to her crew. Of course, Jake's phone wasn't working, so hers likely wouldn't, either. It was so frustrating. "There must be another way." She started in the opposite direction, toward the garage door on the other side of the building where they drove the school's riding lawn mower and the Bobcat in and out.

Jake grabbed her and turned her, blocking her way again. "You can't go out there! Are you crazy?"

"Yes! Clearly! I just had sex with you on the *workbench* in the *storage shed* at our high school class reunion!"

There was an instant change in his expression, and she knew she was in trouble. She didn't know *exactly* what that look on his face meant, but she had the sudden urge to strip her clothes off.

Bad, bad idea.

He reached for her and she stepped back. "Knock it off, Jake! There's a tornado coming."

He paused a moment before letting his hand fall to his side. "Damn." He ran a hand through his hair. "You look at me with soft eyes, all sweet and trusting, and I want you. But you look at me all riled up and spitting fire, and I'm a complete mess."

She stared at him. He'd admitted to being affected by her. She knew—obviously—that he'd been turned on and able to get all the important parts functioning, but hearing that he was a "mess" and, more, that he'd noticed the emotion in her eyes, for some reason seemed like more than simple chemistry.

She liked messing up Jake. Because he sure messed her up.

"Jake, I—"

The sudden loud bang of something crashing into the side of the metal shed made them both jump. Whatever had hit the building was big. Avery's heartbeat leaped into overdrive. Between Jake and the storm, she was afraid she could be in serious cardiac crisis soon.

"Fuck," Jake muttered, and he rummaged in the box again and pulled out two bottles of water. "Come on. We need to get away from the door."

God, they were stuck. She looked around. The shed was solid, heavy. But it didn't have a deep foundation or load-bearing walls like the school building did. Plus, it was full of tools. It wasn't like it was good to have *anything* flying at you at ninety-plus miles an hour, but avoiding sharp things in particular was a good idea.

As if he'd scripted it, a low rumble shook the building, and something else banged into it. It was surely the fact that the shed was made of metal that made it sound so bad, but she couldn't help envisioning the worst.

The sirens were going off, the wind was howling, things were flying around out there. They needed to take shelter with whatever they had at the moment.

She grabbed a heavy blanket from one of the shelves and took Jake's hand. They headed back for the workbench.

It was easily the heaviest piece of furniture in the shed, and there was room underneath it. It wasn't perfect. If a tornado hit the building, the bench wasn't going to save their lives necessarily. But if a tornado shook the building and objects from high shelves started falling, it would keep them from sustaining head injuries. Probably.

Jake crawled under the table first. Avery tossed the blanket to him and started to slip off her stupid shoes. Never again would she wear heels for any reason.

"Shoes on, A." He unfolded the blanket.

"I'm going to break an ankle. If I need to run or climb over something, I'm toast." She was holding one shoe in her hand, the other still on her foot.

"There's going to be debris all over the place," he said. "If you step on a nail or a piece of glass, you'll wish you'd only twisted your ankle."

Dammit. He had a point.

"I have tennis shoes and boots in my car."

He chuckled. "Of course you do."

She frowned. "What's that mean?"

"It means you're the most prepared, in-charge planner and problem solver I've ever met."

She opened her mouth to respond to that. Coming from a sergeant major in the Army National Guard who'd made a name for himself by managing crisis situations, that was some compliment.

He grabbed her hand and tugged. "Get under here."

She crawled under the workbench—no small task in a form-fitting cocktail dress. With one leg three inches longer than the other at the moment, it was impossible. She more or less fell into Jake's lap. He caught her with a little "Oomph."

Avery tried to scramble off his lap, tugging at the bottom of her dress at the same time.

"Now you're being modest?" he asked. "We're a little past being worried about my seeing your underwear, aren't we?"

40

She put an elbow in his gut as she pushed herself off his lap. "Maybe I should strip it off altogether. It'd make climbing around on the floor under a table a lot easier."

"Whatever you need to do," he said agreeably. "Comfort first." His expression was completely innocent, except for the twinkle in his eye and the slight curl at one corner of his mouth.

She stubbornly yanked off her shoe as she tried to figure out how to sit on the floor beside him. She sat on one hip with her legs bent up beside her, but her bare skin rubbed on the concrete. She shifted and tried the other side, pulling the skirt down as she moved. It didn't go down very far. She couldn't sit with her legs crisscrossed with her tight skirt. She couldn't kneel for long on the hard concrete floor. Finally, she tried sitting with her knees pulled up and arms wrapped around them. But the skirt hiked up high in that position.

"Technically, you should be in the safety position on your knees, curled up with your hands behind your head."

He didn't have to sound like he was *enjoying* this.

It wasn't like she needed to be *comfortable*. It was a potentially dangerous situation outside, and she needed to be concerned with her own safety, Jake's, and that of everyone else in town. If she had some scrapes on her knees from this, so be it.

But the dress molded to her like a second skin, and that second skin was restricting in any position other than perfectly upright, and it was annoying the hell out of her at the moment.

With an irritated growl, she reached behind for the zipper and yanked it down, peeled the dress off in one swift motion, and spread it out on the floor. Then she sat on it.

She finally looked at Jake.

He was looking surprised, amused, and maybe a touch impressed. And turned on. Definitely turned on.

Which should not make one bit of difference. She'd gotten her itch scratched. A couple of them, in fact. She'd always wanted to make a guy so crazy that he tore her clothes off somewhere semipublic. Jake had certainly stepped up in that regard.

Still, she couldn't help that her ego liked having an effect on the guy.

A lot.

She leaned forward, elbows on her knees, everything she had on full display. "I should be concerned about flying glass and nails and all this exposed skin."

Jake's gaze made it back to her eyes. "Skin was all I heard."

It was her turn to smirk. "I was wondering what I was going to do about all the flying debris."

"I would be more than happy to inspect every inch of you later to see if there's anything that needs further attention."

Her heart fluttered a little at that—stupid, considering their precarious situation, not to mention that she was really trying hard to remember that Jake was the last guy she should be reacting to. "Wow, you really are a great guy." She knew he'd hear every drop of sarcasm.

There were several seconds of silence.

"A?"

"Yeah?"

"I think you need to cover up."

"You see some flying debris?"

"Nope. I don't see anything other than a lot of places that I'd like to put my tongue."

Heat washed over her and she felt her cheeks get pink. Whenever she thought she had the upper hand, he said something like that.

"Covering up sounds like a great idea."

She reached for the blanket he held, but he pulled it away from her. "We need to use this."

They did. They were in a tornado warning. Things could start flying around. They needed to drape the blanket over them both when things got hairy.

"Here." Jake unbuttoned his shirt and shrugged out of it, handing it over.

Her mouth went dry. She'd had sex with the guy, like, twenty minutes ago, and she still felt wound up and turned on and like she'd never seen a man's bare chest before.

She hadn't seen many—and this one was about a twelve on a ten-point scale—but it was only a chest.

She slipped into his shirt without a word. It was still warm from his body, and it smelled good. She pulled it tight around her and tried not to look at him. That turned out to be very difficult when they were practically sitting on top of each other.

"You're going to have to get closer," he said, flipping out the blanket. "This needs to cover us both."

That was a bad idea. Still, she scooted forward until their knees touched.

Even that much made her far too aware of him. They were nearly nose to nose. And they'd had sex very recently. Not a small detail.

Across the entire gymnasium of the school, she would have felt itchy and restless and hot thinking about it. Inches apart in an enclosed space, both mostly naked . . . yeah, she'd never been more uncomfortable.

They draped the blanket over them both like the tents little kids made out of blankets and couch cushions. Then Jake reached out from under the blanket and pulled something closer, blocking the entrance to their sort-of fort. From the scraping sound it made across the concrete, she guessed it was one of the big plastic totes.

It wasn't like either of them believed that their hiding spot and make-do-with-what-we-have protection was going to save their lives if an EF4 tornado decided to make them a direct target. But she knew they would have both recommended what they were doing to anyone in their situation. Protecting your head and face was first and foremost. Becoming as small a target as possible was important. There were no windows in the shed to worry about, but they were as far away from the door as they could get, and they were as low as they could get, and they were surrounded by heavy objects that could protect them from everyday objects that turned into missiles in the winds of a tornado.

When she focused, she could hear the sirens still squealing and the roar of the wind whipping around the building. Occasionally there was the thump of something hitting the building.

But she had to really concentrate.

Jake filled all her attention if she didn't strain to hear anything outside their cocoon.

"Want to play twenty questions?" he asked.

"Seriously?"

"We have to do something, and the other thing I'm thinking of is inappropriate given the circumstances."

"More inappropriate now than it was before?"

She should have let it go. She should have diverted the conversation. She should have never come to the shed with him and thought she was going to get out of here unscathed.

"I didn't know there was a tornado bearing down on the town before."

"Ah. That's the only thing that makes the sex-in-a-shed thing inappropriate."

He chuckled and she sucked in a quick breath. She liked when he laughed.

"We're two consenting adults, no one saw us, no one was scandalized, we didn't break the workbench—I think we're okay."

Yeah. Okay was one thing she was *not*.

"Twenty questions," she agreed. "You go first."

"Got something in mind."

Her mind made it dirty immediately. "Is it bigger than a bread box?"

He gave her a lazy smile. "Not quite."

"Is it hard?"

This game had never sounded so sexual before.

"Yes."

She swallowed. "Is it warm?"

He paused, and she wondered if a series of hard, warm things was going through his mind like it was through hers.

"Sometimes."

"Thought the answers had to be yes or no."

He shrugged. "Neither is accurate all the time."

Well, she knew where her mind was, and it was *always* warm.

"Does it make noise?"

He grinned. "Yes."

Oh, really . . .

A very ominous noise interrupted them. A loud bang, followed by a groaning from outside. The whole building shook and, in spite of herself, Avery felt a shudder go through her.

She grabbed Jake's hand.

Jake turned up the radio that he'd had sitting next to his hip.

She scooted a little closer, or tried to. Her knees were already pressed against his, giving her very little room to move anywhere but back. She was not backing up. She might hate wanting him and hate how he could reduce her to a brainless twit with a simple smile, but she definitely liked having him under this blanket in this shed with her at the moment.

The air around her was warmer because of him, and his big hands surrounding hers made her feel stupidly safe. She remembered him wrapping his arms around her last year and how she'd been grateful that he'd somehow known she needed that. No one could control the weather, no one could harness and direct a tornado, but if she was going to be in the middle of one, Jake Mitchell was the guy she'd pick to have beside her.

Or directly in front of her, as the case might be.

"A tornado touchdown has been reported in Hall County, two miles southwest of Chance. It is moving northeast at fifty miles per hour. Wind gusts up to one hundred and seventy miles per hour have been reported. If you are in the path of this storm, please take cover immediately."

Winds of 170 miles per hour did put the storm in the EF4 category. Avery gripped Jake's hands harder. She'd been through this before. The whole town had. But rather than making it better, it almost made it worse. Knowing what was coming, knowing what could happen, made her stomach knot.

She worked on controlling her breathing and concentrated on what she was going to have to do when this was over. She needed to contact all her volunteers, track down the mayor, set up a command center, tour the town . . .

"Come here." Jake tugged on her hands.

The action shifted her forward suddenly, and she tipped into his lap. He turned her to sit in the cradle of his legs and wrapped his arms around her. She didn't protest for a moment. Maybe he was cold, maybe he thought she was cold, maybe he was scared . . . whatever. She wasn't going anywhere.

"I can't believe we're together like this for another tornado."

He chuckled. "I've always liked tornadoes best of all the storms, but I have to say, these last two here in Chance have been exceptional."

She shook her head. "How can you say that? Your hometown has been hammered."

"Hot, naked redheads have a way of making everything better."

She blushed, which was silly. He couldn't see her anyway, and he'd seen a lot more than her cheeks getting pink not so very long ago. "I wasn't naked at all last time, and I wasn't completely naked this time."

"You're right. Guess it was a flashback. Apparently it's hot redheads with their tongues down my throat that make things better."

She knew he wasn't making light of the tornado situation and Chance, and she couldn't argue that there had been tongue. Both times.

"Glad I could help," she said lightly.

"I do appreciate it," he said. "And I have a list of ways you could help me in future storms, if you're interested."

She laughed but was interrupted by a clattering on the metal roof that sounded like machine-gun fire.

"Hail," she said unnecessarily.

The howling outside was increasing, and the walls of the shed were vibrating with the power of the storm.

"Heard it before, but it stopped."

"There was hail before?" She hadn't heard a thing.

"When we were . . . busy."

His mouth was right by her ear, and his warm breath washed over her neck. She shivered again, but for a very different reason.

Busy. One word. But it was enough to send every detail of how busy they'd been whirling through her mind. Her stomach flipped and tightened, then a part lower than her stomach tightened.

It wasn't hard to believe that when they were actually doing all the things she was remembering that she'd been so caught up that she'd missed the pounding of a hailstorm. When she was with Jake, she swore the entire town could fall down around her and she wouldn't notice.

She really hoped the entire town wasn't falling down around them now.

"You didn't say anything about hail." Her voice was husky. Dammit.

"There were bare breasts. Hail didn't seem important."

She smiled in spite of herself. "I would think it would take something pretty major to distract an expert such as yourself from a potentially dangerous storm."

The building shook with a suddenly huge gust of wind, and the hail clanging on the roof got louder.

"It would, indeed." Jake tightened his hold on her.

She always felt like her mind was whirling during a storm. It was hard to remember details *during* the tornado. She was always so involved in the preparations and alerts, then had to jump immediately into action afterward, that she didn't dwell on the time during as much.

But she knew this one would be memorable.

Sitting enfolded in Jake's arms while the world went crazy outside.

Yep, she'd remember this.

She decided to concentrate on Jake rather than the fact that her friends and home were outside at the mercy of yet another twisting monster. She could do nothing at the moment but pray. As soon as the storm passed, she'd be all in, doing anything and everything she could.

But right now all she could do was hold on.

Jake was warm. Almost hot. His body behind and under her was solid and strong, and his big hands covered the backs of hers entirely. He was stroking his thumbs rhythmically across her knuckles. His mouth still rested near her ear, his chin on her shoulder, but he wasn't saying anything. She could feel his breath against her neck, faster than normal, and his heartbeat against her shoulder blade—also faster than it should be. Otherwise, there was no sound except the growling and groaning of the wind, and the banging of things hitting the building and the rattling of the hail on the roof.

Then it went quiet.

"Here we go." Jake laced his fingers with hers.

The poets who talked about the calm before the storm hadn't made that shit up. It got completely quiet at times right before the big one hit—there were no birds or insects making noise, the rain and hail let up, the wind died down, the lightning resisted.

Citizens of Chance knew that well. The sickly greenish sky, the eerie silence along with the lonely whine of the siren, the feeling of being stalked and cornered . . .

Right before all hell broke loose.

People often said a tornado sounded like a freight train or the sound of a thousand huge boulders rolling down a mountain, but she'd never thought either of those descriptions quite captured the sound. It was almost impossible to describe. Maybe it was like an oncoming train—the rumbling that grew louder and louder—but there was a wailing that went with it and a crazy *whooshing* . . . but that wasn't even a strong enough word.

It was a sound you never forgot. There was nothing else quite like it.

She hunched forward instinctively as the growling and rumbling outside grew, the rhythm of the thumps and bangs against the building built, and the floor and walls shook. Avery felt Jake's arms tighten around her. He, too, leaned forward, his chest to her back.

There was a horrible *bang* followed by the screeching of metal over concrete. There was a loud creaking, then a *pop* from overhead. She heard the crashes of things hitting the floor from the shelves and a loud *thunk* on the tabletop right overhead. Avery swore she could feel the force of the wind pulling at her like a vacuum, and she gripped Jake hard.

Please, please, please.

That was as much of a prayer as she could utter. She couldn't put more words together than that. She had to trust that the Almighty would know what she needed.

Take the buildings, take the cars, just don't take any people, she silently begged the tornado.

A tornado thirty-some years ago had killed four and injured six. The tornado twelve years ago had seriously injured three. The most recent ones, however, had not resulted in any death or serious injury. Every time Mother Nature came at them, they were more prepared.

The roaring built around them until she was sure she wouldn't have even been able to hear Jake say her name from right behind her.

Then it was gone.

The noise, the shaking, the pressure all disappeared as if someone had thrown the off switch.

It took a few seconds for her to uncoil. Was it really over or was there more coming?

"A?" Jake asked, slowly loosening his grip but not letting go of her completely.

She pulled in a deep breath. "Fine. You?"

"Yep." A second later he let out a long sigh. "Damn."

"Yeah." She couldn't disagree with that assessment. She sat up straighter and let go of his hands. They needed to get out and see what was going on.

Jake seemed to sense her intent because he kept one arm around her waist. "Hang on a sec."

He turned the radio up again.

"A touchdown has been confirmed in the town of Chance," the announcer said.

"No shit," Jake muttered.

"We expect reports of damage will be incoming for the next few hours. The line of thunderstorms continues to move east-northeast, and the following counties remain under a tornado watch: Hall, Hamilton, York, Merrick, and Polk."

Jake took another deep breath. "Let's go see what we've got."

Avery climbed from his lap, immediately feeling chilled, and fumbled around for her dress and shoes.

Jake shone the flashlight on her discarded dress, then their eyes met. For a moment they just looked at each other. They'd shared something unusual, something terrifying and crazy, and it felt like it had changed things between them.

"You know, naked tornado drills could really catch on," Jake said after a minute.

His quip and her smile took her by surprise. "A quickie in the storage shed doesn't make us friends, you know," she said lightly. Because

God knew, in the next few minutes—or days—she was going to need all the lightness she could get.

"How about cleaning up our hometown together after a tornado?"

Her smile faded and she sighed. "That might." She'd loved having him there beside her last time, though it had been too short. Jake had a way of bringing a sense of calm and security with him. She hated that the entire nation needed him, that he was the go-to guy for *everyone*. But she knew why. Jake was the best at what he did.

"Then let's get to it."

He wanted to be her friend? Or was he feeling the bonded-by-disaster thing she was feeling? How long would he be here anyway? A couple of days didn't make a friendship.

She was the first out from their makeshift fort. She straightened and looked around.

One corner of the metal ceiling had been peeled back; cans and bottles and tools littered the floor. A huge plastic jug had hit the top of the workbench and cracked, spilling horrible-smelling liquid all over, while three old paint cans had hit the floor, splattering blue, white, and black paint. The door they'd entered through was now six feet closer to them than it was supposed to be, the entire side of the shed dented in, clearly having been hit by something from outside.

"Guess we're not going out the way we came in." Jake turned to shine the flashlight around the rest of the shed.

"There are the big garage doors on the other side," Avery told him.

"Uh, I think we might be okay," he said.

She followed his gaze and saw that there was what definitely looked like daylight streaming in from the other room. Had a door blown off? That was a scary thought, but at the same time it might be their way out of here.

She slipped on one shoe, then hopped on that foot, trying to get on the other.

Jake watched her struggle. Then he grabbed her arm to steady her and shook his head.

"What?"

"I'm always torn about heels. They're sexy as hell but the least practical things I've ever seen."

"They pinch my toes and kill my arches, too." She completely agreed about the least practical thing. That was why she had exactly two pairs, and she wore them each probably two times a year.

"But you still wear them?"

She got on the shoe and set down her foot. "Tell me they don't look great."

He shone the light up and down from her butt to her heels and back. "Can't argue with that. Especially when you're wearing my shirt."

"Oh my God!" She clutched the front of the shirt. "I almost forgot. I have to get my dress back on."

She started to unbutton, but Jake bent and picked up her dress off the floor. "You're not putting this back on."

"Jake, give me my dress." This was no time to tease.

He shook his head. "It's soaked." He tipped the cracked plastic bottle on top of the bench to look at the label. "Pesticide. No way are you putting this back on."

The bottle of chemicals had spilled on the top of the workbench but had run down behind it and onto the floor underneath. She fingered the material. It was wet and smelled awful. At least the dress had soaked up the spill before it could get to where they'd been sitting together.

"I have more clothes in my car. I'll put this on until I can get to it." Though that definitely sounded unappealing.

"If your car's still out there. And doesn't have a tree lying across it or something," Jake said. "You can't put this stuff on your skin. No way. Keep my shirt on."

Dammit. That dress was brand-new, too.

What she was wearing should be the least of her concerns at the moment. There was her car, various trees lying where they shouldn't be, and potentially a whole host of much bigger problems waiting right outside.

Jake snagged the blanket they'd used to cover up. It was splattered with paint, and the edge that had been near the back wall was also soaked in pesticide.

He tossed it to the side and stalked to the shelving unit where the box of socks was stored. He shone the light over the boxes, then grabbed one, pulling it out and dropping it on the floor. He squatted to rummage inside, and a moment later held up a pair of royal-blue sweatpants with WILDCATS in white block letters running up one leg.

"These will work," he decided.

He started to stand.

"Those are huge," she said with a laugh. "What size do you think I am?"

He looked her up and down with clear appreciation and said, "You're size hot. That's all I know."

She did feel hot with his eyes on her like that. She resisted the urge to fan her face. "Are there small ones in there?" She wasn't built like a teenage girl anymore, but they were sweatpants. There had to be a little stretch to them.

Jake squatted and rummaged through the box again. Triumphantly he held up another, smaller pair of sweats. "Yes?"

She nodded. "Yes."

He tossed them to her, and she did slip her shoes off again to get the pants up her legs. Then she stepped back into her heels.

"Let's go see what we've got." He took her hand and turned the flashlight on the path in front of them.

They stepped around and over cans, bottles, and tools. A little farther and they came to a bucket on its side, nails and screws strewn across the floor. Avery had to slow down and concentrate on where she was walking. She stepped down on one large screw that rolled under her heel, throwing her off balance.

Jake grabbed her arm to keep her upright.

"You got this or not?"

"Sure, great, no problem at all."

He tucked her up against his side instead of holding on to her, hand in hand, as they continued toward the large garage doors on the northwest side of the building.

They stepped through the doorway that separated the storage area and workshop from the room with the bigger machinery.

There was definite daylight coming in, but a door hadn't blown off.

A tree had fallen into the metal building and crumpled the wall, separating it from the ceiling and making a hole. A hole that was about eight feet wide, but six feet from the floor and partially filled with a tree.

Avery and Jake both stopped and stared for a moment.

It was clear what they were both thinking—if that tree had crushed the other wall, the one to the room where they'd been huddled under the workbench, they would have been trapped underneath it. Or possibly squished like bugs under a shoe.

"Damn," Jake said.

Avery couldn't say even that much. Her throat was too tight. What if there were other walls like this around town? What if there were people trapped or . . . worse?

Jake let go of her to examine the wall more closely.

"We can get through, but we'll have to really watch it. There's a lot of jagged metal here, and we'll have to climb over the tree."

Fine, whatever. She felt her adrenaline pumping. She needed to get out there. She needed to know what had happened, who was affected, what needed to be done. She needed to make assignments and assess the damage and—

"Avery?"

She jerked her attention back to Jake. "What?"

"Hold this. I need to see what I'm doing."

Right. They had to get out of here before she could do anything else.

She trained the light on him as he climbed onto the small skid loader so he could peer over the top of the crushed door and through the hole. His muscles bunched and strained, and without his shirt on, she was treated to every detail of his solid, muscular body at work. There was one silver lining to this whole thing, for sure. Wearing dress pants, socks and shoes, but no shirt and climbing on top of machinery, Jake should have looked out of place, but he didn't. At all. He moved with easy grace and purpose. He gave off a vibe of confidence that said he knew exactly what he was doing, or if he didn't, he'd figure it out and not even break a sweat. She was sure he'd also have that sexy grin in place the whole time.

She focused on keeping the light where his hands needed to be, rather than spotlighting the broad chest and sculpted abs that made her mouth water. But she did find the light beam slipping downward slightly . . .

"I'll give you a full show later," he said. "Right now I could use a little more flashlight up here."

Dammit. She aimed the light higher, illuminating the edge of the door so he didn't cut off something important against the torn-up metal. "Don't know what you're talking about."

Sexy grin. Check.

"I get it. You didn't get a good look earlier. Or ten years ago. We keep doing it in the dark. I feel the same way. But it's easily rectified."

He reached high, stretching his long, hard body to grab for the lowest branch. The loader he stood on was a small version, made for the lighter work around the school—and borrowed from time to time for bigger yard and garden projects around town. It was sturdy but not built for having a two-hundred-pound man climbing around on it. The loader started to tip.

"Jake!"

"Fuck." He shifted his weight and eyed the branch above him.

"You live through a tornado, but you break your neck trying to climb a tree?" she asked, trying to keep things light and calm her pounding heart. "I don't think so." She shone the light around the garage, locating a tall ladder lying on the floor a few feet away. "There."

The ladder had clearly fallen from the hooks on the wall behind it. She grabbed the top and dragged it back to the loader as Jake jumped to the ground.

"Sweet of you to care." He took the ladder and propped it against the bent door. He rattled it, making sure it was as secure as possible.

She didn't study the muscles of his shoulders and upper back this time. She was too interested in the tightening of his butt muscles.

"I don't feel like answering a lot of questions if something happens to you when I'm the only witness. There may be some reasons for people to be suspect of that."

He shot her a grin. "Nah, too many people have witnessed us kissing. They know you like me."

She sighed. She could admit that people who'd seen Jake surprise her with semipublic kisses over the past year would believe she was participating wholeheartedly. In spite of her best efforts, she got caught up in the heat. It was the surprise element. If she were given a *choice*, she would never . . .

But that was a bunch of bullshit, too. She'd been given a choice right here in this very shed not so long ago, and what had happened? They were now both half-naked.

So what? It was hormones and chemistry and stuff. It didn't *mean* anything.

But she was sure that wouldn't be exactly clear from a spectator's perspective when they turned a corner and saw her up on tiptoe to get closer, one hand in his hair and the other gripping his ass.

That also wasn't her fault, though. Jake had one of the best asses around.

"I don't like you." It sounded weak, even to her own ears.

"You like me kissing you." He didn't seem concerned. He held out his hand. "Come on."

She stepped up and took his hand, putting a foot on the first rung of the ladder.

As she climbed, she said, "Liking the kissing doesn't mean I like you."

"Uh-huh."

She could feel him right behind her—or below her, to be more exact. She glanced down. And found that he was now staring at *her* ass.

"Jake?"

"Hmm?" He lifted his gaze and grinned unapologetically. "You were saying?"

She couldn't help but tingle a little, knowing he was right *there* and appreciating the view. But still . . . "Since you're back, and we have some alone time, maybe we should talk about the kissing. Or actually about *stopping* the kissing—"

She got to the top of the ladder and grabbed a tree branch.

"Take it easy," he said, now almost directly behind her as he moved up the ladder. "Step out on that branch, but hold on. I'm going to get up right behind you, and we'll go from there."

Avery worked on focusing on the task right in front of her. She grabbed the thickest branch and stepped onto the tree trunk.

It wasn't the climbing or the heights or the fact that once her weight was on it, the tree shifted a few inches—it was the freaking high heels. She would give anything for her work boots right now.

"Okay, easy," Jake said, nudging her forward so he could move off the ladder and onto the trunk with her.

They both held on and held their breaths as the tree shifted again with Jake's weight.

Once it seemed secure again, Jake grasped her hips. "Guess we're going to have to get up close and personal again, Chief."

This day was really not going her way.

Or maybe it was *really* going her way.

She could feel his hips and thighs up against her as he worked to move around her and, in spite of it all, the feel of his hot, hard body against her distracted her. As usual.

Fortunately, he moved around her quickly and, grabbing on to one branch at a time, worked to break off the smaller, lower branches to clear a path for them to climb down. He was dressed for a nice night out, too, certainly not in his usual work clothes, but his shoes were better for the job than hers, that was for certain.

They made their way down the tree trunk, the only sound that of the branches breaking and the occasional creak of metal for a few minutes.

They finally got past the edge of the building and to the wider portion of the trunk, and Jake paused.

He straightened and looked around.

"We might have some other things we need to talk about first," he said.

Avery moved in behind him and looked as well. "Yeah," she muttered. All she could see from here was a lot of debris, a multitude of branches, and a dumpster on its side. She knew it was going to get a lot worse.

She could hear the police and fire sirens coming closer. Which meant that this area of town had been hit. Which meant lots of people would be gathering. Which meant everyone was going to see her emerge from this shed with Jake . . . and without her clothes.

"If I go out there, everyone will think—"

He turned to look at her. "That we were going at it on the workbench?" The damned smirk was back.

"That I'm stupid. Who takes her dress all the way off for a quickie in a shed?"

He looked surprised for a moment, then grinned. "You might get something on it."

"Where are you going to hang a nice dress in a shed? You're going to get something on it, no matter what, but throwing it down on the floor or draping it over a lawn mower isn't a good choice. Keeping it on is the lesser of all the evils."

He chuckled. "Always practical. I like that."

Her stomach flipped. Ridiculous. For one, they were about to step out into the aftermath of a tornado together. Again. For another, they'd just had sex. Again. But hearing Jake say that he *liked* her, or something about her, made her stomach flip.

She was in trouble.

"Let's go." He motioned with his hand that he wanted her to move forward.

She took a deep breath. Inside the shed she could only wonder about what was outside. Once she stepped off that tree, she was going to see the reality. Which could be so much worse than her imagination. Right here, she could pretend things were all right.

"Your town needs you, Chief," Jake said, his voice softer.

She looked at him. He was right. And he was reading her. Which was not a good thing. Nor was the fact it made her feel better that he understood her hesitation.

"Let's go," she finally agreed.

Jake made his way down the tree another couple of feet, breaking branches and clearing the path as he had been, but here it was definitely more stable, and they were both breathing easier. He turned back to her and offered his hand. "This way, milady."

Rolling her eyes, she stepped forward and grabbed his hand, but as she did, her foot turned in her heel. He hauled her up against him, and she had to grab the waistband of his pants to keep her balance.

"Those shoes are a problem."

"Yes, how did I not anticipate having to climb trees tonight when I put them on?"

"With your concern about my pretty neck on that skid loader, I'd feel horrible if you ended up in a neck collar climbing over this tree."

"You have a solution, I take it?" she asked.

"I do. It involves me being your hero, though. I'm damned good at it, but I have a feeling it might rub you the wrong way."

She shook her head. "I'm sure you're right. Not so much because of whatever you're going to do, but because of the way you're going to point it out and congratulate yourself during and after."

She was still holding on to him, and his arm was still around her, pressing their bodies together—his heat and strength soaking into her as they balanced on the tree. She could grudgingly admit that the balancing was much more *his* doing than hers. If he let go, she was going down. And it wouldn't be graceful.

"Maybe if *you* said sweeter things to me, I wouldn't have to stroke my own ego."

"You know what, Jake?" she said *very* sweetly. "You can keep on stroking all of your own things from here on out."

He loosened his grip on her, and she wobbled, grabbing on to his belt with both hands.

He chuckled. "Seems I'm in a very good position for negotiating."

"There's no way you'd let me fall." She was 90 percent sure that was true.

"No, but I could leave you up here and make one of your volunteer firefighters come rescue you. Like a kitten in a tree."

"For God's sake." She bent and took off a shoe. "All I need is to—" But as she put her bare foot down on the tree trunk, she looked at the ground. Glass and pieces of wood, metal, and gravel littered the area. She couldn't step down onto all of that without injury.

She took off her other shoe, feeling more balanced, at least. She breathed deeply and said, "All I need is to ask you nicely if you'll help me."

He grinned. "Yeah, okay. My mama raised me right."

His mama. Avery felt a twinge in her heart at the mention of his mother. Heidi Mitchell had most certainly raised him right. Jake was a great guy—with the exception of his full-of-himself hero complex and the fact that he'd taken all his talents to another city rather than using them in his hometown. But Heidi had done everything right. She was the perfect mother. Avery knew personally. Heidi had been a mother figure to Avery from the time she was four until she left Chance after graduation. Avery had loved her dearly and missed her terribly.

It was worse because Heidi lived only about eight blocks from Avery's house, and Avery saw her in town from time to time.

But they didn't speak beyond general civil greetings and very occasional small talk. Not anymore. Heidi had hurt Avery more than anyone—more than Avery's own mother and grandmother, and they'd never been in the running for parent or guardian of the year. Even more than Jake had.

One positive had come out of that realization, however. Understanding that she'd been more in love with *Jake's family* than with him had certainly helped her get over him.

Avery sighed. She couldn't even say that honestly in her own head. Okay, it had certainly helped her *tell herself* she was over him. For the first couple of years, she'd believed that Jake had been a passing crush, more appealing because of Avery's relationship with his mother than because of him. But now . . . and for the past year . . . it just didn't seem that easy.

"Get me out of this tree, Jake."

"How about a please?" He jumped to the ground.

"I think I'm out of pleases."

He turned to her and extended his arms. "You only said one earlier. Right after the 'God, Jake.'"

"Of course you're keeping track."

"You bet I am. Three of my favorite words when they're in that particular order."

"Such an ass," she muttered. But she leaned forward and put her hands on his shoulders.

His hands went to her waist, and he swung her down from the tree. But he didn't put her on the ground.

Pressed tightly to his body, his hands on her hips, she most definitely felt more inclined to say another please or so.

With a knowing grin, Jake swung her legs so that he was holding her behind her back and under her knees, cradled against his chest.

"You ready to do this?"

She knew he was talking about checking out the damage, but her mind didn't go there immediately. Fortunately, she didn't say what she was thinking out loud.

"I guess." Which would have been her answer even if he *had* been talking about what she was thinking.

He headed around the corner of the building, and Avery found herself squeezing her eyes shut.

She'd deal with whatever it was. She'd do her typical calm, cool, collected, amazing job.

In a minute.

"Oh, boy."

Jake's comment, and that he'd stopped walking, made her eyes open. Which she regretted instantly.

Oh, boy was a pretty good summary.

CHAPTER THREE

There were tree branches of varying sizes everywhere. There were cars that looked perfectly normal, while others had smashed windows and were spun facing the opposite way from which they'd been parked. There was one that had not previously been a convertible that was now missing its top. There was stuff that didn't belong there, lying all over—trash cans, the trash that had previously been inside the cans, plastic bags, a few lawn chairs, a big, plastic multicolored square that little kids climbed on in their backyard, and—amazingly—a barbecue grill.

Then there was the car that had smashed into the side of the shed, causing the dent and the inability to open the door.

And finally, the thing that made her heart nearly stop and tears threaten—the gaping hole in the side of the school. The side where the gymnasium was. The gymnasium that had been decorated for the reunion, full of their friends and former classmates.

"We were having sex in the shed," she whispered.

Jake's hands gripped her harder. "Yeah."

"We're bad people."

"Maybe a little," he agreed.

"Well, there's one more thing we have in common—great sex and incredible guilt."

"Av—"

"Goddammit! I don't believe this!" Whatever Jake had been about to say was interrupted by the arrival of Frank Harvey.

Jake turned, still holding her. "Mr. Mayor."

Avery closed her eyes again briefly, wishing she could disappear. But Frank didn't seem to register or care about her strange clothing or that Jake still held her in his arms.

"Three years!" Frank's face was red, his tie loosened from its knot at his neck, and he was sweating. "Three fucking years in a row. The vultures will be descending any minute."

Avery wondered if she needed to call Dr. Wagner. Frank was in his early fifties, and although he jogged every morning, he also had a penchant for beer and fried cheese.

"Vultures?" Jake asked.

"The media. They're going to have a fucking field day with this. An EF4. Three years in a goddamn row."

Frank Harvey had been mayor for the past eight years. He had been a city councilman for ten years before getting elected mayor, and a small-town business owner before that. He'd been a resident of Chance his entire life. His boys had grown up here, too, and all three lived in town. Frank was a good guy, incredibly passionate about Chance, and could BS with anyone about anything. He was a great small-town mayor.

He also had a voice that could carry across a football field. Or a parking lot.

Especially when he was excited or upset, as he was now.

"Is everyone all right?" Avery asked. They could worry about the media later. She knew that the EF4 status couldn't have been officially confirmed already, but they could make a very educated guess based on the damage done. Frank knew tornadoes. Everyone in Chance did. "Where else were we hit?" she asked. "Is everyone in the school accounted for? There were at least twenty people in there earlier."

Frank nodded. "Everyone from here has been accounted for. They headed for the locker rooms as soon as the siren went off. The gym has the most damage, along with a couple of classrooms."

The locker rooms were easily the safest place in the school—center of the building, no windows, and thick concrete walls. Avery felt some of the knot in her stomach loosen. The people inside had known where to go and had taken cover in time. Thank God.

"The Methodist church was hit," Frank went on. "But only three people were there, and they headed for the basement. They've been dug out. There are some homes still being checked. There's roof damage all over the place, lots of trees down, power lines down in this part of town. Every cop, EMT, and firefighter has been called in, and they're going neighborhood to neighborhood until you and Chief Mitchell make a plan," Frank said, referring to their chief of police. Who just happened to be Jake's dad. Avery was a little surprised he wasn't already there.

Avery blushed hard, the knot tightening again. She'd been half-naked under a blanket in the shed behind the school with Jake while her firefighters and EMTs had been called into action and people had been dug out. She was proud of her team. Of course they were already on the job. She wouldn't be surprised to find that several had been out long before they'd been officially called on duty.

In a small town like Chance, fire departments were largely volunteer. She was the only full-time person in the department, and she had a lot of duties beyond putting out fires. She had two part-time guys on her team, and the rest were volunteers. They all had other jobs in and around Chance, and even in other towns and cities. It wasn't like they all hung out together at the firehouse during their downtime between five-alarm blazes. In fact, Chance had never had a five-alarm blaze. Weeks went by with no calls for fires whatsoever. Much of Avery's job was administrative and focused on training and preparedness as well as being in charge of all emergency-management activities in town and serving on a couple of committees for the county.

But when there was a need—a fire or a motor-vehicle accident or a natural disaster—her guys were on the job and were some of the best she'd ever worked with. She was proud to call them her crew.

"I swear to God, I'm about to start looking into the ancient burial-ground nonsense." Frank ran a hand over his face. "Chief Mitchell is on his way over here. I want to talk to you both and put our immediate plan in place," Frank told Avery.

"Of course."

"Maybe you want to get some clothes on so we can get to work," Frank said.

He had noticed. Avery felt her face begin to burn, and her mind spun with excuses to give her boss. *My dress got caught on a nail. We needed my dress for a tourniquet. We needed it to . . .* But it seemed that *not* talking about it was the easiest way to get away from the topic entirely. Forever.

Avery squirmed in Jake's arms. "Let me down," she hissed.

"I'll take you to your car."

"Jake—"

"For the same reason I picked you up in the first place," he said firmly. "You can't go walking across all this crap."

She sighed. That was, in fact, very gentlemanly. Dammit.

Practicality was always the right decision. She pointed toward her Ford Fusion. Jake started in that direction.

"By the way, your sergeant voice isn't going to work with me."

"Is that right? You might be surprised what I can get you to do with my sergeant *major* voice."

She hated the way her heart thumped when he said stuff like that. Feeling like a pouting child, she didn't talk again until they reached her car.

Where she realized she didn't have her keys. They were inside the school, in her purse—with her phone. And with the fictional condoms.

She sighed heavily.

Chance was a small town, but it was big enough that you locked your car when you were going to be away from it for a while. With a population of more than five thousand, it seemed that everyone knew someone who knew everyone. Still, she kept her laptop with her at all times and had tools in the trunk that she didn't want curious teenagers to have access to.

"Want me to get you in?" he asked.

She had to have her clothes and better shoes, and she couldn't drive home now and leave all of this—and the mayor—behind.

"Yes." Dammit.

Jake set her on the hood, then looked around and easily located a heavy piece of metal something or other—like it mattered—and smashed through her back passenger-side window, grabbed the duffel bag on the seat, and presented it to her with a grin.

"Hero deed number three."

She took the bag and lifted an eyebrow. "Three? You got me off the tree trunk and rescued my clothes. That's two."

"I'd be happy to repeat number one if you've forgotten."

She stared at him, knowing immediately what he was referring to. Orgasms counted as heroic deeds, huh?

In the middle of a disaster, he was still teasing her. And still making her hot.

◆ ◆ ◆

"Jake! Jesus, Jake."

Jake pulled his attention away from Avery and looked over to see his cousin Max Grady striding toward him. Max had a limp from a leg injury sustained from a bad fall when they'd been assigned to Katrina cleanup together, but he looked big and determined as he bore down on them.

Max was home for the reunion, too, but, of course, Jake wasn't surprised that he would dive right into the rescue and recovery as well. It was one reason Jake considered him more of a brother than a cousin or friend. Max had been a part of the Army Corps of Engineers, was now in construction, and was the cleanup-and-recovery specialist for a major portion of the Midwest, extending from western Oklahoma through Arkansas and up into Missouri—a huge portion of Tornado Alley. Max was also a storm chaser, and the men shared an obsession with weather, tornadoes in particular.

"We found your truck four blocks over, and no one had seen or heard from you," Max said.

Jake didn't hug men easily, but Max was one he made an exception for. The men embraced, and Jake thumped his friend on the back reassuringly. "I'm good. We had to hunker down in the shed."

Max's eyes immediately went to Avery. "The shed, huh?"

"We were getting more streamers," she offered weakly.

Jake grinned at that. They hadn't touched a streamer while in the shed.

Max chuckled. "I could use a few more streamers myself."

Avery's face flushed an adorable tomato-red, and Jake felt a stupid surge of . . . something. Pride? Possessiveness? He was the one who'd messed up her hair, smudged her lipstick, and put that pink in her cheeks.

"Block the window." She reached in through the broken window to unlock the passenger-side door and climbed inside.

Jake moved in front of the window, and Max shifted to stand beside him, facing away from the car. Jake knew she was getting dressed, and it took every bit of restraint he had not to climb in there with her.

"What's going on in town?" Avery asked through the window.

"The main damage is here," Max said. "The mobile-home park is upside down, and lots of damage as I went through town."

"Nobody injured?" Jake asked.

"Only scrapes and bruises so far. I checked in with Dillon a little bit ago. He's doing triage at the clinic. They're ready for whatever."

Dillon Alexander was the third of the three cousins and best buddies who had gone off to the National Guard after graduation. Dillon had been a part of the medical branch, but Jake and Max had been fortunate to have him with them in Louisiana. He'd left the Guard for medical school after two years and was now the second in command at the busiest ER in Fort Worth, Texas.

Jake felt Avery's hand on his back, pushing him forward, and he stepped out of the way so she could open the door.

She emerged wearing blue jeans, a T-shirt, and heavy work boots. She'd also gathered her hair back in a ponytail. She looked so much younger. He made a fist and gripped it tight to keep from lifting his hand to wipe the smudge of dirt from her cheek.

If he touched her now, he wouldn't want to stop. As usual.

Plus, that wasn't his place. Even if he *had* been part of the reason for her having dirt on her cheek.

The sex had been awesome. The sounds she made, the way she felt and smelled and tasted. But holding her under the bench in their little tent, weathering the storm, had been—something else. It had taken him all the way back to graduation night. The night when she'd looked up at him like he was some kind of superstar.

God, he'd loved that look from her. Could still recall it perfectly. Other women, other *people*, for that matter, had looked at him with everything from admiration to hero worship over the years, but Avery was the only one who still mattered ten years later.

He shook his head and focused. They had a town to clean up. Their town. Again.

They followed Frank and his entourage toward the school where people were gathering to see what needed to be done.

Jake couldn't help the rush of fondness he felt. His hometown really was a great place. People truly cared about one another here. He knew that Chance would pull together, and going through this as a community would strengthen their bonds.

Driving away from Chance after the twister hit last year had been the hardest thing he'd done. It was always a little hard to go, and over the years it had gotten harder and harder to leave. He loved Chance. He loved visiting and reconnecting, the feeling of home and history he had there. Seeing the rubble in the morning light and getting into his car to drive *away* from it, rather than into the midst where he wanted to be, had torn at him. But it had been imperative that he be in DC that day. That meeting had meant improved procedures for multiple metropolitan areas, affecting the safety and lives of millions. Though it had made him almost physically sick to leave Chance, his little hometown was made up of fewer than six thousand people, and he simply couldn't justify staying there instead. Avery was here. His dad was here. He'd known they would take care of the town.

Honestly, seeing their faces, their sorrow and anger and frustration and fatigue, had eaten at him. There had been no loss of life and no critical injuries, yet seeing his friends and family and neighbors going through the wreckage of their homes and businesses had been harder on him than any of the bigger disasters with higher mortality rates and recovery bills.

So he'd headed out the next morning, feeling like he was abandoning his home and hating himself for it.

As Jake looked around now at the destruction caused by the third tornado in a row, he knew he would be staying for a while this time. But as he surveyed the broken, but not yet defeated town, he wondered, *How much more of this can Chance take?*

"We'll set up the command center at the Lutheran church," Avery was saying. "They have that big social hall."

Then there was Avery. He'd never expected that first kiss to twist him up like it had. But he couldn't leave her alone on his visits after that. Having her respond to him the way she did every time had fed something inside of him that he hadn't even realized was hungry. And now they'd had sex again.

Tornadoes were all kinds of trouble.

"We can set up a shelter at Chances Are and The Jim," Frank said. Chances Are was the old theater where the Community Theater Project performed, and it was the site of most wedding receptions and other big parties. The Jim was a gym . . . owned by a guy named Jim. It was a beautiful workout facility with a large gymnasium that could hold a number of cots, and it had locker rooms where displaced families and cleanup workers could shower.

"Are the school kitchen and lunchroom intact?" Avery asked.

"For the most part," Max chimed in. "We can get it cleaned up and the power back on in the next twenty-four hours."

"Then we're going to need a meal plan until that's up and running," Avery said. "The church kitchens can be used."

"We can put the call out for a potluck," Frank said. "We'll have a town meeting tomorrow at noon. I'll need status updates by then."

The term *potluck* was, perhaps, lighthearted for what they intended, but it worked. Everyone raided their refrigerators and pantries and brought what they could to a central location to share.

"The guys are going door-to-door now."

They all turned as the chief of police joined them.

"Hey, Dad," Jake said in greeting.

"Son." Wes pulled Jake in for a hug.

He was also on Jake's short list of huggable men.

"Glad to see you," Wes said. "Call your mother. She won't calm down until she hears directly from you that you're safe and sound."

Jake nodded. "I'll call her."

"Chief Sparks," Wes greeted Avery.

"Chief Mitchell."

Avery's expression and tone were purely professional, and she met Wes's gaze directly, but her spine was stiff, and Jake noticed her clenching her fists at her sides.

"Hey, Max." Wes turned to embrace his nephew with a firm thump on the back.

"Hi, Uncle Chief," Max said with a grin.

Avery turned her attention back to Frank.

Jake frowned. Was he imagining the sudden tension in Avery? They all had plenty of reasons to be tense, of course, but it seemed that when his father joined them, her edginess increased. And Wes had hugged both Jake and Max but not Avery. She'd spent hours and hours at Jake's house growing up. Her father had never been around, as far as Jake knew, and he'd always assumed Wes was a sort of father figure to her.

Had something happened between them?

His parents hadn't said anything about any problems between the police and fire departments. It wasn't unheard of in a small town. People disagreed on policy and procedure once in a while, and Avery and his dad would have plenty of opportunities to work together and possibly not see eye to eye.

But if there was a problem, Jake was sure he would have heard about it. His father kept him updated on most city business. Max's dad was on the city council, and Dillon's mom was on every committee in town. Jake would have heard *something*.

Jake watched his father. He was looking at Avery with a strange combination of frustration and sadness, and *that* instantly put Jake on the defensive. What the fuck was going on?

They continued discussions about the immediate recovery plan. Avery kept glancing at the school building and was giving only one-word answers to questions—mostly "Yes." She'd wiped her hands on the butt of her jeans, tucked her hands in her pockets, taken them out, wiped them again.

The other men started around to the other end of the school, wanting to check things out from the inside but not trusting the smashed wall on this side as an entry point.

Jake grabbed Avery's arm, holding her back. "Hey, what's going on?"

"What do you mean?" She shook off his grip.

"You're acting nervous and weird."

"I'm not sure you know me well enough to know if I'm acting weird."

Jake felt a bolt of indignation shoot through him. Was that right? He didn't *know her* well enough? He'd known her his entire life. He'd been obsess—*interested* in her for nearly ten years. Especially the last two. He wondered what she'd say if he reminded her that he knew how her inner thigh tasted, and that she bit her bottom lip just before she came, and that her cheeks got red faster when she was mad than when she was turned on.

But instead of any of that, he said simply, "What did my dad do?"

She stiffened, surprise clear in her eyes. "What do you mean?"

"You and my dad must have gotten into it about something. You started acting nervous as soon as he walked up."

"I'm not nervous around your dad."

"Then what is it?"

"It doesn't matter."

That bugged the shit out of him. It clearly mattered. He couldn't explain why it mattered so much to *him* that his dad and Avery were uncomfortable around each other. But it did.

It was, in part anyway, that it underlined the fact that he hadn't been there, didn't know all the details of his hometown and his family's life.

But it might also have to do with the fact that the woman in front of him didn't want to let him get close. He was great. People loved him, trusted him, sought him out for his advice. But Avery wouldn't even tell him something that had to do with his own father.

They'd had sex a little more than an hour ago, and he still felt like she was holding him at arm's length.

He really fucking hated that.

"Avery, either you tell me what's going on or I'll ask him."

She drew herself up tall. "You go ahead and ask him. I'd love to know what he says."

He reached for her again, but she dodged his hand.

"Look, I have a lot to deal with here," she said. "I haven't seen my friends since the tornado hit, my town is in shambles, and I have personal and professional responsibilities to attend to. You and your dad are pretty far down my priority list, frankly. Thanks for your help during the twister, but I need to get to work. You could do the same, big-shot emergency-management specialist."

She turned and walked off.

Jake watched her go, frustration and desire and admiration all warring for his attention.

Dammit, that woman drove him nuts.

There was no way he was going to be able to leave her alone now.

For the next few hours, he kept track of where she was and what she was doing. At one point he'd pushed her into a chair and handed her a bottle of water. She'd looked at him strangely, but she'd taken it and drained the bottle. Then she'd gotten right back to work. But they didn't speak, they didn't share even a smile, they certainly didn't touch, and Jake found his nerves and patience wound tighter and tighter as the night went on.

By midnight, everyone who was supposed to be in Chance, and the eight guests who had been visiting, had been accounted for. There were six head wounds, two broken bones, multiple other minor injuries, and countless bruises, but relatively speaking, everyone was safe and healthy.

Everyone in town had a meal, clean clothes, and a place to sleep—
even if it wasn't their own food, clothes, or beds.

All in all, a successful initial recovery effort.

Jake lounged at one of the long tables in the social hall of the
Lutheran church with Max and Dillon, all of them working to decrease
their adrenaline levels before trying to sleep. He was nursing a bottle of
water and wishing for something stronger.

"You and Avery in the shed, huh?"

Jake glanced at Max. He was surprised his cousin had waited this
long to bring that up.

"Avery?" Dillon repeated. He'd stayed at the ER helping with injuries until everyone was bandaged up and taken care of. "You get your
kiss already?"

Jake, Dillon, and Max had spent nearly every important moment
of their lives together. Their mothers were triplets, and the boys had
been born within two months of one another. They'd gone through
everything from kindergarten to Little League to basic training together.
They knew all about his history with Avery, and if there was anyone he
was going to spill his guts to, it would be these guys.

Jake glanced over at the cot where Avery had fallen asleep, her
friend Liza on the cot next to her.

Avery had sent the firefighters all home with instructions to report
back at eight a.m. She had eventually agreed to go home to shower but
had been back within the hour, and it had taken another hour before
she would finally lie down.

Jake knew he shouldn't know all that. He didn't know if the other
firefighters or EMTs or cops or city workers had showered or eaten or
were sleeping. But he was acutely aware of Avery.

She lay facing him, and he was grateful for the few minutes to
study her like this. She was so damned beautiful, always, but asleep she
looked sweet and peaceful. Those were two things that he rarely saw
on her face. Of course, when he was around she often looked irritated

or turned on—or both. Jake grinned to himself. He liked her sassy. He liked her hot and greedy, too. Even annoyed. Anything but indifferent. That was the one thing he couldn't take from Avery. There had to be emotion between them—any emotion. He knew he was kind of like a strong-willed four-year-old in that way, but yeah, negative attention from Avery was better than no attention.

"We went out to get more streamers," he finally said with a shrug. "And . . . things happened."

"Things?" Dillon cocked an eyebrow.

"Things," Jake told him. "Like a tornado. For instance."

"You kissed her," Max said. He sat forward, leaning his forearms on his thighs and grinning. "During a tornado. Again."

"She kissed me, actually."

They both raised their brows at him.

"Seriously. She initiated it."

"She walked out wearing only sweatpants and your shirt," Max added.

Yes, he was aware.

"That's a . . . long story."

"Are you satisfied now that you got her naked again?" Dillon asked. He was slumped in the chair across from Jake, his elbow propped on the table beside him.

Satisfied? That was definitely *not* what he was feeling where Avery was concerned. "What do you mean?"

"This obsession with her," Dillon said. "Now that you've been able to seduce her again, are you over it?"

Jake frowned. "I'm not obsessed." And he didn't feel over a damned thing.

Dillon and Max laughed.

"I'm not." But he could admit that it might *seem* like he was.

"Dude, you romanced her at prom and took her virginity on graduation night, and you thought that was something amazing and special. Then she told you she was sorry for the whole thing. That's been driving you crazy for years. Then last summer you kissed her again, and you've spent the past year obsessed with proving to her that she's crazy about *you*."

"Come on. It's not an ego thing." It wasn't *completely* an ego thing, anyway. "I like her. She's beautiful. Why wouldn't I want to sleep with her?"

The guys just grinned.

Jake looked from one to the other. "She *is* beautiful."

"She is," Dillon agreed with a nod. "She's also smart and no nonsense and take charge and kind of funny."

"What she is *not*, however, is crazy about you," Max added. "Which is why you're interested."

"You make me seem like an ass," Jake muttered.

"You're sure it's not *you* who's making you seem like an ass?" Dillon asked. "You're the one who's been kissing and teasing her for a year now."

"You've been thinking about that letter for ten," Max added.

That fucking letter. Yes, it had bugged him. A lot. But he wasn't such an egomaniac that every woman he ever slept with had to end up in love with him.

Probably.

But yeah, the letter haunted him. Not because Avery wasn't in love with him after their night together, but because of the fact that she'd believed she wanted a family—his family—so badly that she would give herself to him because of his last name.

Jake hated the idea that Avery would give herself to anyone for anything less than real feelings and true trust.

"I think my favorite part of the letter was when she said she knowingly used alcohol and your hormones against you," Max said with a wink.

Yeah, Jake knew that sounded ridiculous. When he'd first read it, however, he remembered his heart clenching. He'd known she was making excuses, trying to cover the fact that she'd believed there was something between them when he obviously hadn't.

Then again, maybe she really did believe that. She had no other experiences to compare it to. Avery had never had a boyfriend, never been in love, never even been kissed. Maybe she really didn't know that he'd had every one of his faculties fully functioning, and as soon as he'd realized where the night was heading, he'd stopped drinking. He hadn't wanted to miss, or forget, a thing about it. There hadn't been one thing about their night together that he hadn't been fully aware of and participating in 100 percent.

"Oh, *my* favorite part," Dillon said, "was when she apologized for taking her shirt off." He tipped his water bottle toward Jake in a sort-of salute. "I know you were pretty pissed about that."

Jake shook his head. These men were his best friends?

Surely he could do better.

"Time to shut up about the letter," Jake said.

"Fine," Max said agreeably. "How about we talk about you not kissing her anymore instead?"

Jake shifted in his chair. He wasn't going to stop kissing her. He couldn't. But he did recognize that he was teasing her. He lived in Kansas City. He was committed to big things in places far from Chance. Avery was committed to Chance. She wasn't leaving. So messing around with her every time he came home was kind of an asshole thing to do.

But he couldn't leave her alone.

"She's never once told me to stop or pushed me away," he informed his friends. That was something he thought about a lot. "Not once."

Max regarded him intently. Jake shifted again.

"Seriously man, you're over the whole thing now, right? You got her panties off one more time. Nothing to do with her being drunk or naive or in love with your family. Now you're good, right?"

No, he wasn't good. He wasn't good at all. Because he wanted her. Still. Again. More.

"Hey, speaking of Avery and my family," he said, sitting up straighter, "how come she got all fidgety around my dad today?"

Max frowned. "What do you mean?"

"He said hi to her, but he called her Chief Sparks, not Avery. She called him Chief Mitchell."

"So?"

"Then she got all . . . stiff."

"So?" Max asked again.

"There hasn't been any falling out? Any big issues between departments or anything?" Jake was feeling even more restless about the whole thing, now that he was thinking about it again.

"No. Not that my dad's mentioned, anyway," Max said. "They seemed civil today."

Civil. That was a strange word to have applied to Avery's interactions with one of his parents. There had been a time when Avery had been at his house more than he had, and he'd been convinced that Avery was his mother's favorite child, regardless of blood or biology. She'd spent every day after school with his mother—baking, doing crafts, and having tea parties.

Avery had lived with her grandmother since she'd been very young. Her grandma had earned income from cleaning houses around town, and she'd cleaned the Mitchells' house as long as Jake could remember. Ruth Sparks had been a gruff woman, certainly not polished and sophisticated like Jake's paternal grandmother and not warm and bubbly like his mother's mom. She'd rarely smiled, and she had the rough, husky voice and leathery, wrinkled skin of a serious smoker.

For whatever reason—likely the expense of hiring a babysitter— Ruth had taken Avery with her to clean houses until Jake's mother had offered to keep Avery while Ruth was working. Not too proud to accept help, Ruth had agreed, and Avery had more or less grown up in his home from that time on. She'd been like a daughter to Heidi and Wes.

So what the fuck was going on with them now?

"Let the poor woman sleep."

Jake focused on Dillon. "What?"

"The way you're staring at her, it's pretty obvious you want to go over there and grab her. Leave her alone. At least for now. She's been working her tail off."

Jake scowled at him. "I know that. I wasn't going to wake her up."

"But you are going to pounce on her the moment she wakes up on her own?" Max asked.

"I just want to talk to her."

"Uh-huh. The way you're looking at her does not suggest talking."

He did want to talk to her. Among other things.

"You going back to Kansas City on Monday?" Dillon asked.

"I have meetings Tuesday," Jake said absently. The meetings were in Washington, DC, rather than Kansas City, but he wasn't going to tell the guys about the promotion until he'd signed on the dotted line.

Which he would be doing on Tuesday. If he went to DC.

Jake was set to move into a deputy administrator's position with the Federal Emergency Management Agency. It would mean responsibilities on a national level and a chance to have a much greater influence and impact.

It was exactly the kind of job Jake had always wanted. If helping one person was important, helping twenty was better, and helping twenty thousand was even better. An opportunity to make an even bigger difference than what he was doing in Kansas City seemed perfect.

But right now Chance needed him. And he couldn't shake the feeling that things were not okay with Avery. Those two issues were demanding his attention right now.

That this one woman, who tried not to even like him a lot of the time, was taking his focus away from a new job that would land him on a national stage where thousands of people would listen to him and appreciate him and, dammit, *like* him, was mixing him up and kind of pissing him off. But he couldn't deny that he wanted to be sure Avery was okay before he left.

Typically he could go to his parents' house and grill them about Avery over breakfast in the morning, but with the tornado, he knew they'd both be busy first thing. His mother was helping to make breakfast for half the town, and his dad would be back helping with cleanup and overseeing his policemen and women's efforts.

"Then maybe you need to leave Avery alone altogether," Dillon said.

Jake looked at him. "What do you mean?"

"You're leaving the day after tomorrow. You got a little sugar, now let it go. She's going to be swamped with stuff from the storm, anyway. There's no reason to get her all riled up or try to revisit your shed encounter, is there?"

There were all kinds of reasons to revisit their "shed encounter." Mostly that it had been hot as hell and had stirred up a craving he wasn't sure he was going to be able to get rid of. But also because getting Avery riled up was one of his favorite things about visiting Chance.

"Why are you acting all protective of Avery?" Jake asked. "Is there something I need to know?"

Dillon laughed. "You mean, like, do I have feelings for her, or do we have something going on? I promise you, Jake, if that were the case, I would have already broken your nose."

Jake gave his friend an "Oh, really?" look. "Then what's the deal?"

"She's a nice woman," Dillon said. "I like her. I respect her and you're messing with her."

"She's a big girl. If she doesn't want to 'revisit our shed encounter,' all she has to do is say no."

Dillon leaned in. "So you're not trying to get her to fall in love with you now so you can get revenge for her *not* falling in love with you in high school and being the only single, straight female in Chance to not think you walk on water?"

"You failed your psych rotation in med school, right?" Jake shoved his chair back and stood. He didn't need this. It was time to head over to his mom's for a few hours of sleep.

"I did very well on my psych rotation," Dillon informed him.

"You must be rusty, 'cause you're way off. I don't *need* Avery to be in love with me. She doesn't even need to like me. But if she wants to keep kissing me, I'm not going to argue."

"You need everyone to love you," Max said. "You've always gotten off on being 'such a great guy.'"

"The air quotes make you seem sarcastic," Jake said drily.

Max laughed. "I don't want to *seem* sarcastic. I want it to be very clear that I'm *being* sarcastic."

"You'd think some of my greatness would start rubbing off on you guys eventually, wouldn't you?" Jake asked. "But no. I'm still the lone good guy in this bunch."

They just looked at him.

Dammit, they were right. He needed to leave Avery alone.

He sighed. "I'm satisfied. She was totally into me today." Addictingly so. But it was enough. It had to be enough. "That's all I needed to know."

Max nodded. "Good deal. No more sugar. We're both on a strict diet for the rest of our stay."

Dillon and Jake both froze.

"You're *both* on a diet?" Dillon asked.

"No *more* sugar?" Jake followed up.

Max nodded. "Bree kissed me."

"Bree?" Dillon asked.

"Kissed you?" Jake added.

Max and Bree had known each other all their lives. They'd grown up friends, living next door to each other and sharing a variety of interests like dirt bikes and baseball. They'd tried dating in high school, but apparently knowing each other so well for so long meant there wasn't much room for excitement or romance. They'd broken up after only a couple of months and had gone back to being friends.

Max nodded, looking less than thrilled. "She was out watching the twister with me. Got a little close for comfort, so I threw her in a ditch and got on top of her. Saved her pretty ass and got my head bashed in the process."

"You got your head bashed?" Dillon demanded, coming out of his chair.

"It was just a flying branch," Max protested as Dillon grabbed his head in both hands. "Ow! Fuck, Doc," he said as Dillon probed Max's scalp with his fingers.

"You got stitches." Dillon let Max go.

"Yep. No big deal."

"Your head is the hardest of any I know," Dillon said, still frowning. "Stitches and possible concussions are not 'Oh, by the way' topics of conversation, though, got it?"

"Yes, sir."

"That's Dr. Sir to you," Dillon said. "Dumbass," he muttered under his breath.

Max rolled his eyes.

"Are you going to tell us more about you and Bree?" Jake asked.

"Was it good?" Dillon asked.

"Of course it was good," Max said, looking miserable. "Too good. It's so damned . . ." He sighed. "Complicated."

Jake knew all about complicated. "But it was good?" he asked. "That's something."

Max shook his head. "It's not anything. It's just Bree being Bree. She's an adrenaline junkie. The storm got her all riled up, and she mistook that rush for other kinds of . . . excitement."

Bree was, most definitely, an adrenaline junkie. She climbed mountains and went parasailing and jumped out of airplanes. Jake wasn't at all surprised to find that she'd wanted to go storm chasing with Max and that it had gotten her going.

"You'd better be careful," Jake said with a grin. "Tornadoes in Chance have a way of stirring up stuff you don't want stirred up." He was only half kidding. He'd been stirred up about Avery for a year now because of the last tornado, and this one definitely hadn't helped things. "I kissed a girl during a tornado in Chance, and look at how messed up I am." Getting Avery out of his system didn't seem possible.

"People do crazy, uncharacteristic things when they're in danger or feel threatened," Dillon said.

"Exactly," Max agreed with a nod.

But there was something in the way Dillon said it that made Jake suspicious. He knew these men almost better than he knew himself. Something was up with Dillon, too. "What happened with you?"

"Kit Derby," Dillon said sullenly.

"Kit *happened* to you?" Max asked, perking up. "What's that mean?"

"Kit Derby, a storeroom at the hospital, and her damned body lotion happened to me."

"Whoa," Max commented. "Body lotion?"

Jake agreed with the *Whoa*. "And?"

"We kissed."

Max and Jake waited for more. Dillon said nothing.

"Jesus, Dillon, what the fuck *happened*?" Max demanded.

"She smelled good and we were in there alone and we . . . kissed." Dillon did not look happy about it.

"Just kissed?" Jake asked.

Dillon nodded.

"Well, that's . . . okay."

Except that it was—

"Kit Derby," Dillon said.

Yeah, except for that. Kit was not Dillon's biggest fan. And vice versa.

Dillon and Kit had a long-standing rivalry when it came to . . . everything under the sun. They'd been in competition with each other since third grade, when they'd tied for first place in the science fair. And the spelling bee. And the math contest. It had gone on for years until they'd ended up sharing the valedictorian title at graduation. The story of them trying—and failing—to maturely share the podium was still told.

"She kissed you, too, though, right?" Max pointed out.

"Hell, yeah, she did," Dillon said with a scowl.

"I don't know, guys." Jake stretched his arms over his head and linked his hands at the back of his neck. "This was one of the better tornadoes I've been in." There had been no loss of life, the cleanup was going well so far, and he'd gotten lucky with Avery.

Yep, for a natural disaster, this one ranked pretty high.

CHAPTER FOUR

Avery saw Jake before he saw her. He was taking the steps in front of city hall two at a time, and she took a moment to appreciate the view. The guy did nice things to a pair of faded blue jeans. And not-so-nice things to her libido.

Or *very* nice things to her libido, depending on how you looked at it.

That was exactly the kind of distraction she didn't want.

Dang. She had a meeting with the mayor. She couldn't turn around and leave to avoid Jake.

She'd successfully evaded him all day, and considering her day had started at five a.m., that was saying something. Not that she hadn't thought about him. She couldn't help but wonder where he was and what he was doing. And, most of all, how long he was staying in Chance. But her to-do list had been a nightmare from moment one, and she just counted herself lucky she hadn't run into him before this.

Of course, she'd known it wouldn't last. Chance wasn't big, and she was sure he would have an opinion to offer on the recovery effort. But for the morning, anyway, she'd mostly been able to concentrate on her job without his distraction.

Now that was about to end.

She was headed to the mayor's office for a one p.m. strategy meeting. Maybe Jake was here paying a parking ticket or something, but she knew deep down that the idea that anyone would give Jake Mitchell a parking ticket in Chance was ridiculous. Jake was the town's Golden Boy, a big hero, and part of the Montgomery clan, the biggest and most beloved family in town.

He was here for the meeting. Of course Frank would call in the big emergency-management specialist.

If she could set foot in city hall without getting worked up about the last time she and Jake had been in the building together, she would even agree that having his input could be a good thing.

She'd loved seeing him in action last year. He'd been unruffled and assertive, yet concerned and caring at the same time as he surveyed the damage and made recommendations for the recovery effort. He'd made everyone around him feel calm and confident. Including Avery. He not only had made suggestions, but had rolled up his sleeves and gone to work beside everyone else. Just as he'd done last night. Of course, that thought always led to the memory of day two, when she'd arrived at the morning's strategy meeting, excited to see him, only to find out he'd left at the crack of dawn.

She slowed her steps and waited until he'd opened the door and gone inside to continue up the marble stairs and into the long hallway leading to the mayor's office.

But she heard their voices as she approached the door. Jake was in there flirting with the mayor's administrative assistant, Robyn.

The door was open and Avery hesitated outside. Dang, she didn't want to go in there.

Then she heard the giggle. Ah, Shelby was here, too. The mayor's wife. The mayor's twenty-seven-year-old wife.

It was a true testament to how ingrained in Chance and well liked Frank Harvey was that he could weather the scandal around marrying a woman twenty-eight years his junior. Of course, it helped that he'd grieved his wife long and hard after she'd died, and raised his boys through their teenage years on his own. It also helped that Shelby was very hard not to like. She was bubbly, full of energy, a total optimist, and also from Chance. It helped that she was part of the Montgomery family as well—Jake, Max, and Dillon's first cousin. Heidi and her sisters also had a brother, Patrick. In addition to being Shelby's dad, Patrick was president of one of the banks. And one of Frank's golfing partners.

It was weird.

But it worked.

Somehow.

Avery took a deep breath and stepped into the office.

"Oh, good, you're here!"

She was greeted with a warm hug from Shelby.

"Gawd, Avery, you look so cute," Shelby said, stepping back and looking Avery over. "I could never pull off that hot, in-charge look. I mean, you're wearing khaki pants and a white button-up shirt—and those *glasses*—but I look at you and think, 'That girl is totally in charge.'"

Avery subconsciously pushed up her glasses. Hot, in-charge look? She was conscious of the fact that she was a woman in charge of a bunch of men, and yes, she thought about that in how she presented herself. But hot and in charge was not exactly the look she was going for.

"Uh, thanks?" Avery hoped she was the only one who heard the question mark on the end of that.

Shelby turned to Jake. "Doesn't she look like she's ready to take on the world?"

Why was she asking Jake? Avery swung to face him, then regretted it. She hadn't looked at him directly since walking into the room. On purpose.

He lifted an eyebrow, clearly amused, and she knew that not looking at him had been the right choice. She wanted to kiss him. Just because he was standing there.

"I, too, have found Avery to be both bossy and cute at the same time. On more than one occasion."

She blushed. And wanted to kick him. While still wanting to kiss him.

This was exactly why she'd hoped to avoid him altogether.

Of course the first thing he said to—or *about*—her had to be in reference to the shed.

Shelby looked from Avery to Jake and back again with a pleased smile.

That was strange.

"Thank you for the compliment, Shelby." Avery chose to ignore Jake for the moment. "I'm here for the strategy meeting with Frank."

"Of course," Shelby said. "Everyone's waiting for you."

"*Everyone's* waiting for me?" If Shelby was a part of the meeting, it wasn't a straightforward status update and next-step planning session.

"Well, you and Jake."

Yep, figured.

Shelby gave her a smile and turned toward the inner office.

Frank rose from behind his desk as they stepped into his office. And dammit if Shelby wasn't right—*everyone* was waiting for them.

Bree McDermott, one of Avery's friends, but more important, the lead officer on the police force, was there. Kit Derby, the town's psychiatrist, was there, too. Avery gave them both smiles. She wasn't surprised to see them. But in addition to the girls, Dillon Alexander and Max Grady were also in attendance.

Avery shot Bree a questioning look, but Bree shrugged to indicate she didn't know for sure what was going on, either.

"Thanks for coming in," Frank said as Shelby went to stand beside him. He put an arm around her waist, and she snuggled into him.

A lot of people had, of course, thought their relationship was strange and suspect. Some believed Shelby was after Frank's money. Some believed Frank was going through a midlife crisis. An extended midlife crisis, apparently. But no matter how Shelby's perkiness and sweetness made Avery's teeth ache, she had never seen anything other than a love match. She saw how they looked at each other when they didn't know anyone was watching.

Avery wanted someone to look at her like that.

"We're going to burn the first bit of debris Wednesday night," Frank announced.

Avery looked at him, then Shelby, waiting for more explanation.

"You want the department to build and light the fire," she guessed. That made sense. But she wasn't sure it required a formal meeting. They would be burning debris for several days to come.

"Of course. We'll wait until right after dark. The city is providing hot dogs and marshmallows," Frank said.

Avery frowned. "Hot dogs and marshmallows?"

Frank nodded. "Jake suggested we make it a town bonfire. We'll get some music out there, have some food, make it a little party."

Avery turned to look at Jake. He was leaning against the bookshelf that ran the length of Frank's office. He gave her a smile.

"A bonfire?"

"It's a way of turning the negative into something positive," Jake said.

"You think people will enjoy watching their things burn?"

"Their things that have been ruined. It's a way of starting fresh, letting go, smiling even when things aren't going your way."

Avery sighed and turned back to Frank. "I think it's too soon."

Jake pushed away from the bookcase. "It's never too soon to start feeling better."

"I disagree," Avery said, crossing her arms and refusing to look at Jake.

"I'm shocked." He almost said it under his breath. Almost.

Avery felt the tension coil through her body and risked a glance at Jake. Instead of focusing on Frank like she was, Jake was watching her. His eyes held frustration but also a challenge.

Avery gritted her teeth and turned back to Frank. "Let them mourn a little. They need to let things sink in, to process everything." She looked at Kit. "What do you think?" This was her specialty, after all.

"I think people are feeling very downtrodden right now," Kit answered. "I agree that we need something to bring everyone together, to show that we're in this as a community and that they have the city officials' support."

Avery gritted her teeth harder. Dammit. When Kit said it, it made sense. Which meant that Avery was reacting to all this purely emotionally and letting *her* desire to not need Jake for anything affect her decisions for the town.

She needed to pull it together.

And she was sure Kit, as her friend and a shrink, agreed.

Avery gave Kit a wide-eyed look, and Kit mouthed, *"You okay?"*

If she were being honest, she had to shake her head at that. She was definitely not okay.

"We're not talking about burning family albums or books, A," Jake said.

His use of the nickname made her want to smack him. Or maybe it was his placating tone. He didn't need to treat her like a child. Or like one of his team members who needed his guidance. She was his equal here. In fact, *she* technically outranked *him*. She was in charge of emergency management for Chance. He was a visitor.

"We're talking about junk," he went on. "We can make sure most of it's from public buildings if that makes you feel better. But it's a way of bringing everyone together and getting them back on their feet, showing them it's not so bad. They don't need to let things sink in. They've been through this before."

"Yes, I'm aware," Avery said tightly. "*I've* been here the last two times this has happened."

Jake took a step closer to her, a curl to one corner of his mouth. "I was here last year, if you remember."

As if she *didn't* remember. "For what? About ten hours?"

"You're annoyed that I'm giving recommendations about recovery here in my hometown when it's my job to do this for other cities every day?"

"Chance *was* your hometown. You're from Kansas City now, remember?"

"Chance will always be my home."

She wished that he would *act* like it if that were really how he felt. She snorted to cover that reaction.

He arched an eyebrow. "Chief Sparks, is it my recommendation that bothers you or the fact that it's *my* recommendation that you don't like?"

She took a step toward him. "Both. Recommendations are great, *Sergeant Major* Mitchell. Exactly what I would expect, as a matter of fact. That's what you do, right? You recommend, you advise, you write, you lecture, you bask in the attention. But you don't really *do* anything. Long after you've gone home, we'll still be digging out, cleaning up, and trying to rebuild."

He stepped closer. "I bask?"

She lifted her chin. "Yes, you certainly do."

"Is that right? I was getting my hands pretty dirty yesterday."

She blushed hot and hard. "That is not what I'm talking about, and you know it!"

"If you're referring to the shed, then that's not what I'm talking about, either," he said, a smug smile in place.

Avery felt her mouth drop open and her face get even hotter as she realized he was serious. She'd misunderstood his comment because *she* couldn't stop thinking about the day before. And she'd just admitted to him—and to their little audience—that those thoughts were overriding everything else.

Speaking of their audience . . . Avery glanced around, having forgotten for a moment that there was anyone else in the room.

Bree and Max were standing together, whispering while watching Jake and Avery raptly. Dillon was clearly amused and had no intention of intervening. Kit's eyes were wide, but Avery knew the mental-health specialist was analyzing every word. Frank and Shelby looked strangely delighted.

She took a breath, but before she could say anything, Jake went on.

"After I got your pretty butt out of that shed, I was chainsawing and digging and working—"

"One day!" With his one sentence, she was again fully focused on Jake. She took the final step that put her directly in front of him. "It's been *one day*. You'll leave tomorrow or the next day, and we'll still have a lot of chainsawing and digging and working to do."

He stepped in, nearly on her toes. "Why do you care if I'm here?"

"I don't." Or she wished she didn't, anyway.

"You want me to leave right now?"

"I want you to not show up in the first place if it's not to *stay*." She realized she was going to regret some of the things she was about to say, but she couldn't stop herself. "You think you're this big super-hero, but you know what I've always noticed? That when Spider-Man chases that big lizard through the city, he might save a few people from becoming lizard food, but he makes a hell of a mess in the process. Then he smiles and waves and accepts the applause, then goes home and has milk and cookies with Aunt May and leaves everyone else to clean up."

There was a glint of something that looked like anger and amusement at the same time in Jake's eyes. "So I'm like a superhero to you."

Infuriating. That's what he was. "You're like . . . a tornado. You sweep through, touch down for a minute, then leave with a huge damned *mess* behind you."

Oh, boy, *that* was pretty much a huge, obvious confession of her feelings for him. Avery didn't have to look around the room to know that everyone had noticed.

Besides, Avery was too caught up in how Jake was staring at her. There was desire there that stirred something deep in Avery's gut. And pure satisfaction. Like she'd just confirmed something he'd known all along.

Dammit.

"The only person I seem to mess up is you," he said. "Why do you think that is?"

"Why do I even talk to you?"

"Because you can't help it. For the same reason you can't help—"

She narrowed her eyes, daring him to finish. He could say kissing him, he could say sighing when he touched her, he could say taking her clothes off with him in a shed. She couldn't help any of those things. She flat-out couldn't help responding to him. And he clearly knew it. But if he pointed it out now, it would prove that he cared more about his ego than her reputation.

"—wanting to smack me."

She let out a breath. And stared at him. He *did* care about her reputation? Had he just protected her? And why did that make her feel warm at the same time it irritated her? Because the idea of Jake protecting her made her want things she knew she couldn't have. Mostly *him*.

She tried to project the irritation instead of the longing she was fighting. "I should—"

A sudden shrill whistle cut into their argument.

Avery and Jake both froze, then turned toward the sound. It had, amazingly, come from Shelby. Her cheeks were red and she was clearly upset. She had disentangled herself from her husband, and Frank had, probably wisely, taken a step back.

"Enough!" Shelby exclaimed.

"Shel—" Jake started.

"No, I'm going to talk now." The usually bubbly blonde planted her hands on her hips. "This town *is* going to get back on its feet. Right now. We are going to clean it up, it's going to look *better* than it did before the storm, and *everyone* is going to do it with a damned smile on their faces."

Avery risked a glance around the room. The other two women were staring at Shelby with shocked expressions. No one had ever seen the perky, sweet Shelby riled up like this. It was sort of impressive. Even Shelby's cousins stood up straighter at her words, not a smirk in sight, looking like they were about to salute.

"Chance needs to rebuild, and we have to do it quickly," Shelby went on. "The Bronson family from Kansas will be here to see the farm and check out the town in two weeks."

That quickly focused everyone in the room. Shelby was absolutely right. That visit had to go perfectly. Avery had been past the farm that morning. It was a huge mess. Definitely not in any shape to make a good first impression on the Bronsons.

"If we don't get this town put back together, they are going to pass on the farm deal, and we're all going to be screwed. Plus, my favorite aunt is sad," Shelby went on, referring to Gigi Montgomery, the CEO of Montgomery Farms for the past thirty years. "She's sad about the farm and her hometown and the fact that she's letting everyone down because she can't keep up anymore. I don't like Aunt Gigi being sad or feeling bad about anything. So we are going to rebuild Chance, and we're going to make sure that everyone is happy and upbeat and optimistic while we do it."

She looked each of the people in front of her directly in the eye, and Avery felt her spine straightening, too. Damn, this girl had some sass when it came down to it.

Shelby looked a little calmer. "And you all know this is about more than just the farm to the Bronsons. It's about the town—where they're going to live, go to church, send their kids to school. Each of the brothers has a wife, and one has three kids, one has four. We *really* want them to like it here. We *all* really want them to like it here. Right?" She met everyone's gaze again, one by one.

One by one, they nodded.

Avery agreed that making the Bronsons fall in love with Chance was hugely important. No question.

"This town is going to be like a Norman Rockwell painting," Shelby said. "It's going to be that all-American small town where everyone wants to live and work. And *you* are all a huge part of that." She took a deep breath. "You all have jobs that lend themselves perfectly to this rebuilding. However, more than that, you are all models of this community. Everyone here knows and likes you. They look to you for leadership and as a gauge for how things are going. You're young and successful, and you all grew up here and care how this turns out." She narrowed her eyes. "Which means you are all going to be on your best behavior. You are going to act like you like one another. You're going to cooperate and support one another."

Avery felt sheepish. Shelby was right. She and Jake arguing was hardly professional. It wasn't mature, and it was definitely not what they should be focusing on right now.

"You're right," she told her. "Jake and I will make an effort to get along when we see each other."

"Oh, you're going to need to do more than that," Shelby said. "You're going to see each other, a lot, on purpose."

Avery blinked at her, trepidation building without her fully understanding why. "We are?"

"Guys, Frank and I would like to formally ask you to stay in Chance for a couple of weeks to help out. We need the hands, and we can really use your experience in mass disaster situations," Shelby said to her cousins.

The guys all nodded. "Of course, Shel," Max said. "Happy to stay."

"Yeah, you can count on me," Dillon said.

"Me, too," Jake added.

A couple of weeks? No! Avery would never survive two solid weeks of Jake.

"And Avery and I will be seeing each other?" Jake asked. "I believe you said *a lot*?"

Avery had to squelch her first instinct to rise to his teasing. She had *just* acknowledged that she and Jake needed to try to act like grown-ups.

"You're going to be working together. Jake is an expert in disaster recovery. You are *our* expert," Shelby said to Avery. "It makes perfect sense that you would spend time together working on the recovery efforts. It will make the town feel completely secure and optimistic to know that you two are in charge."

She turned to Bree and Max. "Just like it makes sense for you two to work together. Chief Mitchell wants to put Bree in charge of more of the emergency-management efforts for the police department, and Max can teach you everything he knows. Max will be primarily in charge of building inspections and rebuilding, but, as the weather expert, you'll also be in charge of addressing questions about the storm itself."

She finally looked at Kit and Dillon. "Everyone knows that you're two of the smartest people to ever graduate from Chance. And you're both in health care. Knowing that you're teaming up for the physical and mental well-being of the people will make everyone feel completely at ease."

Smiling at them all, Shelby said, "Instead of talking about how they lost their special assortment of Christmas ornaments that they collected for almost thirty years or how they can't find their granddaughter's favorite doll or how their rocking chair was found in their neighbor's evergreen tree, they're going to be talking about all of you—how the guys have stayed to help their hometown recover and how amazing you women are, taking charge and leading the way, and how you've all teamed up to pull us through this. I am *sure* that you can find things to appreciate about each other," Shelby said, her tone indicating that they *would* find things to appreciate about each other.

"Yeah, for, like, an hour at a time," Dillon said.

"More like fifteen minutes," Kit muttered.

Dillon looked over at her. "Really? That's how you remember it?"

She looked down at her nails. "I barely remember it at all."

What was Kit talking about? Kit wasn't looking at her friends, and Bree only shrugged when Avery looked at her questioningly.

"I'd rather have them speculating about you and Dillon in the hospital storeroom during the tornado than wondering if their insurance is going to cover," Shelby said to Kit.

"What happened with you and Dillon in the storeroom?" Bree asked, swinging to look at Kit.

"Nothing," Kit said with a bit too much emphasis to be believed.

Dillon just ran his hand over his face. Max and Jake grinned widely.

In an attempt to save her friend—fully intending to get the whole story later—Avery jumped in.

"But we have a ton of positive things going on already," Avery pointed out. "People helping one another, people supporting one another, the celebration of no lost life. This morning Mrs. Miller found the Garrisons' family Bible under her porch and returned it to them. That's positive."

"Yes, it is. And so is six of the most well-liked and well-respected citizens of Chance making a team of pseudo-superheroes who are going to save their town. You're like Chance's very own Avengers," Shelby said with zeal.

Dillon started to speak again. "Shelby, I—"

She turned to him. "Dillon, if I want you to dress up like a clown and juggle flaming batons in the town square to make Aunt Gigi smile, you will do it and *thank* me afterward for the opportunity."

Dillon raised an eyebrow. "I was just going to say that I'm happy to help."

Shelby nodded, pulled her purse strap up on her shoulder, kissed her husband on the cheek, and started for the door. "I know" were her parting words.

There was a moment of silence. Then the door shut behind her with a resolute *thud*.

"What just happened?" Kit asked.

There was a chuckle behind them.

"You think an EF4 packs a wallop?" Frank asked. "You've been hit by a storm otherwise known as Shelby."

"We didn't stand a chance, did we?" Avery asked.

"Nope," Frank said cheerfully.

Jake didn't mind this turn of events one bit. Working with Avery for the next two weeks? Yeah, he was definitely okay with that.

When Avery said she had to get back to work and started for Frank's office door, Jake gave in to the urge to follow her out.

"I'll find you later," he said to Max and Dillon. "I'll call you," he said to Frank. By the time he got into the hallway, he had to jog to catch up with Avery.

"Hey, hang on." They needed to talk about this, didn't they? Or talk about *something*? The last time he'd seen her—okay, he'd been seeing her here and there around town—but the last time they'd talked, she'd told him he was "pretty far down" her priority list.

Well, that had now changed. They were working together now.

For a moment he remembered the unreturned e-mails on his computer and the three missed phone calls. Those were work, too. If he was staying in Chance for another two weeks, he was also going to need to reschedule the DC meeting.

He should go. He could go to DC and then come back. He could go to the interview and miss only a day of work in Chance.

But he didn't want to miss a day.

He could put off the interview for another two weeks. If they really wanted him, the job would still be there.

"I've got stuff to do." She didn't stop walking.

She also pulled her hand away when he tried to grab it.

Oh, really?

He glanced around and located an open door to an empty room. He reached out and grabbed Avery's belt and pulled her to stop.

"Hey!"

He turned her and pushed her into the room, stepped in behind her, and kicked the door shut.

"Jake!"

It was an empty conference room from the looks of it. He still turned her so her back was against the door so no one would come barging in.

Then he braced a hand on the door beside her ear.

"We're supposed to like each other and get along."

"So?"

"So running away from me doesn't really make it seem like you like me."

Avery slumped against the door. "You put her up to this, didn't you?" she asked. "You asked Shelby to help you come up with some way that I have to be around you all the time and put up with all your . . . stuff . . . so that you can see if I'll keep reacting to you and your . . . kissing and . . . touching."

She was cute when she was so worked up that she stumbled over her words.

Jake leaned in a little and dropped his voice. "Honey, you've been *reacting* to my kissing and touching for a long time now."

He felt the corner of his mouth start to curl at the flash of fury in her eyes.

Yes, he pushed her buttons on purpose.

But it was *so* easy. And the results were awesome.

Avery was a gorgeous woman.

When she was pissed, she became downright mesmerizing.

He would know.

"I thought I could do this. I thought it might be a good idea for everyone to see us working together. But I don't know if it is, after all," she finally said, shaking her head.

"This is absolutely going to work," he told her. "All this requires is you acting like you love everything about being with me whenever we're together. Oh, look, you already do. Piece of cake."

"I do *not* act like I love everything about being with you whenever we're together."

"You sure about that? I could do a public-opinion poll—"

"I have too many other things to worry about," she said. "I don't have time to play around with you the whole time you're here."

The idea of her playing around with him was just too damned tempting.

"You heard Shelby and Frank—this is going to be good for the town to see us getting along and working together. Our relationship is as important—maybe more so—than all that other stuff you think you need to do."

"The things I *think* I need to do?" she repeated, her eyebrows nearly at her hairline. "You mean my *job*? Keeping this town safe? Doing what they pay me to do?"

"No one's asking you to shirk your duties," he told her calmly.

Her pulse was drumming at the base of her throat, and her breathing was quick and shallow. Her cheeks were pink, too. She was worked up, but he knew it wasn't about the idea of not getting all her work done.

It was because of him. Because he was standing so close now.

In fact, he'd maintained the theory for a while that she acted ticked off and frustrated with him in order to hide the physical reactions that came from something else entirely.

He knew how he could prove it.

Jake leaned in. "You still get to be the hot, in-charge fire chief," he told her. "But now you get to hang out with me while you do it. Think of it as a job perk. Handed down from the mayor himself."

Her eyes narrowed, but the pink staining her cheeks deepened, and her lips parted as she breathed in and out. It might look like anger on the surface, but then why did she let him move even closer, and put one hand on her hip, and dip his head, and touch her lips with his without a single protest?

In fact, she sighed as their lips met fully and she put her hand on his chest.

Jake angled his head, increasing the pressure of the kiss, but it wasn't until Avery's tongue licked out along his lower lip that he slid his hand into her hair, held her head in his palm, and *really* kissed her.

Avery whimpered softly and her hips arched into his. Jake pressed her against the door, his fly hard against hers. She wrapped a leg around his, and her hands went to his shoulders, pulling herself up his body until she balanced on tiptoe on one foot.

Voices in the hallway on the other side of the door finally pulled them apart.

He reluctantly let her go, allowing an inch of air between them as Avery settled back on two feet and slid her hands from him.

He didn't give her any more space than that, though. He watched her eyes.

"This is going to work," he repeated. "You like me just fine."

She pressed her lips together. "I'm about to step out of a conference room at city hall with my hair undone, my shirt wrinkled, and my lips red."

Satisfaction coursed through him. Damn right she was. Everyone who saw her would know exactly what had happened in this room.

He got to her. Not her job, not her frustration with Frank or Shelby, not the stress of the recovery efforts—no. What got Chief Sparks breathing hard and itchy was *him*.

"We are working closely together on a project that means a lot to both of us, and we drive each other crazy," he said. "In lots of ways," he added gruffly, his gaze dropping to her lips.

She blushed at that.

"This is going to be interesting and distracting, just like Shelby said," he told her.

"It's supposed to be interesting and distracting to the *town*," she said softly. "Not to *us*."

He felt the smug grin stretch his lips at that mini confession.

"I'll tell you what." He stepped back, watching her straighten her shirt before she turned to open the door. "You don't have to tell me thank you *every* time you have fun while I'm here. One general 'Jake, you're amazing' at the end will be fine."

"Yeah," she said, pulling the door open and stepping into the hall. "You should totally hold your breath for that."

But she did let him fall in step beside her as they left the building and headed out to fix their hometown.

◆　◆　◆

"You're violating one of the top ten rules," Bree said as she scraped a chair away from their lunch table at A Bar and plopped into it.

She was out of uniform so was apparently no longer on the clock. Of course, since the tornado had hit, everyone was technically on call 24-7.

Kit took her seat. "I don't know what you mean," she said calmly.

Kit did everything calmly.

As usual, the contrast between the two women she called friends struck Avery, and she shook her head. Bree scraped and plopped; Kit was graceful and calm. Bree was in a wrinkled T-shirt and cutoff denim shorts with flip-flops, her curly blonde hair in a messy ponytail. Kit was dressed in a red pencil skirt and a red-and-white blouse. Her dark hair was straight and sleek, and her makeup was flawless.

"You *do* know what I mean," Bree said. "Something happened between you and Dillon, and I want to know what. You *have* to tell me. One of the top ten rules in girl friendships is you *always* dish about the guys. Hell," she said, sitting back, "that might be rule number one."

"I'd just like a break from everything," Kit said. "I was hoping for a nice lunch with the only two people in this town who might be able to talk about something other than the tornado."

"But we're still teaching Avery how to have girlfriends," Bree said. "You're being a terrible role model, Kit."

The idea that Avery needed to be tutored in how to have girlfriends had started the night they'd first drunk margaritas together almost three years ago. After the third margarita—or had it been the fourth?—she'd confessed to not knowing how to be a friend to a woman her own age. They'd decided to teach her—including lessons in how to gently tell your friend her new hair color was horrible; how to be properly sympathetic about an unexpected weight gain; and when to drop everything, gather the chocolate, and show up on someone's doorstep even when the someone said she wanted to be alone. Over the years it had become an inside joke, but in all honesty, their lessons were some of the best things in Avery's life.

"Maybe there's nothing to tell," Kit said as the waitress set their regular drink orders down.

Bree snorted at that. "Please. The sexual tension in Frank's office this morning was . . . wow. *I* almost needed a cold shower after."

Avery laughed, then took a deep, contented breath and felt some tension unwind from her shoulders and neck. She couldn't believe this was the first time she'd had a chance to sit down with her friends. Things had been crazy in town, and though they'd exchanged quick phone calls and texts, they had all been fully focused on the immediate needs of Chance. But no matter what else blew into town, she could always count on Bree and Kit to be exactly what she expected.

Bree was outgoing and direct and funny. She was that friend who would tell you honestly if your new jeans made you look fat. But she was also the friend you could tell to back off, and she would do it and not be the least bit offended.

Kit, on the other hand, had been a little tougher for Avery to warm up to. Kit was, frankly, intimidating as hell. She was the smartest woman Avery had ever met, and she was cool and sophisticated. She was even a little prissy—something Bree told her all the time.

They both amazed Avery. She loved the way Kit always had her shit together, but she equally loved that Bree didn't . . . and that Bree owned it.

Avery liked to think she fell somewhere in between the two personalities. She was neater and more organized than Bree, but she was never as put together as Kit.

Kit sipped her iced tea. Then she took a breath. "Fine. We kissed. In the storeroom at the hospital."

Bree slapped her hand down on the table. "I told you I had a sex dream about Max, and you didn't tell me that you'd *kissed* Dillon?"

Avery sat forward. "You had a sex dream about Max?"

Bree nodded. "After we made out in the ditch."

"You made out in the ditch?" Avery repeated. "What ditch? When? *What?*"

Bree grinned at her. "Look who's suddenly chatty," she teased.

Avery was definitely the quiet one of the group—though with Bree around it was impossible to be the loud one.

"What ditch, Bree?" Avery asked.

"You didn't say you'd made out," Kit added.

"I was going to tell you, but Frank's office was the first I'd seen you, and then everyone was there. But I wanted to tell you," Bree said. "I *needed* to tell you."

"Are you okay?" Kit asked.

Bree laughed. *"Yes,"* she said with enthusiasm. "I want to do it again."

"The making out in a ditch?" Avery asked.

Bree grinned at her. "Well, the making out, anyway."

"It was good?" Kit asked. "With Max?"

"It was," Bree said with a nod. "But don't for one second think that you're going to distract me from the fact that you and *Dillon* kissed." She turned to Avery, *"That* is not cool. We get to know about kisses and stuff, got it?"

Right. Great. Avery was very ready to talk about kisses and stuff.

"It's not a big deal," Kit said. "We were in the same storage room taking cover, it was a small space, and our emotions were running high. It was a stupid, spur-of-the-moment thing."

"But was it good?" Bree asked, a twinkle in her eye.

Kit rolled her eyes but said, "It was Dillon Alexander. He's good at everything." She definitely sounded more put out than turned on by that.

Bree and Avery shared a grin.

"I'm sure you were good, too, honey," Bree teased Kit, patting her hand. Kit had to be good at everything, too. Especially the things that Dillon was good at.

"So now you're going to tell us more about you and Max?" Kit asked Bree, clearly trying to redirect the conversation.

"How much detail do you want?" Bree asked. "I can give you length and girth measurements if you want." She held up a hand, fingers curled to make a circle. A big circle.

Kit laughed. "Not necessary."

Avery grinned in spite of her whirling thoughts. Bree was the proverbial open book. There were very few thoughts and emotions she didn't express. Avery wished she could be a little more like that. She was learning. The longer she knew Bree, the easier it seemed to get. But she wasn't quite to the point where she would just blurt out, *I had sex with Jake*. As much as she wanted to.

"Well, I cannot give *you* length and girth measurements. Let's leave it at that." Kit lifted her iced tea again.

Bree grinned and grabbed her bottle of beer. "I'm sorry to hear it." She took a big chug.

Avery chewed on her bottom lip. The girls would never believe that she wanted to talk. About boys. She barely believed it herself. But she'd been hoping this lunch would go like their usual ones. Bree would notice something was up with Avery and would coax everything out of her with a barrage of questions and humor. Kit would listen to all of it and then ask thought-provoking questions that would lead Avery to understand something about herself she hadn't before.

Now it seemed that Bree and Kit were both pretty distracted by their own stuff. And Max and Dillon.

Avery couldn't help but grin at that.

"I finally ordered that new couch," Kit said, setting her tea down and opening a menu.

"The urine-yellow one?" Bree asked, also grabbing a menu.

"Yes." Kit didn't let Bree's brashness get to her. Which was fortunate. Bree had a lot of brashness.

"Are you going to paint the room?" Avery asked. She had to participate in the conversation, even if this was not the topic she'd been hoping for. She was the quiet one of the group most of the time, but they'd know something was up if she said nothing at all.

"Yes," Kit said.

"Please tell me you're going to use blue or green. Something interesting," Bree said. "Your house cannot take one more beige wall, Kit. Seriously."

"I was thinking about a teal color," Kit said.

"Yes, thank God," Bree said enthusiastically.

"A *soft* teal. Light. Nothing too bright," Kit said.

Bree leaned in. "Let me pick it out."

"No."

Bree bounced in her chair a little. "Come on. Trust me. Throw caution to the wind. Tell you what, I'll do the painting. You let me pick the color and I'll do the whole room. You can leave the beige wall behind when you go to work, and when you come home, your life will have some color in it."

Kit shook her head, but she was clearly trying not to smile. "I don't think so."

"This way you won't have to work up a sweat or risk chipping a nail," Bree said, getting into her pitch.

"I'm hiring painters," Kit said.

"What?" Bree slumped back in her chair. "No. Come on. I'll charge you *half* of whatever they're making you pay."

"You would charge me?" Kit asked, obviously amused.

Bree tipped her head. "Cookies. You can have me for cookies."

Kit laughed softly. "Does Max know that?"

Bree gave a mock scandalized gasp. Then grinned. "Doesn't everyone know that?"

The waitress arrived to take their order, after which they chatted about silly things—Kit's new shoes, Bree's split ends, the fact they all deserved a full-body massage and pedicure followed by a sixteen-hour nap.

Avery felt her nerves building minute by minute. She wanted to talk about Jake. More specifically, she wanted advice about Jake.

Finally, as Bree stole a third fry from Avery's plate, Avery took the plunge. "So, I don't want to break any girlfriend rules."

Bree nodded as she chewed. "Good girl. What's up?"

"Jake and I had sex in the shed behind the school during the tornado." Okay, so maybe she could blurt it out.

Bree started coughing, and Kit pushed her water glass closer as she gave Avery a look that was surprised and concerned at the same time.

"You and Jake had *sex*?" Bree rasped before Kit could say anything.

Avery bit her bottom lip and nodded.

"*During* the tornado?" Kit asked.

"Actually, right before it," Avery clarified. "We were . . . done . . . and got under the workbench during the actual tornado."

"You stayed out in the shed?" Kit asked. "That doesn't seem safe."

"That's what you're focusing on?" Bree asked her. "Seriously? Clearly they made it out alive. Let's get to the good stuff."

Avery felt the tight band around her chest loosen. This was what it felt like to have girlfriends—people who cared about your safety during sex and during a tornado, and especially when the two were combined.

"So you're not surprised?" Avery asked.

Bree laughed. "No. Are *you*?"

"*Surprised* is not the word, no," Avery said honestly.

"What is the word?" Kit asked.

Avery thought about that. "The first word that comes to mind is *stupid*."

"Stupid?" Bree asked. "The sex was stupid?"

"The sex wasn't stupid," Avery said with a grin. She was so thankful that these women could make even this topic seem better. "My giving in to the sex was stupid."

Kit seemed to be considering that. Then she shook her head. "I don't think so. I think it's a good thing."

Avery perked up at that. "Really?" She would kind of like to think that sex with Jake was a good thing.

"Yeah, I do. The last time—the only time—you slept with him, it was your first time, and you had this big thing about his family and forever built up. It was huge. I think you've been carrying that around, and it's allowed Jake to get to you and to even hurt you more than it should. And he's been messing with you for a year. Now you've had sex again and you realize it's no big deal, nothing major is attached to it, it's just great sex. And now, Jake won't be able to get to you anymore."

Avery took it all in. She had to admit that part of her was leaping for joy and saying, *Yes!*

If only the other part of her that was saying, *He still gets to you*, and, *It's still big*, would shut up.

Kit squeezed Avery's hand. "Jake Mitchell is just a guy."

Avery nodded.

"Say it, Avery," Kit said.

She took a deep breath. "Jake Mitchell is just a guy."

Bree was watching them both with narrowed eyes. "Okay, now how about you, Doc?" she said to Kit.

"How about me, what?" Kit asked, focusing on her straw and stirring her tea.

"How about a little 'Dillon Alexander is just a guy'?" Bree prodded.

"Of course Dillon Alexander is just a guy," Kit said. But she didn't take her eyes off the straw.

"Uh-huh." Bree looked from Kit to Avery. "I think you're both full of crap. At least I own the fact that this tornado was more fun than I've had in a while."

Kit scoffed at that. "And I was just thinking that as far as tornadoes in Chance go, this one was one of the worst."

Avery didn't know what to say.

They were both right.

All she did know was she needed dessert.

CHAPTER FIVE

"Actually, it would be fantastic if the governor didn't come for a visit," Jake said into the phone Monday morning. It was already his third call of the morning, the state patrol was waiting to meet with him, and he had a message to return a call to his mother about how the ladies at the Methodist and Lutheran churches could be involved.

It was busy and crazy and chaotic.

And he loved it.

And Jake was fairly certain that the number one reason Frank Harvey was happy to have him in town was that Jake was willing to make and take the phone calls and meetings Frank didn't want to deal with.

Frank was a hands-on guy. If there was cleanup to do, he wanted to be right there beside the people he led. It wasn't a ploy to get votes. It was who he was and the reason he would never have to do anything more than say, *Sure, I'll be the mayor*, to get reelected. Sitting in meetings wasn't Frank's thing, and he'd pointed out that all of this—coordinating resources and agencies, identifying needs and getting things mobilized and in place—was Jake's expertise.

Indeed, it was. Though Jake worked primarily for the state of Missouri and more specifically for the city of Kansas City, he consulted with other cities and states on a regular basis. He had the contacts, the knowledge, and the experience. So Jake had taken a seat behind Frank's desk, picked up the phone, and gotten to work.

He'd already talked to the local and state-level Red Cross and had plans to call the governor's office and Nebraska National Guard directly if his current call was unproductive. Jake wasn't afraid to use his friendships and his history with the Guard.

"You're kidding, right?" said Andrew Pierson, who was Jake's counterpart in Nebraska as the director of emergency management for the state. The men had met a number of times and had a good working relationship.

"We're looking to downplay all of this," Jake said. "We don't want the tornado to get any more attention than it's already gotten."

Unfortunately, it was impossible to keep the local and state media from covering the tornado and its aftermath. Chance had been on the news for the past day and a half, and that morning's *Omaha World Herald* had a full-page story on them.

Jake hoped the Bronsons weren't subscribers.

Of course, The Weather Channel had sent a reporter as well.

Thankfully, Max was the perfect guy to talk to the media. Jake knew about storms and the destruction they caused, but Max was the cloud-formation, air-current-updraft guy.

"It's an EF4, the tenth in the same town." Andrew chuckled. "I think it's going to get attention."

"It will get less if the governor stays away," Jake snapped.

"I'll tell him. But it's an election year."

Right.

Photo ops, especially of the governor being supportive and encouraging to a downtrodden little town, would be precious. But Jake knew Governor Mike Thomas. Jake had spoken about emergency preparedness and disaster management at summits and in one-on-one meetings throughout Tornado Alley. He had bonded with the governor of his home state over football and crop talk, and Mike had called Jake for a second opinion on some things Andrew had been pushing when the Missouri River had flooded two years ago.

"I've got the troops on standby," Andrew said, referring to the National Guard. "You can have fifty soldiers this afternoon."

Jake shook his head. "I need a hundred. We've got most of what we need covered. We've got food and water and shelter taken care of. But we need utilities back on and cleanup done fast."

If the director of emergency management told the governor that Chance needed more National Guard in, it would happen. This was procedure. But Jake was happy to put the call in himself.

"A hundred?" Andrew asked. "We sent 250 into Kearney four years ago."

Kearney was six times the size of Chance, and Jake understood what Andrew was saying. But Chance needed those troops. "If you want to send 250, I'll put them to work."

Andrew chuckled again. "They'll be tripping over one another in Chance."

Jake smiled. "I'll settle for the hundred, then."

"How about I come out tomorrow and check things out?"

Jake's smile died. They didn't need support from the Guard for *security*; there was no looting going on in Chance. They didn't need search-and-rescue or temporary shelter or ready-to-eat meals. The city's water was still on. There were areas without power, but more than half the town was still connected. Jake worked with the Guard all the time and knew they had any number of things to offer a community in crisis. Fortunately, Chance didn't need most of their resources.

But Chance needed bodies and their ability to use power tools and put stuff together. Besides, Jake loved the feel of having the National

Guardsmen on scene. The uniforms alone brought a sense of security and comfort. When a local unit showed up, people knew these were men and women from the area, and they brought a sense of community and hope with them. They were there to make things better, to do whatever needed done. Simply being there mattered.

"No offense, but no matter how good you are, you can't take the place of fifty National Guardsmen. I'm telling you, if we're not back on our feet in two weeks, this town won't survive." He paced to the window and filled Andrew in on the economic impact to Chance if the town and farm weren't cleaned up fast. "Help me get this done."

"Fifty can help you get that done," Andrew pointed out.

"You're right. If I didn't have a tight timeline. But I need this all done in two weeks. Less if possible." Jake sighed. He knew a hundred National Guardsmen was a lot to send to one little town that was, more or less, already getting back on its feet. "Look at it this way—you send a hundred now, they get done fast and they're out of here in half the time it would take fifty to get done. It's the same amount of money and resources either way."

"Fine," Andrew finally agreed. "A hundred it is."

Jake felt the triumph surge, but he said firmly, "Tomorrow."

"Yes, tomorrow."

And that was why Jake Mitchell was called upon when things needed to get done.

They disconnected, and Jake watched the activity in the town square below Frank's office window. There was a long folding table set up under some trees, manned by volunteers from one of the churches. The women behind the table had multiple sign-up sheets in front of them. Some were people offering assistance, others were for requests for assistance. Things like clothing, tools, and trucks were being offered up, along with time and muscles. All useful, valid things. But the disorganization was making Jake a little crazy.

He had to grin, however, when he saw Max on the steps of the gazebo. He'd been roped into meeting with a group of students from the University of Nebraska. Max had thought he was going to be talking to, and showing off for, a bunch of wannabe storm chasers. In actuality, they were science students interested in meteorology who wanted to study the weather phenomenon around Chance and make a short film.

"There is no weather 'phenomenon,'" Jake had heard Max say to the group on Jake's way into Frank's office. "These tornadoes have formed like any other. There is no scientific explanation for why Chance keeps getting hit. There's nothing unusual here in the topography, the geology, the atmosphere, nothing."

Jake had grinned and quickly gone several yards out of his way to avoid walking past the group. His cousin would have most definitely tried to pull him into that conversation. Then left him there alone with the students.

But Max wasn't fooling anyone. He loved to talk about that stuff, and it didn't matter the audience.

Jake's phone rang and he glanced at it. He'd been using Frank's lines for most of the Chance-related calls, but several of his contacts had his cell number.

This call wasn't about Chance, though. This was a DC number.

He took a deep breath and accepted the call. He couldn't keep avoiding them completely.

"Mitchell," he answered.

"Sergeant Major Mitchell, this is LeAnn in Senator Conrad's office."

Conrad was one of the senators from Missouri. "'Morning, LeAnn," Jake said, making sure his voice sounded friendly. He'd met LeAnn on a couple of occasions and knew that charm would go further with her than the firmness he'd just used on Andrew. "How are you?"

"Fine, thank you." He could hear her smile. "Senator Conrad would like to confirm that you'll be in DC tonight as planned. He would like to meet you for dinner."

Nick Conrad was thrilled that Jake would soon be in the FEMA deputy administrator's position. He'd been a fan of Jake's for a long time. Not only would it look good to have a guy from his own state's emergency-management department moving up, but Nick knew that Jake was the best man for the job.

No doubt Nick intended to give Jake a pep talk as well as some advice for his interview.

"I'm sorry, LeAnn, I'd planned to call you later on. I won't be coming to DC this week, after all."

"Oh, the senator will be sorry to hear that. Can I tell him why?"

Jake told her about Chance and the tornado and that he hoped to reschedule the interview.

"I'll be sure to let him know," LeAnn told him.

"Yes, and also mention that I'm swamped here. I probably won't be answering calls on this number for the next couple of days." Jake knew Nick would be calling him immediately after hearing that Jake was postponing the interview. He would, no doubt, ask Jake a bunch of questions Jake didn't know how to answer. Like why Jake was so sure this tiny town in a state where he was not on the payroll couldn't survive without him for twenty-four hours.

He disconnected with LeAnn and silenced his phone's ringer as he paced to another window that looked out over Main Street. Multiple buildings had windows blown out and pieces of their roofs missing. Trees had been uprooted, street signs bent, and two cars overturned. But even shaken up and broken, the sight of the street that represented the heart of his hometown sent a powerful wave of nostalgia through him.

The signs of recovery and healing also made his heart swell. The cars were now back on their wheels and being towed, the missing windows were boarded up, and replacement glass was already going in down the block. A group of roofers climbed over the tops of the buildings across from city hall, and others took chainsaws to the trees.

Jake shook his head, shaking off the feeling of homesickness that had hit him.

It looked like a lot of work was going on, but it was unorganized, and efficiency was suffering. For instance, to get the cars off the street, the trees had to be moved. But the tow truck was there anyway, hooking up the cars and then sitting and waiting for the chainsaws to do their work.

There were people boarding up windows in the building right next door to where the glass was being replaced. Rather than putting wood and nails to use there, they could have been helpful in rebuilding the doorway to the florist shop that had crumpled when one of the flipped cars crashed into it.

Jake sighed. There were a lot of people working hard, but they weren't working smart.

It was going to make him nuts.

There was a knock at the door, and Sheriff Blaine of the state police came in.

Jake and the sheriff talked briefly, but they needed little support from the state patrol. Troopers were keeping their eyes on people coming to town—reporters and gawkers and volunteers from other towns alike. One of the highways into town was being detoured because of some farm equipment that had gotten tossed onto the road, but that would be cleared up by the end of the day. When Blaine left, Jake went to the window again.

The guy with the tow truck sat watching three guys work on the trees blocking his path while a woman two doorways down was struggling with a ladder.

Heaven forbid the guy get out of his truck and lend a hand.

Jake jammed his cap on his head and stomped out of Frank's office. Enough phone calls for the morning. There was work to be done.

His first stop was across the street, where he not only positioned the ladder for the woman at the flower shop, but also climbed the ladder, unhooked the torn awning, and pulled it down for her. Then, with a glare at the man in the tow truck, Jake headed for his truck.

The initial work that needed to be done was pure physical labor. Cutting, hauling, loading, digging. Streets needed to be cleared first so they could get vehicles moving around town to load debris and gather furniture, clothing, and other salvageable items from family homes.

Jake manned a chainsaw and loaded and unloaded his truck for a good four hours, but he eventually found himself back at Command Central. Big surprise. Sure, he wanted to be a part of the effort and yes, this was where the food was. But more than that, the command center in the gazebo in the town's square was where Avery was.

He'd been thinking about her all day in spite of how busy he'd been. He knew she'd been working nonstop as well. As the fire chief and primary emergency-management director in Chance, Avery had a lot to do. She was coordinating the cleanup efforts, inspecting the damage, keeping track of what had been done and what was left, prioritizing tasks, and assigning personnel from her crew and the rest of the city departments.

But he missed her. And he now fully intended to remind her that Shelby and Frank had essentially ordered them to work together. He wasn't in the town square now because he needed a new assignment or a sandwich. He was here because he was drawn to her—over and over again.

It was a pleasure to watch her work. Not just because she had a glow about her as she organized and strategized. Not just because she had tied up her hair in a quick, messy bun that made him think about how her hair would look first thing in the morning after being kept awake a lot of the night. Not just because he loved the contrast between the woman in the white button-up shirt and khaki pants today and the woman wearing the silky, hardly-there thong Saturday night in the shed. But because it was clear she loved what she was doing.

She was good. When he'd been a civilian-affairs specialist in the Guard, his expertise had been in identifying the needs of citizens affected by combat or crisis situations and delivering personnel and supplies effectively and efficiently. There wasn't anything about Avery's decisions in directing the emergency responders and the volunteers that he would have done differently. It was rare he found someone whose capabilities he could trust as completely as he trusted his own.

The disorganized array of requests for, and offers of, assistance was now divided up into work teams, each focusing on a different portion of the cleanup and orchestrated so that they could efficiently get their work done in a way that would assist the other teams, keep the teams out of one another's way, and avoid duplication.

He was impressed. All he would need to do tomorrow when the National Guard showed up would be to plug them into the established teams, giving them more manpower and expanding what they could get done.

Or maybe he'd let Avery plug them in. Not only her crew and city employees, but everyone working cleanup and recovery was listening to her. She was creative and personable even as she was making demands, she gave more praise than she did direction, and she listened as much or more than she talked. All the signs of a good leader.

That was why he found her interesting. That was the only reason he was intrigued.

Yeah, sure.

But she was doing a hell of a job.

It seemed clear that his father agreed.

Wes had, as expected, been out of the house that morning by the time Jake had come down for coffee and cereal. But Wes now stood off to one side, listening as Avery outlined a plan to gather debris that could be burned in one of the pastures about a mile from the high school where the fire department would oversee the process.

Jake made his way to his dad's side. "How's it going?"

"Good." Wes put an arm around his son's shoulders. "All things considered, of course."

"Right."

They listened to Avery and a few of the crew talk about some chemical-spill cleanup needed at the school and in one of the mechanic garages downtown.

"She seems to be on top of things," Jake commented casually.

Wes nodded. "As usual."

It was a compliment, of course. The kind of thing that Jake would have expected his dad to say. But Jake itched with the sense that something wasn't right between Avery and his parents. And he intended to find out what was going on.

Avery's mom had been very young when she'd gotten pregnant and had left Avery with her mother to raise. Heidi had stepped in to help with Avery fairly early on. Jake didn't remember a time when Avery wasn't a part of their household. He and Avery had never been close. They'd barely even been friends. But Jake had been thankful for Avery.

She'd made his mom happy and, frankly, had distracted Heidi from Jake and his shenanigans. He'd had the freedom to ride horses, swim in ponds, dig in the dirt, and go on adventures with Max and Dillon. He loved Heidi dearly, but he had no desire to spend time baking or gardening or talking about books or watching old movies. Avery, on the other hand, had eaten it all up. She'd been Heidi's little shadow, and his mother couldn't have been more thrilled.

Jake knew he'd been a miracle baby. His parents had had a difficult time conceiving and had almost given up when his mother's morning sickness had started. He'd been cherished and spoiled since day one. But they'd always wanted more children, and Heidi had made no secret of the fact that she would have loved to have a daughter, too.

Avery had been that daughter.

"She's doing a good job as chief?" Jake asked his dad.

"Absolutely."

Jake looked at his father. There was something in Wes's expression that looked almost like pride.

"Do you ever tell her that? I bet she'd appreciate it." If Avery had questionable motherly influences growing up, she'd had *no* father figure other than Wes. She'd spent most of her time with Heidi, but Wes had been around, too, giving Avery the unconditional support he was known for.

Wes shifted, his arm dropping from Jake's shoulder. "I congratulated her after she was elected chief. Your mom and I showed up at the reception. Avery didn't have time to talk."

Jake frowned. That sounded absurd. "She didn't have time to talk? What do you mean?"

"I mean, she said thank you after I said congratulations and then told us she didn't have time to talk and walked away."

Jake looked at Avery, then back at his father. "Did something happen between you and Avery?"

Wes sighed. "Things are different than they used to be," he admitted.

"Different how?"

"She and I work together, of course, but she's always very professional, always focused on the job. She and your mother will have small talk if they run into each other. But it's clear Avery doesn't want the relationship we used to have."

"What *happened*?" Jake insisted.

"Everything changed when she left Chance."

"When she left Chance?" Jake repeated. "That was *ten years* ago."

Wes nodded, watching Avery instead of his son. "She chose fire-fighting. Went to fire school and started working in Omaha. She didn't come back to Chance until she found out your grandfather was retiring."

"But she's been back for two years, Dad. Every time I've asked you about her, you and Mom have given me vague answers, but you always made things sound okay. When I pushed once to know more, you said that there was nothing to worry about."

Wes didn't say anything to that.

"Do you know what I thought that meant?" Jake asked. "I believed that everything was good. That *she* was good. That you saw her . . . that you were looking out for her."

Wes swallowed hard. "I know. And I promise you, I *was* looking out for her."

"But you didn't see her. She didn't come to dinner. She and Mom didn't shop or bake. Or talk."

There was a long pause before Wes said, "No, she and your mom don't do any of those things."

"*Why?*"

Wes shook his head. "It's been Avery's choice."

"But Mom—"

"Jake." Wes cut him off. "Avery should be the one who tells you. If she wants you to know."

Jake looked at the gorgeous redhead across the room.

He'd been so focused on making sure she couldn't ignore *him* when he was around that he hadn't paid much real attention to her.

And he'd made a lot of assumptions. Because those assumptions made him feel better.

Jake had imagined Avery at his mother's dinner table on a weekly basis. He figured they had lunch and shopped together occasionally. He'd pictured her in meetings with his father, making joint decisions about Chance. He'd also imagined his father putting his arm around her and telling her she was doing a great job, and her flushing with pleasure at having made Wes proud.

Basically, he'd pictured her having the ongoing, loving, supportive relationship with his parents that she'd always wanted. That she'd hoped to get by dating him even back in high school.

He'd imagined her having everything she wanted in spite of the fact that he'd left and gone on to his own things.

Her relationship with his parents had never included him before. Heidi and Wes were part of the foundation of Chance and were never going anywhere. Now that Avery was here, an integral part of Chance herself, why couldn't she have all those things she'd dreamed of—Christmases with them, birthday dinners, Wes helping her with car repairs, Heidi giving her advice about home decor?

She could have had it all. Even without him.

What the hell was going on? It made him feel . . . unsettled . . . to know that there were things about his family—and yes, Avery—that he didn't understand.

He didn't like that one bit.

"Gentlemen." Max joined them.

Jake wasn't sure if he was disappointed by the interruption or relieved. This was a lot to delve into, and if his dad said it was Avery's story to tell, then Wes wasn't going to tell Jake anything.

It was quickly evident that Max wasn't his usual jovial self. He wasn't grinning; he wasn't cracking jokes or saying inappropriate things.

Seeing a chunk of your hometown leveled took a little bounce out of a guy's step, and Max had been out in the thick of it all day. After escorting the students around town, he'd helped with some of the building inspections—homes and businesses alike—ensuring they were safe for people to return to or tagging them as unsafe.

Apparently there were more that were unsafe than he'd hoped for.

Max definitely knew how to be serious. He'd been in New Orleans after Katrina, he'd seen his share of tornado cleanups, he'd consulted twice in California after earthquakes, among many others. But all that serious stuff made him even more determined to have a good time and see the fun, positive things in life whenever he could.

"How far did you get?" Wes asked.

"Not as far as we wanted," Max admitted.

That was the other thing that got to Max, to all of them—not getting things done the way they wanted to. They all understood, maybe better than most, that there were a lot of things out of their control. Weather, for one. The choices and actions of people intent on hurting others, for another. But that only made them all want to control anything and everything they could.

"I can give you a couple of my guys tomorrow," Wes said.

"We'll take them."

"How are things going with Bree?" Wes asked.

Max straightened. "What do you mean?"

Jake and Wes shared a wide-eyed, amused look.

"She was excited to learn more about building inspection and repair from you," Wes said. "Has she been helpful?"

Max evidently realized he'd overreacted to the initial question. He cleared his throat. "Fine. It's all . . . fine."

Wes chuckled. "With anyone else, I'd warn them that Bree can be a handful, but I don't have to tell you that." He clapped Max on the shoulder.

"Yeah, thank—"

Someone yelling cut off Max's response.

"Chief Mitchell, you have to help us!"

Jake, Max, and Wes swung toward the young voice.

Wes stepped toward the panting young boy who had clearly come running, literally, to find Wes. "What's going on?"

The boy looked to be about twelve. There was another, slightly younger boy behind him, looking nervous, too. Jake knew who they were immediately. They looked like their dad, Tim Hubert, the star shortstop on their championship baseball team their senior year.

"Chief." This voice was female.

Bree, in full uniform and full frown, had come up behind Wes. *When it rains, it pours,* Jake thought.

Wes turned from the boys. "What's up, Bree?"

"Altercation on Main. A tow-truck driver got into it with some guys who are doing the tree removal."

"Okay, I'll be right there," Wes said before looking back to the little boy. "Brody, what do you need?"

"Kayley won't come out of our house."

Wes's frown deepened. "What do you mean?"

"She thinks our dog is still in there."

Wes sighed.

"We can help Brody out," Jake said, indicating him and Max.

Wes nodded. "Brody, this is my son, Jake, and his friend Max. They went to high school with your mom and dad. They're soldiers. They're going to help you and Kayley."

Brody's eyes had widened at the word *soldiers*. They got that a lot.

"Thanks, son," Wes said as he started toward Main Street with Bree.

"No problem." Jake turned to Max, who was watching Bree go.

Max clearly had it bad. Jake shook his head. He knew the feeling.

"Let's go." He looked at Brody. "I'm going to grab my bag from my truck, then we're right behind you."

Brody nodded, his wide eyes filled with concern and fear.

Jake and Max each ran to their trucks to retrieve the backpacks that they both had in their trucks at all times, which held the essentials, including flashlights, water bottles, and hand tools.

"We're ready," Jake told Brody a minute later. "Let's go."

He didn't like that these kids had been out running around by themselves. There was a lot of debris that probably looked like it would be fun to climb on or in but that could end up being very dangerous. There were also a lot of structures that needed to be cleared before *anyone* walked under or in them.

"What are you guys doing out tonight?" he asked as they jogged along with Brody and the other boy.

It wasn't late, but it was starting to get darker, and with all the trucks and skid loaders roving the town, the drivers wouldn't be thinking about looking out for kids.

"I'm supposed to be babysitting them," Brody told them. His voice was laced with worry. "Our mom's helping with food at the other church, and Dad is out of town until tomorrow. We're supposed to be asleep at the church."

Ah. They were out of their house and sleeping on the cots in one of the makeshift shelters. That sucked. It sucked for everyone, but maybe especially for the kids. Kids needed the comfort of familiar surroundings and routine.

Oh, who was he kidding? Everyone needed that to some extent.

It was going to be a while before there was anything like a usual routine in Chance. Jake knew the town wouldn't fully settle down until things were back to normal. People would work in shifts, but there would be around-the-clock activity. Everyone would have trouble sleeping.

"Kayley snuck out?" Max guessed.

"Yeah," Brody said. "But I know where she went. She won't stop talking about Cooper."

Cooper was, Jake assumed, the dog.

"We couldn't find him after the storm. She thinks he's stuck somewhere in the house."

"How old is Kayley?" Jake asked.

"Six."

Dammit.

Two minutes later, they all skidded to a stop in front of a big two-story house four blocks from the square.

To the untrained eye the house looked fine. But Jake and Max knew that the twister could have shifted the house on its foundation even though it still stood. A few inches would be enough to make it unstable.

Max pulled a high-beam flashlight from his bag. "Nobody goes in but me."

"I'm going with you. It'll be faster," Jake said. He also pulled out a flashlight and some rope. If there was a dog in that house, it might be tough to "convince" the animal to come with him.

"Just give me a minute."

"If that little girl's in there, it's not gonna matter if you think the place is unstable," Jake told him. "I'm going in there to get her."

Max sighed. "Fine."

"Stay here," Jake told the young boys in a voice that had commanded National Guard units. The boys nodded dutifully.

Jake and Max approached the front door with caution. "So far, so good," Max commented.

The front door seemed to be level and shut tightly. There were no cracks or obvious shifts on the porch, doorway, or the windows on this side of the house.

Max checked the door. It was locked.

He glanced back at the boys. "How'd she get in?"

"From the back," Brody said.

Max and Jake exchanged a look, then headed for the other side of the house.

"I'd like to edit my assessment of the situation," Max said as they rounded the corner.

"Glad we have your expertise here," Jake said wryly. "Otherwise how would we know when a house is structurally unstable?"

Where the front of the house had looked untouched, the back was an entirely different story. For one, there was no back of the house any longer. The house looked like one of those dollhouses that had no back wall so you could see into the rooms. The roof had been lifted off, and the sides of the house were angled in. Windows were broken; furniture, clothing, and belongings were scattered; and most of the second floor was resting on the first.

"Dammit." Max started forward.

Jake was right behind him.

"Kayley!" Jake called as he neared the rubble blocking the living room. He scanned the pile of debris, gauging the best way to go over it. In the descending dusk it was hard to know if there were nails or ragged pieces of metal or glass. He wanted to find the girl, but he preferred to do it with minimal bloodshed.

"Kayley!" Max shouted. "We're here to help you!" Max looked over at Jake. "Do you smell any gas?"

Gas leaks were a very real poststorm threat. As were frayed electrical wires. Add them together and a tornado wasn't the only thing that could level a house.

"No, but it's pretty wide open here. Are the gas and power shut off in this area of town?"

Max lifted his phone to his ear and asked that very question of whoever answered. He shook his head at Jake. "Damage was limited here. They recommended shutting off each house rather than the whole section of town."

"Can we find out if that was done?" Jake put a foot up gingerly on a big piece of drywall. He pushed gently with the toe of his boot and found it was solid. He stepped up on it.

"We can try." Max pulled on work gloves and shoved two wooden beams out of his way.

"But we don't want to wait for that," Jake filled in. "Right."

They intended to find the little girl and her dog and get them away from the house. They'd worry about electrical wires and such when the sun was up and visibility improved. As long as there were no people—or dogs—in the house, the gas and power were secondary concerns.

"Kayley!" he called loudly. "Are you here?"

"Help!"

Jake and Max both froze.

The little girl's voice came again. "Help!"

"Kayley! Where are you?" Jake called out, climbing over the pile of junk under him with less care now. Some of the debris shifted, and his ankle twisted slightly. He fell to the left, catching himself with an out-stretched arm on the seat of a kitchen chair. Well, half a kitchen chair.

"I'm under the stairs!"

Dammit. Jake's eyes and flashlight beam both focused on the staircase.

Well, half the staircase.

"Kayley, don't move!"

The top several steps had been stripped off and thrown across the yard. The banister had been split down the middle, the top half hanging precariously, still attached by a few splinters and nails.

There was a little door that opened into the storage space under the steps, but the shift in the staircase had crumpled the door. However, there was no need to go through the door to get into the space—there was a gaping hole at the back where the rest of the staircase should have been. Unfortunately, that gaping hole was blocked by what appeared to be a bed. An entire king-size bed, complete with thick oak frame and headboard, on its end, blocking all but about three inches of the hole.

He got to the bed and shone the light into the space behind it. "Hi, I'm Jake," he said to the little girl who peered out at him.

She stared at him. She was a miniature version of her mother, Kristine Tompkins. Jake had taken Kristine to the homecoming dance their freshman year.

"I'm here to help you get out."

"Something else might fall and hit me," Kayley said.

"You were already in there when the bed fell?"

She nodded. "I thought Cooper was hiding in here."

Good lord, that bed could have squished her like a bug. Thank goodness she'd been out of the way. The intact portion of the staircase was a fairly secure place to be. Unless a bathtub or something decided to plummet from above.

"Cooper's in there with you?" Jake put a shoulder against the bed and shoved.

The bed was heavy. And jammed against the wall on the other side. Fuck.

Her big eyes welled with tears, and she shook her head. "No. I can't find him."

Dammit. "No problem. We'll get him." He turned away from the bed. "Max! We're going to need a saw over here."

"Got it!"

"Cooper will come back here." Kayley sniffed. "He'll be scared and try to come home."

"Then we'll keep coming back to check," Jake said. "But honey, you can't stay here."

"He'll be scared if we're not here."

"But he's smart," Jake told her. "He'll know that you can't stay in a house that isn't safe. He'll be coming back here to check on you, and he'll be glad you're not here."

The tears ran down her face.

Dammit. He hated when girls of any age cried.

But before Jake had to come up with anything else, Max showed up with a chainsaw and a crowbar.

"This is going to get loud," Jake told her. "I need you to move up to the front of that space and then turn away and cover your head. We're going to get you out."

Kayley did as she was told, and Jake applied the saw to the thick wood bed frame. He cut through the headboard and one corner of the frame, then Max took hold and yanked. They opened a gap big enough that Kayley could slip through.

"Okay, sweetheart, come on," Jake called into the opening.

She didn't reply.

"Kayley? Time to go, honey."

He heard a sniff, but nothing else.

Awesome. They hadn't cut a big enough opening for him or Max to fit through.

"Kayley," he said firmly, "you have to come with us. Now."

He heard a shuffling and shone the light into the space. She'd turned to face him. Her eyes sparkled with tears, but she started taking steps toward him.

Huh, looked like his sergeant-major voice worked on one female, at least.

Kayley stopped out of arm's reach. He sighed.

"What about Cooper?" she asked.

"I told you, he wants you to be safe."

"I want him to be safe, too."

"I know you do. But I need *you* to be safe right now." Jake stretched his arm though the gap. "Come on, Kayley. I'll buy you ice cream."

"I don't want ice cream. I want Cooper."

Jake sighed.

"Tell her you'll find the dog," Max hissed to him.

Of course that seemed obvious. Tell the scared, sad little girl that the big, tough, in-charge man would find her dog. She'd believe him. She'd trust him. She'd come with him.

But then he'd have to find her dog.

"What if I can't?" Jake hissed back to Max.

"At least she's out and safe."

Fuck. He'd done this before. He'd made promises in the heat of the moment, when that was all he had, when he didn't have any other options. Then he'd failed to keep his promise. The family had gotten out safely. Their grandson had not.

"Kayley," he said, putting as much confidence in his tone as he could, "I will do everything I can to find Cooper. But I can't do anything until you come out here with me."

There was a long pause, then she took two steps, putting her close enough that he could grab her hand and pull her the rest of the way out.

Kayley wrapped her arms around his neck and let him pick her up and carry her out of the house.

"Thanks for finding Cooper for me, Jake," she said against his shoulder.

Dammit. He'd said he'd *try.* But yeah, she'd heard what she needed to. Women learned that selective-hearing thing early.

"You bet." He ran his hand over her hair. What was he going to say? What was he going to *do?* Try to find her dog, of course.

"Let's get you home," Max said, taking her from Jake's arms.

She wrapped her arms around his neck, too. "You're going to tell my mom about this, aren't you?"

Max patted her back. "Yeah, kiddo, 'fraid so."

They made it back to the church, where Brody and the other boy, Danny, got Kayley settled onto her cot as their mother showed up. It was easier relating the story, since the happy ending was right in front of her. Still, Max and Jake got hugged again.

"Thank you, guys," Kristine said, her voice thick. "God, I shudder to think what could have happened."

She was dirty and clearly tired from helping with the recovery efforts.

"That's what we're all here for," Max assured her. "To help one another out, right?"

She gave him a wobbly smile. "Right."

Kayley was nearly asleep, but she lifted her head as the guys said good-bye.

"Jake?"

He leaned over her. "What is it, honey?"

"We're goin' to my gramma's tomorrow. When you find Cooper, will you keep him safe for me till I get home?"

She blinked her big green eyes at him and gave him a sleepy smile, and he sighed. He was a sucker for big green eyes.

CHAPTER SIX

He had to be trying to find a little girl's puppy, didn't he?

Avery got into her car, resisting the urge to check her reflection in the window or her hair in the rearview mirror.

She was ticked at herself for being all stirred up over Jake. She could at least cling to her delusion that she didn't care how she looked tonight.

It was Wednesday, and he was supposed to be back in Kansas City, and she was supposed to be getting over his most recent visit. But no, he was still here, and she was on her way to meet him at the bar for a drink.

She'd only agreed because he'd asked her in public with witnesses. She couldn't turn him down. They were supposed to be getting along, working together, putting the town back together.

Truthfully, he'd only said he wanted to talk to her and that they should get together before the bonfire. She'd been the one to suggest a public place. Otherwise, they would have had to meet at her house or his mom's. There was no way she was letting him into her house. The last thing she needed was to make memories of him in her personal space. His mother's house was completely out as well. Avery couldn't possibly set foot in Heidi's home and not break down sobbing.

So, she was on her way to the bar.

It wasn't until after she'd suggested it that she realized she couldn't win. It didn't matter if she saw him in the town's square, or in Frank's office for the daily update meetings, or at someone's house, or in the bar, or in his mom's house—it was *all* messing with her.

Yes, all her pushing and tensing and sarcasm were to cover her real reactions to him. Big shock. She even suspected he knew it. But she was very comfortable with pretending that she didn't know that he knew that she was completely affected by him.

Not only had she been anticipating seeing him tonight, she'd been hearing about him, seeing him, *thinking about him* all damned day. Jake couldn't simply cut trees, haul debris, or shovel dirt. No, he had to go around town doing all of those things *and* trying to find a little girl's puppy.

God.

It would be far too easy to fall for a guy like that.

Avery had held herself together as the third person asked her if *she'd* seen the dog as she'd been surveying the town. She hadn't rolled her eyes; she hadn't sighed in exasperation; she hadn't said, *Of course not. If I'd found a dog, I, too, would have been sure to return it to its owners.*

But if one more person—especially a female person—commented on how *sweet* it was that Jake was combing the town for little Kayley Hubert's dog, Cooper, Avery was going to scream.

Because, yeah, it really was sweet.

But it wasn't like Jake was the only person capable of doing something nice around here. Or heroic. There were heroic things happening everywhere they looked, but everyone noticed Jake. Jake, who approached every situation with an enviable combination of calm, confidence, and humor.

Anyone in town could cut trees and load pickups. But Jake made people laugh and look on the bright side as they did it.

She'd run into him at Crystal and Jay Singer's place. Jake had looked at the leveled garage and said, "I think this is the perfect time to get that three-stall garage you've always wanted, Jay." When Jay had mentioned that he didn't have anything to put in the third stall, Jake had said, "Then it's also the perfect time to buy yourself a golf cart."

He'd also been at Mary Wilson's on Cranberry Lane when Avery stopped over. Jake had told Mary that she should build a gazebo where the toolshed of her late husband, Cliff, no longer stood. Jake had added he thought a birdhouse and birdbath would be perfect by the gazebo, since Cliff had loved birds.

Avery had gotten a little choked up as Mary cried and kissed Jake's cheek.

He'd build the damned gazebo himself if needed, she was sure.

Avoiding him as much as possible seemed like a great plan. When she was around him, she was supposed to be his professional colleague, his teammate in rebuilding Chance, maybe even his friend. She understood why all of that was important. But truthfully, she was most comfortable when she was acting like she couldn't stand him. Or when she was having sex with him. This in-between stuff, the making nice but not making *out*, was going to drive her nuts.

But avoiding hadn't worked. At all. He'd been at the high school when she'd stopped there, too. She could have sworn he'd planted a GPS on her somewhere to keep track of her. Except that he only gave her a simple wave when he saw her. He didn't rush to her side, he didn't say anything flirtatious, he didn't make a point of speaking to her at all.

Not that she cared. In fact she preferred it. Acting unaffected was much easier when she wasn't near him. She'd convinced herself that she was happy to not have his attention when she'd made her next stop at the city park and sporting complex where they were going to have the bonfire. He wasn't there. It was the first place she'd been where he hadn't shown up.

Which was great.

But then, just as she was believing she was relieved to have a break from him and his charisma, she'd seen his truck at the Methodist church. *Of course he'd be there.*

She'd pulled in. Not because of Jake's truck, of course. One of her crew members had asked her to stop by. But she didn't *mind* that Jake was there, too.

Then he'd brought her a sandwich.

Instead of the simple wave he'd been giving her all day, he'd approached her when she was done talking to Jeff and handed her a sandwich.

"I'm guessing you haven't eaten all day," was all he said.

She thought that was all it was going to be, but then he'd leaned in and kissed her cheek.

The sandwich was ham salad and *not* her favorite. Yet there she stood, watching him walk away, feeling a little . . . affected.

Avery pulled into the lot and parked her car beside the restaurant and bar known simply as A Bar. The real name of the place was Sorry Mom, We Bought A Bar, the tongue-in-cheek name the twin-sister owners had come up with when their mother said, "Can't you do something more important with your life?"

Avery stayed in the car for a moment, breathing deeply. This was going to be fine. She didn't disagree that Chance could use some fun, something positive to get caught up in, something to take their minds off the cleanup and insurance claims they were dealing with. Just that morning, she'd seen a reference to Chance on the news. Words like *devastation* and *heartbreak* had jumped out at her.

Was a bonfire with toasted marshmallows only a few days after the twister too soon? Maybe. Did it seem that they weren't taking the disaster seriously and were making light of the losses? Possibly. Was a truck driving around town, filled with ice, bottled water, and Gatorade and blasting fun party music as people cleaned up a little overboard? Yes. But was Chance devastated or heartbroken? No. Chance was a wonderful place with warm people who'd been hit by a wave of bad luck. Period.

Avery could get behind anything that made the people of Chance smile and hope for the best. And if that included having a drink with Jake in the most public place in town and being civil, respectful, even *friendly*, then she was in. No matter what havoc it might play with her emotions. Not to mention her hormones.

Avery finally got out of the car and started up the sidewalk from the parking lot to the front door of the bar.

As long as she and Jake kept their hands to themselves in private, things would be fine.

Or avoided being in private together. Yes, that would be even better.

She shook her head.

Jake was just a guy. A good guy. A hot guy. But just a guy. There were other good, hot guys in Chance. More important, Jake was a good, hot guy who lived three hundred miles away, who visited Chance four times a year, and who had a reputation and personality that would no doubt take him even farther from Chance in the future. Jake was destined for great things. Big things. Things much more important than Chance. And her.

She needed to *not* let him under her skin. She needed to not daydream about his kisses. She needed to not get all tingly when she saw him smile, or go all soft when she heard he was looking for a puppy. She needed to—

"Hey."

She needed to *not* feel all warm and . . . affected . . . when he said one-syllable words.

She took a deep breath and turned. "Hey."

"We need a story." He took her upper arm in his big, warm hand and pulled her around the far corner of the building.

She was, of course, instantly reminded of the way he'd backed her up against the door in the conference room.

That had been kind of private. As was this.

"A story?" She had to keep her cool. Jake had always picked up on the slightest sign from her that she was reacting, that he'd had an effect.

"About what happened in the shed during the tornado."

She met his gaze, the memory of what had happened in the shed playing in her mind like an erotic film.

Dammit.

If she let her guard down and got any closer—and she'd essentially promised the mayor and Shelby that she would do exactly that—it was going to really suck when Jake left town.

Because he would leave.

And she'd still be here.

"Why do we need a story?"

"There were a lot of people at the school who saw us go out to the shed together and then come out with you in my shirt and me without a shirt."

She was instantly assaulted by the memory of how Jake had looked—and felt—without his shirt on. Why did his voice have to get all sexy and husky like that? And why did he have to smell so good? And stand so close?

But she made no move to push him away.

"We have a story," she said.

The corner of his mouth curled slightly. "We do?"

"Yes."

The streetlight on the corner was the only illumination, but Avery somehow *felt* Jake respond.

"You want to use our real story?"

She shrugged. "I think sticking with the truth as much as possible is a good idea, don't you? Less room for error, less chance for one of us saying something the other doesn't."

He leaned in. "What are we saying about the shed?"

He's just a guy. Just a guy. Just a guy. She kept up the internal mantra as she said, "I think we tell everyone we were out there to get streamers and then took shelter when we realized the storm had kicked up."

"What if someone asks why you came out wearing my shirt?"

Was it her imagination or was Jake's voice a little raspy? She smiled. Okay, so she could understand the fun in getting a reaction. As long as she *had to* pretend to like him, she might as well enjoy it.

"We'll let them fill in their own blanks," she said.

"You don't mind if they say we were having a quickie on the workbench?" he asked with a full grin.

She lifted her shoulder again. "We *were* having a quickie on the workbench."

"You're an upstanding part of this community." Jake lifted a hand and brushed her hair back over her shoulder. "You're okay with them knowing what you're willing to do in a shed?"

She felt the goose bumps dance down her arm from his touch. "But you're Jake Mitchell."

He leaned in and put his lips against the side of her neck he'd exposed. "What's that mean?" he said softly against her skin.

Her whole body seemed to say *Jake's back! Jake's back!* when his tongue flicked out against her neck for a moment, before he kissed the spot.

She let her head fall back against the bricks of the building behind her. "It means you're a god here, and no one would expect me to resist you. I'm not worried about other guys thinking they would get the same result in the shed."

Yeah, her voice was a little breathless now, but she couldn't help it.

He trailed his lips to her collarbone, then up to her jaw and over to her mouth.

"Since no one would expect you to resist me, and because I've made no secret of the fact that I like to kiss you, no one would be surprised if your lipstick got a little smudged before we went inside, would they?"

Avery snorted over that ridiculousness. Or she tried to. With his mouth so close to hers, it came out more as a sigh. "I'm sure they wouldn't."

"Good." He sealed his lips over hers and pressed her back into the wall of the bar with his hips.

Avery wondered briefly if maybe the god thing was true, because *she* didn't expect her to resist him. Maybe if he hadn't been trying to find that little girl's dog. Maybe if he hadn't made Mary Wilson cry. Maybe if he hadn't given Avery a sandwich. Maybe she would have been able to resist him if even *one* of those things hadn't happened. But they had all happened. Jake *was* a good guy. Who could certainly kiss like a god.

She wrapped her arms around his neck and went up on tiptoe, deciding to blame it on the ham salad.

One of Jake's hands cupped her butt, the other braced against the wall so he could fully lean in to her.

Avery felt the evidence of his arousal, hard and hot behind his fly, and felt that thrill of affecting him again. He was kissing her like he was starving for her, and holding on to her like he wasn't ever going to let go.

In a flash, she wished for a big king-size bed and plenty of light.

Light, in particular.

She'd been with Jake twice. Had sex with him a total of four times. Still, she had yet to really see and appreciate this big, hot body. The first time, they'd been on a blanket laid out on the grass, but she hadn't been experienced enough to know what she wanted to do.

Now, she definitely knew what she wanted to do.

She wanted to undress him, slowly undoing the buttons of his shirt, then the fly of his pants. She wanted to see him stretched out on the bed, his clothes half-on and half-off, exposing his chest and abs. She wanted to trace the hard planes of his chest and stomach with her tongue. Then she wanted to lean over him and tease him with her hands and mouth on his cock while she watched his face. She wanted to see his eyes heat; she wanted to see his chest rising and falling as his breathing grew ragged; she wanted to hear him saying her name, begging, needing her.

Jake tore his mouth from hers and stood staring at her for a long moment. "There's a difference between your lipstick being smudged and your clothes being ripped from your body."

That voice—the gravelly, turned-on voice that said she'd managed to get him going, too—she also really liked that.

She focused on his mouth again and started to lean in.

He put both hands on her shoulders. And pushed her back.

"Whoa, hang on." He gave a little chuckle. "What's gotten into you?"

She blinked and shook her head. Then blinked again and made herself focus on his face. What had gotten into her?

Him looking for a puppy. And ham salad.

Apparently.

"Nothing." She cleared her throat. "Nothing. I'm fine."

"That was a hell of a kiss."

That was a hell of an understatement.

She smoothed the front of her dress, pressed her lips together, and cleared her throat again. "I don't know what you mean. It was a kiss. Like all the others you've forced on me over the years."

She started to step away from the building, but Jake's hand went to the bricks behind her again, his arm blocking her way. "Uh, no. That was not like all the others."

How did he know? How could he possibly feel the difference? Sure, most of the other times their kisses had been spontaneous, and shorter than this one. But there was no way he could tell that this time she *liked* him.

Erin Nicholas

Deep down, she supposed part of her must have always liked him. She'd admired him, for sure. She'd been attracted without question. But she'd never let herself *admit* that she liked him.

She didn't want to like him.

He took his family for granted; gave his energy, time, talents, and money to other towns; and had a tendency to butt in—to conversations, projects, even cleanup efforts—without an invitation, assuming everyone would be thrilled he was there.

But everyone *was* always thrilled he was there.

"We should get inside," she said, attempting to push his arm out of the way. Avoiding private time with him was a very good plan.

"Yep, in a minute. As soon as you tell me what was going through your pretty head during that kiss."

She licked her lips. She could make something up. Tell him she'd been thinking about what scent car freshener she wanted to try next. Something to put him in his place. Because there was no way she was going to tell him that she *liked* him.

Or she could tell him part of the truth.

"I was thinking about pushing you down on a bed, stripping you bare, and licking you all over."

If turning him on was fun, shutting him up was almost better.

He stood gaping at her, his expression a funny mix of surprise, amusement, and lust.

She ducked under his arm and made it all the way to the front door before he caught her.

He grabbed her arm. "A—"

She looked over her shoulder. "We should go in."

He pulled in a breath through his nose. "Fine. But we're going to talk about the licking thing later."

A tingle raced through her. Sleeping with him again was a bad idea. Licking him all over was a very bad idea. She'd never recover.

"We'll see." She started to pull the door open.

"If you don't promise to talk to me about it later, I'm going to bring it up inside this bar. With an audience."

She closed her eyes. He would. Of course he would.

"Fine."

"Great." He reached past her, pulled the door open, and escorted her through it like a perfect gentleman.

CHAPTER SEVEN

The place was packed.

"Jake!" A collective greeting went up as they stepped through the door.

"Hey, everyone," Jake said good-naturedly with a big smile. He hardly seemed surprised by the enthusiastic welcome.

Avery was sure he *wasn't* surprised. This was probably typical for him. She wouldn't be surprised if he walked into congressional meetings in DC and the senators did the same thing.

"Seriously?" Avery muttered.

Jake must have heard and understood what she meant, because he chuckled behind her. He was close enough that she felt the rumble. She also felt his hand at her lower back nudging her forward.

Well, if they wanted to show the town that they were spending time together and getting along, this was the place to be seen together. It seemed like the whole town was here.

Being the center of attention was not the norm for Avery, and she found herself leaning back into Jake's touch. For the first time, maybe ever, Jake's proximity calmed her a bit.

They walked through the crowd together, with Jake acknowledging people throughout the room as they made their way to a booth toward the back. He smiled, shook hands, but never moved his left hand from her lower back.

Avery smiled as well, returned greetings, and generally tried to look like she was thrilled to be here. She was, however, *honestly* grateful to see Brenda and Becky, the twin sisters who owned A Bar, standing next to an empty table, holding two huge drinks.

The drinks were green and had yellow twisted straws sticking out of them.

Avery didn't care what they were, as long as they had liquor in them.

She took one and sipped.

Delicious.

"Tornado straws?" Jake asked, accepting his.

Becky grinned. "Of course."

Avery eyed the straw. That hadn't even occurred to her. Wow, talk about going with a theme.

"What else would we put in the Twisted Sister?" Brenda asked.

"You invented a drink for the tornado?" Jake asked, taking a taste.

"We did. What do you think?"

"Delicious."

"You invented a *drink* for the *tornado*?" Avery repeated.

"We did a whole menu. We've got the Storm Warning. It's lemonade with a kick . . . starts out sunny and sweet and then boom, hits you."

Jake laughed. "Awesome."

"We've got Hailstones, too," Brenda added with a grin. "It's a brandy slush. And Liquid Lightning—a whole bunch of stuff goes in that one, but it definitely gives you a jolt."

Avery sucked harder on her straw. This was fun. It would give people a smile. It wasn't like drinking something called Liquid Lightning would make people complacent about the storms or that they'd hear "warning" and think lemonade. She needed to lighten up.

"Hi, you guys!" Shelby seemed to appear out of nowhere. Her smile was huge. "I'm so glad you came out tonight!"

Avery worked to give Shelby an equally bright smile, but her face felt stiff. "Hi, Shelby."

It wasn't like she never spent time at A Bar. She and Bree and Kit got together for lunch and drinks all the time. When Liza could get a night away from her six kids, she joined them. But either the rest of the people in the place paid her no attention when she was with the girls, or she was so at ease with the girls that she didn't worry about what other people were thinking. That was an ease she didn't feel with Jake.

But when Jake suddenly took her hand, she had to admit that the way she felt wasn't *bad*. He made her feel jittery, like all her senses were working overtime, but it wasn't exactly unpleasant.

In fact, as the heat from his hand seeped into hers, she started feeling . . . comforted. By Jake.

She might be in big trouble here.

Then he squeezed her hand and she felt instantly better.

Definite trouble.

"Come on. Sit with Frank and me," Shelby said.

They should *definitely* do that. Because they were professional colleagues who needed to talk about some of the recovery strategy while happily socializing with the town over optimistically tornado-themed drinks. Sitting with the mayor would seem much more professional . . . and much less like a date.

Not that this was a date.

Except that with Jake holding her hand, the heat of his big body never more than a few inches away from hers, and the sensations from the kiss outside still humming through her bloodstream, it really *felt* like a date.

Those thoughts vanished a moment later when she stepped through the doorway into the back room. "Oh. My. God." Avery stopped short and felt Jake bump into her. But she couldn't even fully appreciate the him-against-her feeling.

The sight in front of her was too distracting.

In the middle of the room, on top of the hardwood floor they used for dancing during wedding receptions and parties, was a tornado.

Or a crazy, crafty model of a tornado, anyway.

A twisting contraption of chicken wire, tissue paper, and twinkle lights.

Twinkle lights.

"I don't remember it being so sparkly," Jake said near her ear.

She laughed, maybe a little hysterically. "Me neither."

If it had ended with chicken wire and twinkle lights, things might have been okay. Or at least *mildly* crazy instead of completely crazy. But there was more.

On the walls of the party room were huge blown-up pictures from *The Wizard of Oz*. Dorothy standing on her farm in Kansas adorned one wall, opposite the wall that boasted the floor-to-ceiling photo of Munchkinland. Straight ahead as you stepped into the room, in all its sparkly green glory, was, of course, the Emerald City.

"You've got to be kidding," Avery muttered.

"We're definitely not in Kansas." Jake nudged her forward, and not having a better idea, she started after Shelby and one of the booths in Munchkinland.

There were sparkly red shoes in the middle of each table. As Avery drew closer, she realized they were plastic and held twisted pretzel sticks, green fruit candies, and square gold-foil-wrapped chocolates.

Shelby slid into the booth next to Frank. She picked up a pretzel, a green candy, and a piece of chocolate. "Tornadoes, emeralds from the Emerald City, and bricks from the Yellow Brick Road."

Jake took a seat across from Shelby and Frank.

"What is all this?" Avery asked, looking around the room.

"They had a party for the kids today. A lot of the people doing cleanup have young kids who are getting in the way or who are having a hard time dealing with going through their ruined stuff. Kit suggested we have some of the high school kids entertain the young ones today, and she was here to lead some activities and talk to the kids one-on-one. They played games, had snacks, and watched *The Wizard of Oz* and *Cloudy with a Chance of Meatballs.*"

"Storm themes?" Avery asked. Was it too soon for the kids? But she shouldn't worry. Kit was handling it.

Then Jake reached out, grabbed her hand, and pulled her into the booth next to him. He put his arm over the back of the booth behind her, and Avery kind of lost her train of thought.

Shelby nodded. "Movies with fun, kid-appropriate plots and a happily ever after."

"They made their own meatballs for spaghetti at lunchtime, and everyone made a scarecrow or a tin man to take home," Jake said.

"You knew about this?" she asked.

His thigh pressed against hers, and she tried to scoot away, but there was nowhere to go without ending up on her butt on the floor next to the booth.

Which he knew, judging by the grin he gave her. She was surrounded by him—his body, his heat, his scent.

She needed a drink. She started to take a pull on the straw in the Twisted Sister she still held but was surprised to find her glass was empty.

That wasn't good. But she lifted her hand to signal the waitress, anyway.

"They decided to leave all the decorations up?" Avery asked.

Shelby looked around with a smile. "Everyone's getting a kick out of it. Kit's making it a weeklong event. The kids will come every day, which will help out their parents a ton, and she can work with them, help them through their emotions about all of it."

Avery looked at the humongous tornado sparkly and twinkling in the middle of the dance floor. It was the centerpiece, for sure. And when they only had to walk out the door to see the results of the real tornado front and center, it seemed like a bit much.

But, then again, there was no ignoring or denying that all this was the focus right now. Maybe making it sparkly and twinkly, adding chocolate, and associating it with fun was a good thing. For the kids and adults alike. Adding the liquor for the grown-ups was absolutely a good idea.

The waitress set Avery's drink down, and she immediately sipped.

Yep, a really good idea.

Jake chuckled and squeezed her shoulder. "Nobody's thinking about the cleanup outside or the fact that their electricity is still out or that they may never find their grandmother's jewelry box or their wedding album or their daughter's stuffed duck."

She pressed her lips together. He was right. This was ridiculous and over the top and gaudy and loud and . . . everyone was having a great time. Ridiculous seemed to be what they all needed.

Frank and Shelby were distracted for a moment by a couple of city-council members, and Avery wiggled in her seat. She needed to get even a centimeter of space between her and Jake so she could *think* and not be completely distracted by how rock solid he was.

His hand settled on her shoulder. "I love sitting in booths. They're so cozy."

She elbowed him in the side, keeping an eye on Shelby and Frank so she wouldn't get caught. "You're taking up more than your half," she said quietly.

"Yep." He pressed his hip more firmly into hers. "I'm the same way in bed."

Heat rushed through her even as she glanced at the men talking with Frank to see if they'd overheard.

"Stop it," she hissed.

Jake leaned in close and said in her ear, "You *will* play up that we're friends. You will get into this. You will help me keep their spirits up. Or you haven't even begun to imagine the crazy-assed drama I'll stir up to keep them gossiping while they clean up, and laughing while they rebuild this town."

He was threatening her. And bossing her around.

Still, she felt her heart warm as she looked at him and saw the determination in his eyes. This mattered to him because the town mattered to him.

Yeah, well, they had that in common.

But she was definitely affected. For sure.

She took his chin between her thumb and fingers, making sure he was looking directly into her eyes. "I'm going to go along with it so convincingly that even *you* will start wondering what's true and what's an act," she said as Shelby turned back to them. "But," Avery added, running her hand along his jaw and loving the little shiver that went through her as her skin rasped over his early-evening stubble, "not because you're telling me to. But because they matter to me, too."

His gaze glued to hers, he took her hand from his face and pressed a hot kiss to the center of her palm.

A definite jolt of electricity shot through her, and she thought briefly that if Brenda and Becky could bottle that into Liquid Lightning, they'd make a killing.

"Then I guess we're in cahoots." Jake slid his fingers between hers and rested their hands on his thigh.

"You two are so cute," Shelby said with a huge grin that showed every one of her perfectly straight, pearly white teeth.

"We are?" Avery asked, aware that she'd been fully sucked into the Jake Mitchell bubble and had, again, forgotten there were other people around. And suddenly pretty sure she was going to regret that more than usual.

"I *love* how the two of you get all wrapped up in each other and the charge in the air around you," Shelby said. She picked up her drink and sipped, a mischievous sparkle in her eye. "The whole town loves it."

Avery sat up straighter and looked around. "What do you mean?"

Shelby laughed. "Everyone knows that all of your bickering and snapping is just a crazy form of foreplay. And everyone is just waiting for it to explode."

Avery swallowed hard. Oh, boy. That wasn't good.

She glanced at Jake. He was grinning smugly.

"It's definitely interesting and distracting," he said. "Wouldn't you say, Shelby?"

Shelby nodded happily. "Definitely."

Avery narrowed her eyes. "So this . . . foreplay thing . . ." She hated that she stumbled over it. "That's what you meant about how *interesting* we are when we get together?"

Shelby nodded. "Of course."

"You've noticed that before?" Avery asked.

"Of course," Shelby said again.

"And that's why you wanted Jake and me working together. Not for the good of the rebuilding or town morale?" Avery asked, her voice rising slightly.

Shelby didn't look a bit apologetic. "This *is* good for town morale. *Everyone* has seen this thing between you before."

Avery slumped back in her seat, very aware of Jake's arm behind her now. "You should have told us that," she said.

Shelby leaned in, a suddenly serious look in her eyes. "Don't get me wrong for one second, Avery Sparks. You and Jake working together is good for *many* reasons. You're both passionate, intelligent leaders who love this town, and having you side by side makes everyone feel more secure. The fact that everyone is waiting for Jake to dip you back and kiss the hell out of you in the town square just makes it that much better."

Avery stared at her. And told herself that she did *not* want Jake to do exactly what Shelby had just said.

They were in something, all right. But Avery was afraid *cahoots* was way too innocent a term.

Jake would very gladly dip Avery in the town square and kiss the hell out of her. He'd go along with just about anything if it meant he got to sit with his arm around her, with her side pressed up nice and tight against his.

No complaints from him at all.

He knew Avery was far less comfortable with being the subject of town gossip, but he thought it was good for her. She deserved the attention. Not necessarily the what's-she-doing-with-Jake-behind-closed-doors type of attention, but the more eyes that were watching her with him, the more people would see how amazing she was and how great she was at leading the town through the recovery.

He hoped the whole town paid very close attention for a long time.

"Excuse me, I have a couple of people I need to talk to." Frank left the table, and Jake had to admit A Bar was a good place for the mayor to hang out. In Chance everyone stopped by A Bar at some point. It was a very efficient way to conduct business. Especially at a time like this, when everyone in town needed to work with everyone else. A Bar was the location of what could easily be called a town meeting. All Frank needed was his gavel. Though, honestly, he was getting everyone's undivided attention faster with the mugs of beer he was handing out.

"Crap," Avery muttered.

Jake had been stroking his thumb up and down the side of her neck, and now he felt her tense against him. No one else in the room could see where his thumb was or what it was doing, but he was taking complete advantage of the fact that Avery couldn't slug him for touching her.

He loved her skin. He liked feeling it against his lips and tongue and lots more of *his* skin than just the pad of his thumb, but he also liked how she'd been relaxing into him, as if the stroking were comforting.

Now he looked up to see what had caught her attention and saw it immediately.

His aunt Gigi was headed for them.

He kept his hand on Avery's shoulder, sensing that she wanted to bolt.

"You'll do the talking, right?" Avery whispered to him.

She was suddenly leaning into him hard. Which was completely fine with him.

"If you want me to."

"But I reserve the right to pinch you or elbow you if you start making up some crazy thing," she added.

He grinned. With his aunt's attention on them and their shared desire to lift everyone's spirits, it was tempting to make this into a really juicy story.

He had no doubt Avery would pinch. Probably hard. But it might be worth it.

The thing was, they had a pretty juicy story anyway, and he didn't mind sharing it. For the sake of the town, of course. The town he wanted to see shine again. The town he wanted the Bronsons to love as much as he did. The town that was a part of him.

The town he'd left ten years ago for bigger things. Which he'd found.

Why, then, did every trip home make it harder to leave?

"I really fucking hate tornadoes." Gigi squeezed in next to Shelby.

Jake pushed his thoughts and emotions about Chance down deep and pasted on the smile he'd perfected over the years of being interviewed and giving speeches. It wasn't exactly fake, but it also didn't allow people to read much into his expression. "Hi, Gigi."

Without looking at her, he knew Avery wasn't smiling. He squeezed her shoulder.

"Good to see you sticking around for a while, Jake," Gigi said in her smoke-roughened voice.

"My pleasure," Jake told her.

"The suits decide they could survive without you?"

The suits. Jake swallowed. He didn't really want to go into all that right now. Because no, the suits did not think they could survive without him, and he was getting pretty regular phone calls and e-mails emphasizing that point.

"They know Chance is important to me," he said. That was true. He had his answer down pat by now—*This is my hometown, and I need to stay until the people are back on their feet.*

"Chance is doing really well," Gigi said. She gave Shelby a nod. "Things are looking good."

"I think so, too," Shelby said enthusiastically. "We're right on schedule. Thanks in part to Jake, Max, and Dillon being here."

Jake appreciated his cousin's acknowledgment, but Gigi's comment did bring up something he'd been stubbornly ignoring—Chance *was* doing well. Everything was on track for the Bronson visit if things continued the way they were.

But he still didn't want to leave.

As Avery squirmed against him, he also had a pretty good idea why.

Gigi grabbed the bottle of beer the moment the waitress set it down and took a long swig. She swallowed with a satisfied "Ah," then looked back and forth between Jake and Avery. "So you two are heading things up, huh?"

Jake nodded. "With Max and Bree and Dillon and Kit."

Gigi nodded. "Sounds like a good team. Things going well from your perspective?"

"Very well," Jake said. "Avery and I are pretty great together."

He felt her try to elbow him, but they were sitting so close that it was really more of a nudge. But she'd clearly caught his innuendo. He smiled and took a long drink of his Twisted Sister.

Gigi looked intrigued. "Is that right? Is this the first time you've been great together?"

Jake fought the laugh that threatened to escape. Was Gigi onto his second meaning as well? It wouldn't surprise him.

He cleared his throat. "Actually, no. We've definitely been great together before," he said.

He felt Avery tighten her fingers on his in warning.

"I mean, Avery and I have known each other for most of our lives," Jake said before Avery could reply.

"I know you graduated high school together," Gigi said.

This was Chance. Nearly everyone who lived here had gone to school together since kindergarten.

"Yes. But we knew each other way before high school. Avery was my savior when we were kids."

He knew *that* would get Gigi's attention. Avery's, too.

"How so?" Gigi asked, clearly intrigued.

"Avery spent a lot of time with my mom when we were little. They hung out together in the house while I ran wild outside." Jake gave Gigi a grin. "Mom was so caught up in the craft and cooking projects she and Avery did together, she barely noticed I didn't get all my chores done and left the back door hanging open and borrowed her good silverware to dig in the dirt."

Gigi smiled. "I know you were close to Heidi," she said to Avery.

Avery was nearly vibrating now from holding herself so tight. Jake tried to pull her closer, but it was like trying to cuddle up to a two-by-four.

"Heidi babysat me while my grandmother worked," Avery said with a nod. "She was always very . . . nice . . . to me."

Jake felt the frown he'd fought earlier slam his brows together.

Nice? His mother had been *nice* to her? His mother had loved Avery. Heidi had practically adopted Avery. To hear her refer to their *years* of time together as "babysitting" made him frown even harder. What the hell was that?

"Did you have a crush on Jake?" Gigi asked.

"Not exactly."

"Are you sure?" Jake said. Surely he'd flirted with her. At least.

But for the life of him, he couldn't come up with any concrete memories between just the two of them before the night he'd asked her to prom. And that had been his mom's idea. He'd been planning to go as a bachelor with Max and Dillon, who'd also sworn off girls, knowing they were heading to basic training a month after the dance.

He remembered praising her cooking almost constantly. She'd gotten even better than his mother. He had a hard time recalling a time when Avery wasn't present in his parents' kitchen after school. She'd helped make nearly every dinner he'd eaten growing up.

He'd noticed she was cute, in a sort of passing way, like he'd notice if the weather was nice that day. But she'd been quiet and seemed to like being in the background. She'd smiled much bigger when Jake's father had praised her cooking anyway, so Jake had always figured she didn't care what he thought.

Which was also why, when she'd looked up at him at the river on graduation night with hope in her eyes and said she'd never been kissed, he couldn't resist.

He'd been addicted ever since.

"I'm sure," Avery told him. She looked at Gigi. "He barely noticed me. Until Heidi told him to ask me to prom."

Jake looked down at her, surprised. "You knew that my mom suggested I ask you?"

She rolled her eyes. "Of course. You never would have asked me otherwise."

"That's not—" But it was. "I didn't know you knew that."

"She never *told* me," Avery said. "But she and I had just been talking about prom, and she'd been upset that I'd never been and didn't plan on taking my last chance to go. Three days later, you asked."

And he thought he'd been so sweet and suave, making her feel special and like he was happy to be there with her. But he *had been* happy to be there with her. He just hadn't known that he would be ahead of time.

Avery shrugged. "Anyway, that was the first night there was ever anything between us."

Jake started to protest. That didn't seem right. But he couldn't argue. It was true the night at the dance had been the first time he'd felt . . . anything . . . for her.

But damn. It seemed like once he made her laugh, he was addicted. She was sweet and smart and funny and interesting. He'd been hooked. Then there had been graduation night at the river. It had been like a blowtorch to dry straw. The fire had ignited and taken over so quickly that it seemed ridiculous there had been nothing there before.

"You had a spark back then but are just figuring it out now?" Gigi asked. "What happened?"

"He left."

Avery said it bluntly, flatly, without hesitation. Jake felt her *lack* of emotion hit him almost harder than everything else he'd been feeling.

Shelby looked at him, one eyebrow up. "You left? What's that mean?"

"Enlisted." That word seemed better. "In the Guard. Remember? That had been the plan all along. The prom . . . wasn't." He said it with a little grin—a fake little grin—designed to lighten the moment.

"Without saying good-bye."

Avery's input was almost too soft to hear. But Jake heard it. As did Gigi and Shelby.

"You didn't say good-bye?" Shelby asked him. "Wow."

"Hey, I had every intention of seeing her when I finished basic," he protested. "Until I got her letter."

There. If they were going to out everything that had happened, he wasn't about to look like the bad guy. Or at least not the only bad guy. Leaving without saying good-bye had been a crappy thing to do. But he'd still been processing that *anything* had happened between him and Avery, not to mention that it had been something big. Not the sex. Not *just* the sex—though that had been an absolute shock. And big. And awesome. But the fact that he really had wanted to see her when he came home. He really had dreamed about her while he'd been gone. He really had mentally prepared a great homecoming where he went to her house the minute he hit town.

Until the letter came.

That fucking I-only-liked-you-because-of-your-parents letter.

He forced himself to relax and not dig his fingers into her shoulder.

"Not a Dear John letter?" Gigi was clearly into the story.

"Broke my heart," Jake said with some truth.

Gigi turned to Avery. "Why did you break up with him?" There was a definite note of protectiveness in her voice, but her eyes were wide with interest.

Avery snorted. "He's kidding. There was nothing to break up. We sort of dated for, like, a month, and then fooled around one night. Then he left without saying good-bye, and I realized what I thought was maybe there . . . wasn't."

Jake felt his fingers curl into her shoulder for a moment before he consciously relaxed.

"Then we saw each other again here in Chance, and I convinced her there *was* something there." This much was true—no matter what else had happened, no matter why she'd written that letter, when he kissed her, it was real. Which was one of the reasons he'd kept doing it.

Besides liking it. A lot.

Shelby was clearly enjoying this drama immensely.

"Those encounters over the years added up, and the other day, things . . ." Shelby trailed off meaningfully.

"Things definitely . . ." Jake mimicked her down to the lift of one eyebrow.

When Avery nudged him this time, it was much harder.

Shelby laughed, and Jake squeezed Avery up against him.

"You do make a cute couple," Shelby told them. "The sparks are so obvious. I'm glad you're finally doing something about it."

"I'm a lucky guy," Jake said. "Avery's the whole package—she's beautiful, smart, tough, talented. She's the first female chief this town's ever had. But even more than that, I know she can refinish a wood floor, knit me a scarf, and she's a hell of a cook. I think I fell for her over her lasagna when I was about nine."

Jake felt Avery tense even more, and he stroked a hand up and down her arm. He'd pissed her off. On purpose. Though none of that was an outright lie. Her lasagna was amazing.

He was trying to make a point. Relationships couldn't be summarized like that. His mother had not just babysat Avery, he hadn't screwed around with her at the river just because he was going off to basic the next day, and his feelings for her were not just about his favorite pasta dish. Just like she hadn't screwed around with him back then—or in the shed—because she liked hanging out with his mom.

For God's sake.

She was trying to make things simple because it was easier to dismiss a babysitter, a high school fling, and a pan of noodles. But that didn't explain at all why she wanted to dismiss any of it in the first place.

"I think this is all very . . . interesting," Gigi said. She tipped her beer bottle again and finished it off. "Max said you were heading to my place tomorrow to work on the roof," she said, changing the subject suddenly.

Jake nodded. "That's the plan."

"Good. The shed could use a little help, too. But my workbench is nowhere as big and sturdy as the one at school. You've been warned." She gave them both a wink and slid out of the booth.

That caught him by surprise for a moment before he chuckled. He glanced at Avery. She was still staring after Gigi.

More people came over to talk to Shelby, and while her attention was diverted, Avery leaned in to Jake.

"You might want to think about toning it down a bit."

"Toning what down?"

"The whole been-crazy-about-each-other-for-ten-years thing. The being crazy about my cooking. All of it."

"We're supposed to be getting along."

"Which means you should stop trying to annoy me."

"I'm not trying to annoy you." But he did feel mildly amused at the moment.

She shook her head. "Well, there's kind of a big spectrum between getting along and secretly in love for a decade."

Yeah, there was. And he knew which end of that spectrum he was closer to.

She sighed. "Just take it down a notch."

"Maybe I'm trying to make up for your clear lack of enthusiasm toward our relationship."

"Are we talking about our past relationship or our current one?" she asked.

"You had enthusiasm for our relationship when we were at the river and you were naked and underneath me and—"

She elbowed him again. "Knock it off. I was a horny, tipsy teenager. Jeez, Jake, if you want me enthusiastic like *that*, maybe you need to break out the peach schnapps again."

This was getting damned old. There was no way in *hell* she'd been thinking about Christmas dinner at his parents' house during any of the orgasms he'd given her.

He hadn't been a virgin at the river, but he hadn't realized until he'd been with several more women that orgasms didn't always happen that easily, and certainly not without some concentrated attention from him. But sweet virgin Avery had come apart in his arms three times that night. Three damned times.

She could claim whatever she wanted about her motivations that night, but the cold, hard facts said she'd been worked up because of *him*.

Why did she insist on denigrating all her relationships? At least, her relationships with his family?

"I don't recall there being any schnapps involved in the shed a few days ago."

Avery shifted on the seat next to him so she could face him more fully. "A *relationship* is about more than sex and lasagna. That's what we have—sex and lasagna."

"And you and my mother just had crafts and cookies?"

That made her pause, and she swallowed hard. "Yes."

"So all these years you've been under the impression that my mother, what? Needed the extra cash so she picked up a babysitting job?"

"Of course not."

"Then what? Why would she give you all that time and energy?"

"She felt sorry for me." Avery took a deep, shuddering breath. "She felt sorry for me and my grandmother, so she took me off Ruth's hands while she worked."

Jake stared at her. How could she believe that? How could she think everything Heidi had given her had been out of pity?

"Is that what you think the river was?" he asked her, his voice rough.

She pressed her lips together and stared at him.

"Jesus, Avery, you think I slept with you because I felt *sorry* for you?"

She lifted a shoulder. "You had a bunch of schnapps, too."

"The river was not about pity or fucking schnapps," he snapped.

"What about prom?" she shot back. "You took me to prom because your mom told you to because *she* felt sorry for me. Did she tell you that? Did she tell you how much I wanted to go, and how I had a dress all picked out, and how sad I was that I wasn't going to get to wear it?"

He stared at her. "No," he said gruffly. "She didn't tell me any of that."

Avery seemed surprised. She took a breath. "Well, trust me. She most definitely felt sorry for me."

"*I* promise you that sorry is not on the rather lengthy list of things I've felt for you." Another thought occurred to him. "But if you thought that, how could you let me do what I did in the shed? You should *never* let someone close to you like that without pure emotions. Even lust is better than pity."

She choked on a laugh. "It took you a year to fully wear me down, but I can't resist you. And you know it."

Her voice had risen, and the space between them had grown, and suddenly Jake became aware of the fact they had an audience. Literally.

Well, great.

He glanced across the table at Shelby and the two women she'd been talking to about meals for the workers the next day. Frank had also returned to the table and had Martin Carver, the city's attorney, with him.

"See? *That* is what I'm talking about," Shelby said ardently.

Avery sighed, then gave a soft but heartfelt "Crap" and bolted out of her seat.

She headed for the nearest door—the emergency exit.

The alarm squealed the moment she hit the door, but she didn't slow at all.

Jake took one second to find amusement in the fact that the fire chief had just set off the fire alarm in the bar. Then he took off after her.

◆ ◆ ◆

Well, *that* had been mature and professional.

Avery shook her head as she paced to the end of the sidewalk. The heavy, humid June air pressed against her, doing nothing to relieve the heat in her cheeks or the weight of her embarrassment.

She *was* mature and professional, dammit. Until Jake came around.

She kept her head on straight, her crap in order, her emotions under control. She put out fires, put together safety action plans, and put people at ease because they knew she was in charge. Until Jake came around.

Since he'd shown up this time, she'd set fire to a tablecloth and set off a fire alarm in a public building and blurted out her biggest heartbreak—or at least part of it.

The man made her lose her mind.

There was no other explanation for how she acted when he was in town.

Avery ducked around the side of the building. They'd get the alarm shut off. Two members of her crew were in there with plenty of witnesses to attest that there was no actual fire or need for alarm, so she didn't need to stay.

But Jake would be following her, she knew.

She heard him approach and turned, her arms crossed over her body.

"We need to work on that thing where we get so wrapped up in each other that we forget there are other people around," she said drily.

"Yeah, well, you're about to be all wrapped up in me for the next several minutes or more," he said. "Get used to it."

"Excuse me?" She drew herself up tall. If he thought what had happened inside A Bar was some kind of strange verbal foreplay, he was sadly mistaken.

"Enough of this, Avery." He took her by her upper arm and started toward his truck.

"Hey." She yanked her arm from his hold. "Enough of what?"

He sighed and bent at the waist, put his shoulder into her gut, and stood with her hanging halfway down his back like a sack of potatoes.

"Jake!" She squirmed, but he simply tightened his hold around her thighs. "What are you doing?"

"Finding out once and for all what the hell is going on with you."

She stopped squirming. She should have known this was coming. She'd let her emotions run away with her—as usual, when he was around—and she'd said that stuff about his mom feeling sorry for her. Of course he'd want to know what she was talking about.

"Nothing is going on with me," she said, striving to sound calm. "I'm fine. I was just nervous in front of your aunt, and my mouth ran away with me."

He stopped by his truck, hit the unlock button on his key chain, and let her slide to the ground.

Down the front of his body.

Slowly.

When her feet touched the pavement, she took a second before stepping back.

Part of Jake was happy to have her up against him, too. Maybe she could distract him from all of this with sex.

"Jake—"

"Don't you dare," he said gruffly.

"Don't dare what?"

"Look at me like that. Say something sexy. Tempt me. You know I'm a damned sucker for you looking up at me like that, but we've got some talking to do."

She stepped in, running her hand up his chest. "Apparently I'm a sucker for you admitting you're a sucker."

He caught her wrist before she could sink her fingers into his hair. "You haven't been a sucker for me for one minute. Ever."

Damn. She dropped her hand.

"I very much doubt you've ever been a sucker for anyone." He leaned past her and opened the passenger door to his truck.

Oh, she'd been a sucker. A big one.

"I don't suppose it has occurred to you that this is none of your business?" she asked.

He put his big hands on her waist, picked her up, and tossed her onto the seat in the truck. "Nope."

CHAPTER EIGHT

She could climb out, of course. He couldn't *kidnap* her, after all. But she didn't. She sat staring out the windshield, chewing on her bottom lip.

Heidi had, obviously, not told Jake anything about her relationship—or lack thereof—with Avery. Jake had, obviously, not asked. Even a simple "Have you spoken to Avery lately?" would have brought up the subject. She and Heidi had absolutely *not* spoken lately. Or for about ten years.

The fact that Avery had, clearly, not come up as a topic of conversation at all between Heidi and Jake in *ten years*—including the year where Jake had been going around town kissing Avery every chance he got—kind of pissed her off.

By the time Jake rounded the front of the truck and climbed behind the wheel, the *kind of pissed off* had already turned into *really pissed off*.

She crossed her arms and scowled out the window as he drove them across town to where her department would be lighting and supervising the bonfire later on.

They had about an hour until anyone else showed up.

Plenty of time to hash out ten years of hurt and humiliation and anger.

"Did you know your mom and dad more or less supported me and Ruth from the time I was four to the day I left Chance?" she asked before he could jump in and direct the conversation.

In her peripheral vision she saw him turn to face her, but she didn't look over at him.

"What do you mean?"

"I mean, my grandmother cleaned your house once a week for fourteen years. At every other house in town she made about fifteen dollars an hour. Your mom paid her three thousand dollars a month."

Jake shifted on his seat. She still wasn't looking at him, so she couldn't read his expression.

"You're serious?"

"Yes." She took a deep breath. "I didn't know until the day I left town. But, yeah, all those years, they basically supported us."

"Why?" But then he shook his head. "Never mind."

She glanced over. "You know why?"

He shrugged. "Your grandma didn't have much money, Avery. That was a fact. My parents loved you. I'm not surprised they helped take care of you."

Avery felt her stomach tighten. Ruth—she'd given up calling her *Grandma* a long time ago—had never made a secret of the fact that taking in Avery had been a burden. Ruth hadn't wanted to raise her granddaughter. She hadn't really wanted to raise her own daughter. Avery had heard all about it. Over and over. Ruth had gotten pregnant young and could barely make ends meet then. When Avery's mom, Brooke, finally moved out, Ruth was relieved. Brooke had been only sixteen when she'd taken off with her boyfriend—and eighteen when she'd come back with her baby girl.

Ruth hadn't shared all the gory details with Avery until that May morning when Avery had come back to the trailer after her night with Jake. But her grandmother spared no detail in filling Avery in on the fact that Ruth had kept her only because of the paycheck from the Mitchells, and now that Avery was eighteen and had graduated, the money train had run out of track.

"Ruth took advantage of their generosity, that's for sure," Avery said drily, focusing on the pile of wood and burnable debris they'd be setting on fire later. "When I was finally eighteen and had graduated, your parents were relieved. They could stop the checks without worrying that I would suffer because Ruth couldn't afford to take care of me. I was an adult and able to be out on my own. I could get a good job; I could qualify for lots of different kinds of assistance. I wasn't their responsibility anymore."

"They stopped paying when you graduated?"

Avery nodded. "They stopped giving *Ruth* money." This was humiliating, but she couldn't resist a glance in his direction. Jake was staring out of the windshield as well, his grip tight on the steering wheel.

"Tell me what happened, A," he said. The soft tone of voice was in contrast to the way the muscle in his jaw ticked. "How did you find out?"

She pulled in a deep breath through her nose. It was still painful to think about that morning, even ten years later. She'd never told anyone the story before.

But fine.

If Jake wanted to know, maybe it would help prevent any awkward moments with Heidi and Wes surrounding their pretend relationship. Avery could pretend to be in love with Jake—that wasn't much of a stretch anyway. But she wasn't sure she could make nice with his parents without crumbling.

"I picked up my car at your house the morning after the party." She'd left her car there and ridden with him to the river.

He nodded.

"When I got to the trailer, all my stuff was packed up in boxes and sitting in the front yard."

She was fascinated to see his grip tighten further on the steering wheel. But he said nothing.

"Ruth came out and said, 'Have a nice life.'" Avery breathed deeply, waiting for the twinge of pain to pass. *She'd* been ready to move out, to leave the trailer in her rearview mirror, but to have her grandmother initiating the move had truly surprised her. She chalked that up to being eighteen and naive and trusting in spite of everything. "I was shocked. Which, looking back, was stupid. Ruth had a calendar hanging by the kitchen table where she crossed off each day to graduation with a big red *X*. She was obviously looking forward to it."

"Jesus."

The word was quiet, more of a mutter, but Avery heard it. He sounded pissed. Something about that made her stomach unknot slightly.

"Ruth told me that your parents would be giving the money to *me* from that point on. They'd made arrangements with the college for a scholarship that would cover everything from tuition to room and board and books. They set it up so I would be the only recipient. They were paying my way to college, and Ruth was pissed because she wouldn't be getting any more money."

Jake ran a hand over the back of his neck and let out a long breath. He didn't say anything.

"I was shocked by the whole thing but also relieved," Avery went on. "I was out from under her thumb, and I knew I had a safety net in your parents. I knew I could show up on their doorstep and they'd take me in."

"You showed up on their doorstep?"

She pressed her lips together and nodded. "*Your* doorstep."

"The morning after."

She nodded again. "The morning after we'd really committed to *our* relationship. Or so I thought. Imagine my surprise when your mom answered, and it looked like she'd been crying."

"She'd just said good-bye to me," Jake filled in. "I left within an hour of getting home that morning."

"Yeah." Avery had been stunned, then hurt, then angry. Jake had hurt his mother, too, and that had ticked Avery off. She hated seeing Heidi cry.

Jake hadn't told his parents his plans before that morning, either—that he was going to basic training for the next ten weeks.

"So Mom took you in, and then what?"

Avery felt her heart tighten. "She didn't take me in."

"What?"

They were facing each other now. Avery shook her head. "She wouldn't even let me come into the house." She felt the stab of pain, remembering the way Heidi had stood in the doorway, blocking the entrance. "I asked if I could come in and talk for a little bit, and she said no."

She couldn't remember Heidi ever saying no to her before that.

Jake frowned. "Did you tell her what happened with your grandma?"

"Of course. It didn't matter."

"What did she say to you?" Jake's voice had gotten dangerously low, like he was barely containing his emotions.

"She said she thought it would be best if I headed for Virginia that day. The sooner, the better."

"*Virginia?*" Jake repeated. "Why?"

Avery laughed humorlessly. "That's where the college was that had offered me the scholarship."

"But *Virginia?*"

She nodded. "Far, far away from Chance."

"But . . ." He trailed off, clearly without words.

"I was eighteen. They'd felt sorry for me growing up, but once I was legally an adult, they didn't have to worry about Ruth not taking care of me. I could take care of myself."

Jake sat without saying a word, seeming to process all that for a few minutes. Then he said, "My dad told me the other day you never went to Virginia."

She shook her head. "I didn't."

"You didn't want to go far away?"

That and . . . "I didn't want your parents' money to pay for college. I figured if they didn't want me, I didn't want them—or anything to do with them."

He swallowed. "They were trying to help you."

"They got in over their heads," she said flatly.

"What do you mean?"

"I was this cute little girl from a poor home, and your mom had always wanted more kids. She felt bad for me and bought me a few books and toys, then some clothes, then gave Ruth a little extra cash, then a little more. It snowballed on her, Jake. It was like feeding a stray cat—pretty hard to stop after you get it dependent on you."

His frown was deep and immediate. "You can't honestly believe my mother thought of you as a stray cat."

She knew that sounded bad and maybe wasn't completely accurate. But it *felt* accurate. "I wanted to be a cop."

Jake looked confused for a moment with the seeming abrupt shift in conversation.

"I wanted to be a cop and work with your dad. My plan was to end up back in Chance. Or never leave. I could have gotten my criminal-justice degree in Kearney or Hastings, and the Law Enforcement Training Center is in Grand Island. I could have lived here while going to school." Kearney, Grand Island, and Hastings were all within an hour of Chance, with multiple opportunities for classes and training. "Your dad was the one who told me all about the requirements to go into law enforcement. I planned to buy a little house your mom and I could paint and decorate together. They knew all of that."

She focused on the crease in his jeans at his knee instead of his face as she went on.

"I figured we would see each other all the time; we'd have dinners together and shop. Your mom and I had even laughed about how we should decorate cakes for weddings and stuff together on the side."

Avery looked up at him. "The plan was for me to stay close. At least, I thought that was the plan. But when graduation came around, I guess they realized it was real. That I was never going to leave them alone. They did what they could to get me away from here."

"Avery." Jake's voice sounded tight and his expression was pained. "They loved you. This can't be right."

"Come on, Jake," she said quietly. "I'm not their daughter. I'm not related at all. I was a pathetic little girl who became their charity case. I'm sure they felt good about helping me but . . . I was a burden on them, too. Your mom gave me so much time, not to mention the things she taught me and the money they spent. Then I started talking about being around all the time forever? I was the annoying houseguest who had overstayed her welcome. They saw a chance to be free, and they took it." She shrugged. "It hurt, but I don't blame them. They lasted a lot longer than anyone else."

Jake's expression changed quickly. Now he looked mad. "What's that mean?"

Avery felt her eyes widen. "What's your problem?"

"What do you mean they lasted longer than anyone else?"

"They put up with me longer than anyone else ever did."

He pulled in a breath, then reached out and grabbed her arm, hauling her across the seat and into his lap. "Don't say stuff like that," he practically growled.

She scowled at him. No one had ever been as physical with her as Jake was. He put his hands on her as if it was his right. And it didn't upset her as much as she thought it should. Which upset her.

"It's true. My mom lasted two years, but I was never more important than the boys and the drinking. Ruth would have thrown me out long before she did if it weren't for the money." She narrowed her eyes. "You lasted one month before you found something more important than me."

His eyes narrowed as well. "That's why you wrote the letter. You lumped me in with all the people you thought were throwing you away."

Her heart thumped, and she couldn't tell if it was because he'd hit close to the truth—people really had thrown her away her whole life— or because he looked genuinely pissed she would think that.

Maybe it was a combination.

Jake was making her feel crazy. As usual.

She lifted her chin and met his gaze. "It wasn't like I was enough to make you stick around."

"I had *enlisted*. That wasn't something I could just undo."

She knew that. In the rational part of her brain, she knew that. She also knew Jake had been as surprised at what had happened between them on prom night and their night at the river as she had. To turn his life upside down because of some accidentally great sex with a girl he'd barely noticed before he took her to prom as a favor to his mother would have been stupid.

But the emotional part of her brain—the part that was much bigger and more insistent than she wanted it to be most of the time—was still hurt.

"Maybe, but you never called or wrote me while you were gone."

"I was in *basic training*. I was overwhelmed. By the time I settled in, I'd gotten a letter from *you*. A letter telling me you were *sorry* for what had happened and that you'd used me."

She pressed her lips together. He was mad. That was clear. And she knew he had a right to be. But there was something else in his tone. Exasperation, yes, but also . . . affection? That couldn't be right.

"I was eighteen, Jake. And shook up. And scared. I didn't handle everything the way I should have or the way I would now. But I did use you. I loved your parents; I had this big dream of living this perfect life in Chance. It's completely stupid, and I blame it on being a teenage girl who sucked down too many Fuzzy Navels too fast, but yes, you kissed me and I started picking out bridesmaid dresses in my head."

"It wasn't about me at all?" Jake asked.

She became aware that his thumbs were under the hem of her top and that they were stroking back and forth over the bare skin at her waist.

She also became aware that she was sitting on his lap. He'd put her there, but she'd been so caught up in the emotions and memories, she hadn't been *aware*. Now she was. It seemed Jake was very *aware* of her, too.

Still, she shook her head. "It wasn't about you."

"All the *Oh, yes, Jake*s were about getting to decorate cakes with my mom?"

His thumbs had moved higher and were now stroking over her ribs.

She pressed her lips together and nodded.

"All the *More, more, more*s were about getting to drink the crappy coffee at the police station every day?"

She nodded again, but her breathing hitched when his thumbs met the underwire of her bra.

"How about now?" he asked gruffly. "Now you're a kick-ass fire chief who's decorated her own house and has plenty of other people to go to lunch and shopping with. What are you using me for now?"

Avery focused on his mouth. "Orgasms."

His mouth curled into a grin. "Uh-huh. Well, keep in mind I've been *not* over you for about ten years. My mom and dad might have been a part of your life for fourteen years, but I've held on for ten even after you tried to push me away. I think that should count for something."

She shook her head. The too-big, too-hopeful-in-spite-of-everything, emotional part of her brain really liked the point he'd just made. However, the rational part of her brain was small but mighty.

"That's because your ego is stronger than any other force in the universe."

His smile died, and she looked up into his eyes. He was dead serious now. "That's what I would have said yesterday, too," he told her. "But now I realize it's because you came back to Chance as a firefighter in spite of everything."

She frowned. "What do you mean?"

He gave a soft snort-chuckle, but he still didn't smile. "All of these people were pushing you away, dumping you out on your own, making you feel unimportant, but instead of leaving Chance forever and giving up your dream, you did exactly what you'd wanted to do anyway. You put yourself through school, got your master's on your own, came back to Chance, bought a house, and made your life. And you gave them the middle finger by becoming a firefighter instead of a cop. Don't think for a second my dad doesn't realize he lost out on one of the best officers he would have ever had."

Avery stared at Jake, emotions flooding through her, too fast and too many to name or concentrate on.

"You didn't even know this story. That's not why you've been kissing me for the past year."

"I've been kissing you because I really fucking like kissing you." He shifted her on his lap, emphasizing the bulge under her right butt cheek. "But I also like ruffling your feathers. Because it's hard to do. I didn't have to know the story to know you're tough and confident and strong. Trust me, making a woman like you melt in my arms is a rush I'll never get enough of."

Emotions choked her and she couldn't respond.

"I've never thrown you away, A," he said gruffly. "I'm very happy to say I'm smarter than that. I hated your letter. I've hated it every day since I read it. Once I kissed you again . . . I've been trying to get close to you for a year."

But he'd leave again. He was going back to Kansas City eventually. He wasn't enlisted this time. This time when he went it really would be because she wasn't enough to keep him here.

Still, he was here now.

"Melt in your arms?" she asked, forcing cockiness into her voice and lifting an eyebrow.

His intense expression smoothed into a mischievous grin in a snap. "Yeah. Something like this."

He slid a hand around her rib cage, grazing her breast as he did it, and up between her shoulder blades, sending tingles throughout her body. Then he brought her in for a kiss.

If the kiss outside of A Bar had felt different because she'd admitted that she liked him, this kiss—with the story of the past and the heartbreak and the anger out in the open—felt like a whole new world.

Jake's kisses had always heated her blood, made her crave things she couldn't even name, and put a yearning in her gut that made her think of nothing but getting closer to him.

Now, it was all that and more.

She couldn't open wide enough for him, she couldn't touch enough of him, she couldn't press close enough.

He seemed to feel the same way. Tongues stroking, their breathing heavy, he turned her to straddle his lap. He pushed her shirt up and pulled the cups of her bra down, his fingers rolling and tugging on her nipples.

Her hand didn't fit adequately between them, but she itched to touch him, to stroke and squeeze, to feel him pulsing in her grasp.

"Jake. Please."

"I know, I know." He kissed her again. "We should . . . go somewhere."

"We should definitely go somewhere."

They kissed again, their hands roaming, the frustrating inability to really do anything about their hunger ratcheting up the emotions to a near frenzy.

"I want you so bad."

"I want to taste you."

"I need to feel you."

"Now, please."

A hot rush of jumbled words and emotions filled the truck.

Until they heard the rumble of another engine.

The fire truck. The crew was here to prep for the bonfire. Avery sat up straight on Jake's lap.

His hair was mussed from her fingers, his lips wet from hers, and his eyes heavy with lust.

"Wow, you look good like that," she said as she pulled her bra and shirt back into place.

He grinned. And looked even better.

"Ditto."

"Let's skip the bonfire."

His eyebrows rose. "The fire chief is going to skip the bonfire? I think people might notice."

"It'll give them even more gossip to keep their minds off things. Especially after my spectacular exit from A Bar."

He chuckled. "That it would." His gaze went to something over her shoulder. "But we've already been noticed."

She pivoted to look and saw that not only was the fire department present, with two big trucks, but so was the police department. Specifically, Chief Mitchell.

Along with his wife.

Avery slid from Jake's lap, all of the endorphins from their make-out session seeming to evaporate at once.

"So, I heard your whole story and I . . ." Jake trailed off and gave a heavy sigh. "I'm not happy. I'm still processing the fact that I want to yell at my mother and punch my father."

Avery ran a hand through her hair. She was certain Jake had never even thought about doing either of those things before. She'd witnessed his family's interactions for years. They were damned near perfect.

The fact that he felt those things now, because of her, made her want to climb right back into his lap no matter who was outside.

"But," Jake went on, redoing the buttons Avery had gotten open so she could run her hands over his chest, "I don't really want that to be part of the town's entertainment tonight."

Avery nodded. It wasn't fair to make Jake deal with an awkward scene between her and his parents. "I'll stay out of your way."

"No."

His emphatic response surprised her. "No?"

"No. You will not be staying out of my way. Spending time with you tonight is more important than dealing with my parents."

She didn't miss that he'd used the word *important*. He *had* been listening to her tonight. Her heart melted a little.

"You can't avoid your parents entirely, Jake," she said. "People will notice if you give them the cold shoulder."

"I'll say hi before I find a way to lose them."

The idea of Jake trying to "lose" his parents was crazy. This was the Mitchells. One of the most perfect families in town. Maybe the world. "That will hurt your mom's feelings," Avery said.

"Well, that's her fault," he said with a frown.

Avery bit her bottom lip. It was kind of Heidi's fault, yes. Heidi had broken Avery's heart. And she really liked Jake being protective of her. A lot. But part of her hated the idea of Jake being angry with his mom. It didn't make complete sense. Maybe it was a product of her being older and more mature now. But she didn't want to be a wedge between Jake and Heidi. She cared about them both too much. Even after everything.

"I can make small talk for a little while."

Jake looked at her for a long moment. "You'd do that for me?"

She nodded. She'd do a lot for Jake. But she wasn't quite ready for him to know that.

"I don't want you to be hurt, Avery," he said quietly.

And she believed him. Which made her able to say, "It will be okay."

He leaned over and pressed a quick kiss to her lips. "Let's get this over with."

They got out of the truck at the same time, and Jake met his father at the front bumper.

"Son."

"Dad."

Wes turned to look at Avery. "Chief Sparks."

"Chief . . ." She trailed off and looked at Jake. "Wes," she amended.

Jake's dad was clearly surprised by her greeting. He started to respond, but Heidi appeared at his side at that moment.

"I heard an interesting story about the two of you at the bar," were Heidi Mitchell's first words to Avery since congratulating her on her election to chief.

"Later," Jake said, taking Avery's hand. "For now, you're going to let it go. You're going to let it *all* go."

Heidi and Wes both looked from Jake to Avery and back.

Avery held her breath.

Finally, they nodded.

She let out her breath. Of course they'd nodded. This was Jake. They would always have Jake's back.

They headed toward the bonfire like one big, happy family.

Everything Avery had always wanted.

Now she wanted to cry.

Jake couldn't remember ever being angry with his mother.

He also couldn't remember ever not enjoying a bonfire.

But it took everything he had to smile and chat and roast marsh-mallows and act like he was having a great time, act like everything was fine . . . and that he didn't want to use swear words with his mom.

Jake didn't swear around Heidi. No one did. She was the ultimate lady. She was sophisticated and conservative.

Yet he was biting back a good *What the fuck, Mom?* the entire time they watched the town's storm debris literally go up in smoke.

That didn't last once he stomped into the enormous kitchen in his childhood home after the bonfire.

"What the fuck, Mom?"

Heidi turned from the stove and her teakettle.

"Pardon me?"

Jake took in the details of his mother's perfect appearance. She was dressed in blue jeans, as was appropriate for a town bonfire. She also wore a T-shirt—a hot-pink T-shirt with a black twister in the middle that sparkled with silver glitter, much as the faux tornado with the twinkle lights had to be specific. Yet somehow, Heidi made the T-shirt-and-jeans ensemble look classy. It wasn't the bracelets and earrings she'd added, or the expensive leather boots she wore, or the black scarf she'd looped around her neck. It was how she carried herself.

Heidi had fallen in love with and married a hardworking blue-collar guy who'd gone into law enforcement and community service, but she came from money. On both sides of her family. Jake's maternal grand-parents, Jacob and Nita Williams, were natives of Chance. They owned the local dairy. His paternal grandparents were the Montgomerys. Heidi had always been involved with the family business. Her participation had grown in the past few years as her father gave up more and more work and focused on his golf game and fishing.

Thinking about it now, Jake suspected most of the money Heidi had given to Avery's grandmother had come from the Montgomery bank accounts. No way would his father's paycheck have been able to cover an extra three grand a month.

Instantly, Jake's anger was back.

"Avery told me about how you shut her out after she graduated and Ruth threw her out," he said bluntly. "What the hell? She trusted you. She *needed* you."

Heidi didn't react initially. She calmly turned and shut off the burner under the teakettle. Then she took a deep breath and faced Jake again. "You and Avery are getting close."

"Yes, we are."

Heidi's eyebrows rose. "I don't want you messing with her, Jake."

Now his eyebrows rose. "Pardon me?" he asked, mimicking her words to him.

"Avery . . ." She trailed off and needed to clear her throat.

Jake frowned.

"Avery needs stability. She needs people who are sincere with her. She needs people who will be there for her. I think you need to leave her alone."

Jake's eyes widened and he felt his mouth drop open. "*You're* telling me *I* need to leave her alone?"

Heidi crossed her arms and regarded her only son through narrowed eyes. "I would be thrilled if something would bring you back home for good. I'd be thrilled if you were the one to give Avery the stability and family she needs. Are you telling me that's what's happening?"

Back home for good.

The words hit him in the gut, and he had to pause a moment before responding. Home. He missed it. The town, his family, his friends.

Kansas City was a long way from here. Washington, DC, was even farther.

He loved his visits to Chance. They always seemed too short, and they didn't happen frequently enough. The first few years away from home had been good—he'd been busy with the Guard and training and then work. Max and Dillon had been there with him for part of that time, too, which helped. Then the first couple of years in Kansas City had been a thrill—the recognition of his talents, the attention to his work, important people calling him for input. But it wasn't long before it became harder to say good-bye when the visit to Chance ended. His condo had started to feel lonelier, his social life had started to feel routine, and he'd found his thoughts wandering to Chance more often.

This past year had been the hardest of all. He didn't think it was a coincidence that he'd kissed Avery again just before the yearnings for home had gotten stronger.

He loved his mom and dad. He missed them. But he was equally eager to see Avery when he came home.

That admission, however, would open a huge can of worms he wasn't quite ready to deal with.

Jake shook off the softer thoughts of Avery and focused on the newer information he'd been given—namely, that his mother had broken Avery's heart. "I want to know why *you're* not giving her the family and stability she needs."

Heidi looked at him for several seconds, a myriad of emotions crossing her face. "I thought it was the right thing to do at the time."

"Turning her away when she needed you the most? Cutting her off? *Hurting* her? How was that possibly the right thing to do?" he demanded.

Heidi's eyes filled with tears. "She needed to get away. Ruth was neglectful, at least, and emotionally abusive, at worst. I wanted Avery as far from that woman as she could get."

Jake's anger dissipated a little. He hadn't known about Avery's relationship with her grandmother in any detail, but the bit he'd heard tonight had him agreeing with his mother.

"But you wouldn't even let her in the house? You told her to get in her car and leave."

Heidi pulled in a shaky breath. "I did not handle that whole situation well at all," she admitted. "I know that. I've regretted it so many times over the years. You had just left. Maybe thirty minutes before she showed up. I wanted so badly to grab her and hold on and beg her to stay. But I knew she would do exactly that. I knew she'd never go. She never had dreams, Jake, because her grandmother told her over and over that she wasn't important, that how she felt and what she wanted didn't matter, so she didn't think she deserved to dream. She had to get out of this town and have a *chance*. But I knew I wouldn't be able to *let* her go if I didn't push her at that moment."

Jake felt his throat tighten as his mother's story came spilling out.

"I knew I'd never go if we talked about it ahead of time," he said. He'd told her the same thing that morning. "If you had cried and asked me to reconsider even a week before that, I would have."

Heidi nodded again. "I know. And I might have done that. The next day, when I was adjusted to the idea, and your father and I had talked, I realized the Guard was perfect for you. I was so proud." Heidi brushed a fingertip along her lower lashes, catching the tear that had formed there. "I immediately regretted what I'd said to Avery. I never wanted her to think she wasn't wanted or loved. But later I talked myself into thinking it was the right thing to do. She did need to go. She needed to have a chance at something more, something bigger. She needed to know she could do whatever she wanted."

Jake shifted his weight and worked on not going to her and hugging her. He needed to get the rest of the Avery story, and he needed to make sure his mom understood that she would *not* hurt Avery again.

He wanted to make Avery smile and blush and laugh. He wanted to kiss her some more. A lot more.

If he had to keep her away from his parents to make sure this was good for her, he would.

But he really wanted to heal all this. For Avery. For his mother. Not so they looked like a happy family to the town or the Bronsons when they came to visit, but because these two women meant a lot to him, and he hated to see them hurting. He hated to see them hurting each other. He fucking hated that he'd had anything to do with any of it.

If he hadn't asked her to prom, he wouldn't have realized how amazing she was, and she wouldn't have dreamed up the fantasy of becoming a Mitchell. If he hadn't left the next morning for the Guard without any warning or real conversation about it with his parents, his mother wouldn't have overreacted when Avery showed up on her doorstep.

"She had a plan," Jake said, his voice scratchy. "She had everything worked out in her head. She was fine leaving her grandmother's. She was ready to move on."

"But she was focusing on short-term training programs and staying here, afraid to spread her wings and realize her full potential. She'd never let herself think beyond the boundaries of this town."

Jake felt a bubble of anger rise again. What was wrong with being within the boundaries of this town? "Becoming a cop, taking care of her neighbors and friends, being a part of this community—that *you* love and give back to—how is that not realizing her full potential?" Jake asked, incredulous. "She basically wanted to be *you*."

Heidi nodded, looking miserable. "I know."

"How is that possibly a bad thing? How can that be something to push her away from?" He, too, had looked at his parents and wanted what they had. People looked up to Heidi and Wes; they were respected and liked and would have the backing of anyone in town. *Everyone* in town, if needed. They were part of the core of Chance.

"Your father and I love this town and our life here. But we didn't choose it. My future as a part of my family's business was predetermined, and your father couldn't afford to leave to go to college. The police academy was great for him, and he loves his work, but we're blessed it was something on the very short list of possibilities. My parents bought the house for us, and we got pregnant young, even though we had to try for a while. Our path was essentially drawn for us."

She took a deep breath.

"A very selfish part of me that loved you and Avery both so much wanted you to stay. To make your lives here. To live down the street, and have dinner with us three times a week, and sit with us in church, and let me take care of the grandkids after school," Heidi admitted.

Jake felt a streak of—something—go through him. He couldn't define it exactly. It felt like surprise, but it also felt like enlightenment or realization or awareness or something equally existential. "You wanted Avery and me to be together? To have kids?"

Heidi's eyes widened. "No. I mean, I wanted you to have kids. Each of you. Not necessarily together. I never thought about the two of you together."

Jake watched his mother stumble over her words, torn between amusement, because he'd clearly flustered her, and irritation. Maybe it was strange to think about two people you considered your children being together like that. But why wouldn't she have thought of him and Avery together? She didn't think they would make a good couple? She didn't think Avery was good enough for him? Or possibly—and more likely—that *he* wasn't good enough for Avery?

He crossed his arms and waited for his mom to continue.

Heidi shook her head as if to clear all that out. "But another part of me—thankfully, a bigger part—wanted you to each *choose* your path in life. If you ended up back here, it would be because you wanted to be here, not because you didn't have a better option."

Jake took that in and admitted what she said made sense. They were the thoughts and actions of a loving mother.

"But *Virginia*?" he had to ask. "You couldn't have pushed her out of the nest a little closer to the tree?"

"They were willing to work with us on the financial arrangement because I was an alumnus."

"Surely you could have set up a scholarship somewhere else."

"The school called it a scholarship at our request, but it was us paying the bills. Everything she needed was sent to us, and we paid it."

"You could have—"

"Yes, we could have done things differently," Heidi interrupted. "But we wanted her to get as far from her grandmother as possible, to see another part of the world, to truly be out on her own."

Jake felt his chest tighten at the thought. "She didn't want to be out on her own," he said. "She'd essentially been on her own since she was four. She wanted a home. A family."

Heidi drew herself up tall. "She had a family. From the time she was four. She was *my* family."

Jake looked at his mother, saw the defensive set of her spine and the possessive look in her eyes.

"Then how could you let her believe that you didn't want her for *ten years*? How could you not reach out to her? How could you not talk to her about all of this?"

Heidi looked miserable. "I tried to find her. But she didn't go to Virginia, and she didn't tell anyone where she did go. After trying to track her down for a few months, I finally went to Ruth. I had hoped to never speak to that woman again in my life, but I had no other option. I asked her for Avery's address and sent her a letter that basically told her everything I just said to you."

"And?" Jake asked.

Heidi shrugged. "She never responded. I assumed that meant she couldn't forgive me. Then, when Ruth died and Avery moved back a couple years ago, I ran into her on the street one day. I was so happy to see her. It *hurt* to not be able to hug her and tell her I'd missed her."

"Why didn't you? God, Mom, she needed to hear that." Jake couldn't believe the frustration that had his body wound tight from head to toe.

"I started my apology, but she cut me off. She said if I cared about her I would just leave her alone." Heidi wiped her eyes again. "And it's funny—even though she's pushed me away, part of me is so happy that she's stood up for herself. I want her to be strong and sure and to always cut toxic people out of her life. She dealt with her mom and grandma for eighteen years. Now I only want her to have people around who love her and make her happy. If I'm not one of those people in her mind, then I'm proud of her for pushing me away."

Jake shook his head. This was so complicated.

"She's not pushing you away, is she?" Heidi asked him.

"No, she's not."

"I'm glad."

He was, too. But he wanted her to have more. He wanted her to be happy, but he also wanted her to be healed.

Finally, he said, "We're going to make this *all* better. Starting with dinner. Here. Friday night."

CHAPTER NINE

"You actually said the word *fuck* to your mother?" Dillon asked as he threw old shingles from the roof to the ground.

"My mom would have knocked me into next week. Still. Even at my age." Max was kneeling, pounding new shingles into place on Gigi's roof.

Jake had to grin at that. Max was six foot three and solid muscle. His mother, Jodi, was barely five feet five. But she was tough. Jodi swore like a sailor; laughed loud and often; and when she yelled, her voice could be heard for a five-block radius. A fact that had been proven numerous times when the boys were growing up.

"I know," Jake said of his swearing at his mother. "It wasn't my best moment." He pulled another stack of shingles over between him and Max.

It was Thursday. Five days after the storm. They'd worked on the farm all day yesterday and were now getting started on repairs to Gigi's house.

The 110 Army National Guard troops who had arrived on Tuesday had truly been a godsend. The town and the farm were nearly cleared, most windows and roofs had been repaired, and rebuilding was under way all over.

If they could get the school finished up, all the big stuff would be done in time for the Bronsons' visit. There were residential areas that needed more work, but if they could keep the Bronsons' tour restricted to the farm, school, and other places that were most pertinent to their decision to move to Chance, there would be more time to spend on the hardest-hit neighborhoods after they left. But that was risky. If the damage in those areas scared the Bronsons off, Chance was screwed in spite of the hard work being put in. That would be almost more deflating than being hit by another tornado.

"Sounds like Avery's got you pretty worked up," Dillon commented.

His tone was casual, but Jake knew better.

"Yeah." What was the point in denying it?

"I wish I could remember what it was like to be really worked up about a woman in a *positive* way," Dillon muttered.

Max laughed. "You're not *positively* worked up about Kit?"

Dillon threw more shingles to the ground. "Is wanting to strangle her at the same time you want to kiss her positive?"

Jake and Max both pivoted to look at him.

"Still want to kiss her, huh?" Max asked with a grin.

"And strangle her," Dillon said. "You heard that part, right?"

Max nodded with an even bigger grin. "I heard."

"That's . . ." Dillon trailed off, clearly unsure how to finish the thought.

"A pain in the ass," Jake filled in. He knew exactly how Dillon felt.

"*Yes,*" Dillon said.

Max nodded. "For sure."

"I'm distracted, I'm swearing at my *mother*, I'm restless, I'm—" Jake broke off, swore—much as he had at his mother—and raked a hand through his hair.

"Not getting anywhere," Max guessed.

Jake frowned at him. "What?"

Max sighed and stretched to his full height. "You thought that what Avery needed was your attention, some flirting, some hot sex. But turns out she needs more, and it's something you're not sure you can fix, and that's going to make you crazy. Because you always need to fix everything."

Jake frowned at Max. But couldn't deny the words. "You know that's pretty much the pot calling the kettle black."

Max nodded. "Takes one to know one."

By "one" he meant a hero. Jake, Max, and Dillon all loved being heroes and had spent their lives seeking those opportunities. It came from the cousins' grandfather, who'd been the fire chief in Chance for fifty years, and their fathers—Jake's was a cop; Dillon's was a doctor; and Max's was a city councilman, volunteer firefighter, EMT, and volunteer . . . anything anyone in Chance needed a volunteer for.

"The hero thing is always harder with people you know," Max said, prying up more shingles and tossing them to the side. "We've talked about this before. It's why you're in Kansas City, remember?"

There were two people on the planet who knew all of Jake's issues. And he was facing them both in the hot sun on top of their aunt Gigi's roof. Fuck.

"I remember." Of course he remembered. He was *not* in Chance on purpose. Chance was small. And it was full of people he knew and cared about.

He had an irresistible drive to fix things and to help people, and he'd sought out bigger and better ways to do that. He'd gone from Chance to the National Guard, then got involved in emergency management for a big city, and was now, potentially, moving on to even grander things on a national level.

He knew it seemed that he was looking for a bigger stage and spotlight, more people to help, more amazing things to do, but there was more to it.

Helping strangers was easier than helping his hometown. Because it didn't always work out. It sucked when that happened and he had to deal with a certain level of anger and guilt, but it wasn't like it would be if it didn't work out for someone he personally knew and cared for.

"Maybe I am fixing things for her," Jake said. He really needed that to be true.

Whether he liked it or not, he was very personally involved this time in Chance. And not just with the cleanup. He could have fixed it if there was a hole in Avery's roof or the tree in her front yard had been uprooted. But no, her house hadn't had a single shingle out of place.

All her damage went a lot deeper.

"Oh?" Max raised an eyebrow again.

"We're having dinner with my parents tomorrow night."

Both of Dillon's eyebrows went up. "You're getting them back together."

Jake had shared with the guys the whole revelation about what had happened between Avery and his mother after graduation. They knew everything about him, and they were helpful and insightful. Once in a while.

"They miss each other," Jake said. "They need each other."

Max looked concerned. "What if it doesn't work out? Then there are *two* people for you to worry about."

"Why wouldn't it work out?" Jake asked, irritated because the thought had been nagging at him, too.

"I'm just saying it's been a long time. It's not like Avery is a poor, needy little girl anymore," Max said.

No, she didn't seem to be. She was, in fact, pretty kick-ass. Jake pulled his hand through his hair again.

He just could not shake the memory of talking with her in his truck at the bonfire. She'd never felt important to anyone. At least she'd never felt important *enough* to anyone. Including him. She'd been haunting his thoughts for a decade, but she hadn't felt important. That damned word kept echoing in his mind.

This was why he was helping Max with the roofing project. It was physical labor that didn't require a lot of thought and understanding. He'd been looking to work off some of his agitation and feel productive.

It had been working. Until Max started talking.

"What if being friends with my mother again isn't enough? Is that what you mean?"

"Exactly."

Continue to bug her until he figured out what *would* make her better. Then do it. Or buy it. Or *be* it.

The temptation to *be* what Avery needed was way too strong to be healthy.

"I'm hoping the hot sex will start working," he finally said, going for glib rather than honest in this case. These guys knew him. They would worry about his desire to be everything Avery wanted and needed.

"You failed to mention there had been more hot sex," Dillon said.

"Well, there hasn't . . . but . . . never mind."

Both men laughed.

"No wonder you're worked up," Dillon said, tossing Jake a bottle of water from the cooler they'd brought up the ladder with them.

This state of horniness wasn't *helping* anything, that was for sure.

Jake rolled the cold condensation from the plastic bottle over his face.

"What about you and Bree?" Dillon asked Max. "You still wondering what that would be like?"

"I knew what being with Bree would be like back in high school," Max said, suddenly *not* grinning.

"And in the ditch the other day," Jake pointed out, watching the face of the man he knew so well.

"The ditch was . . . complicated," Max said. Again. That seemed to be Max's favorite word when it came to Bree.

"Funny," Dillon said. "A lot of my patients tell me those near-death moments are the simplest—things get clear, you realize what's important. Your words and actions in those moments are driven by the purest emotions and intentions."

"That's so interesting," Max said in a tone that indicated it was definitely *not* interesting to him. "I didn't think of or feel anything for either of *you* in those moments."

Jake and Dillon both snorted. They weren't too worried about whether they were important to Max or not. They were. Dillon and Max were Jake's brothers in every sense of the word but pure biology, and they shared enough family traits for that to be a gray area at best.

"Just so you know," Max said to Dillon, "your psychoanalysis skills do suck."

"Or are they so good that they hit so close to home that you can't even face all the deep, secret things I know about you?" Dillon asked.

"That's creepy," Max told him.

Dillon shrugged. "The human mind is a scary place."

"Some more than others," Max added.

"For sure," Dillon said, pointing a finger at Max's nose.

Max grunted. Then he eyed the work Jake had done on the roof so far and grunted again.

Jake looked from the shingles to Max. "What?"

Max lifted a shoulder. "You're good. If you ever decide to leave that fancy desk job in KC, let me know."

"Fancy . . ." Jake trailed off. He knew damned well Jake didn't spend all his time behind a desk, and it wasn't fancy. He dug through debris, much like he was doing now. He oversaw rebuilding projects. He slopped through mud, and worse, at times. Sure, he also saw a lot of boardroom tables and podiums. Yes, he'd been to the White House and the Pentagon and lots of office and capitol buildings around the country. But he could, and did, get dirty with the best of them.

He surveyed the roof, then the view of the town he had from this vantage point.

He felt a definite sense of contentment.

Working to help strangers was easier because there were fewer emotions. Less guilt and remorse. But the emotions he missed out on included good ones, too, like pride and triumph and satisfaction.

He was putting Chance back together with his own two hands. He could see the progress from his high vantage point. It was like a healing wound, and it filled him with an unmistakable feeling of fulfillment.

Which was followed quickly by the thought that he'd really love to see the same progress and healing in Avery. Progress he could claim being a part of.

Fuck.

"I'm not moving to Oklahoma," he told Max, trying to get his mind off Avery for even five minutes.

"What about back here?"

Jake froze. Had he heard Max right?

"What are you talking about?"

Max nodded. "Roger Swanson wants to retire. He asked me to buy him out."

Roger had owned the local construction company for as long as Jake could remember. He was easily in his sixties, and Max, a hometown boy with an interest in and skill for building, was a logical choice to take over. Provided, of course, that Max wanted to come home.

"You serious?" Dillon asked.

Max nodded. "I love what I'm doing but . . ."

"This is home," Dillon said when Max trailed off.

"Yeah."

Jake felt his heart twist. None of them had ever stopped referring to Chance as home. That fact wasn't lost on him.

"The hospital board president asked me about staying, too," Dillon said.

"No shit," Max said. "You gonna do it?"

Dillon took a second to answer. "I think I want to."

Jake breathed out. Max and Dillon were both coming home.

"Our mothers are going to freak out," Max said.

Dillon grinned—something he didn't do enough of anymore—and said, "And grandma and Gigi and Shelby."

The town. The whole fricking town would freak out.

Jake knelt and picked up his hammer again, trying to ignore, or at least hide, the sharp sting of jealousy.

His cousins and best friends were coming home. They'd have barbecues together and get beers after work. They'd see their families regularly. They could pursue whatever was going on with Bree and Kit. Maybe it wouldn't work out, but at least they could try. There would be no what-ifs. The fucking what-ifs could make a guy insane.

They could also serve on the school board together or coach Little League or . . . a thousand things. A thousand seemingly small things that shouldn't be important next to the work they were each doing in their respective cities, but that still made Jake green with envy.

Of course he could consult with emergency-management officials, do presentations, write and blog from Chance. He could also work with Max. Jake loved working with his hands. He loved building things. There was a definite satisfaction in creating something where there had been nothing before or repairing something that had been damaged.

But if rebuilding tiny Chance could give him this incredible sense of gratification, then he couldn't ignore that he was being given an opportunity to do the same thing on a much larger scale. The job in DC was something Jake had always wanted, and he'd be damned good at it. He couldn't forget that working with FEMA meant he would help to support places like Chance all across the nation.

He could stay in Chance and build it up and support it and make it great. Or he could go to Washington and build up and support thousands of Chances and make the *nation* greater.

It wasn't that Chance wasn't important; it was just that he needed to look at the bigger picture.

And damned if even the *thought* of the word *important* didn't make his heart begin pounding.

Were strangers' lives more important than the people he'd grown up knowing and loving? Was sitting in meetings discussing policies and strategies for all of FEMA more important than nailing shingles back on his aunt's house with his own hands? Was having dinner with the head of Homeland Security and the president of the United States more important than having burgers with Max and Dillon?

Was being *important* to millions by doing something he was unquestionably good at more meaningful than being important to a woman who didn't trust or love easily and who made him work for every smile?

Yeah, Avery was teaching him a few things about feeling important.

Jake focused on hammering, but he couldn't ignore the hammering in his chest, too.

"We can get burgers at A Bar on Wednesdays like we used to," Dillon said, moving across the roof to a new spot.

"And take turns eating at our moms' houses all the other days," Max joked.

"I have missed your mom's chicken and noodles."

Jake tuned out their conversation and hammered another shingle into place.

Building with Max, burgers with Dillon—those were stupid things to be tempted by.

But he was.

Among other things.

Avery pulled up at the curb across the road from where Jake was helping repair the roof on his aunt's house. He was up on the highest peak—because where else would Jake be—and his back was to her.

He wore faded blue jeans that clung to his butt and legs like—well, like *she* would cling to his butt and legs given half a chance—and above the loving fit of the denim was a lot of smooth, bare, tanned skin and bunching muscles.

Watching him bend and reach and stretch and pound, her palms itched with the desire to slide all over that skin and those muscles.

She pulled in a deep breath.

She was in trouble.

Ever since the bonfire last night, she hadn't been able to forget how angry he'd gotten when he'd heard what had happened between her and Heidi. It had made her feel safe and cared for. And if his muscles were tempting, his protectiveness toward her was more so.

Even once they were with Heidi and Wes, he'd been tense. He wasn't the laid-back, charming, happy guy he usually was around his parents. He'd scowled at his dad twice and had physically put himself between Heidi and Avery. He'd also directed the conversation, keeping them chatting about nothing important or personal at all.

She could tell he was trying to shield her, and part of her definitely liked that. Too much.

Then she'd gotten a voice mail from Heidi telling her dinner was at six.

Tomorrow night.

The voice message from Heidi had been a shock. For about two seconds. Then she'd realized Jake had talked his mother into inviting Avery over.

She wasn't sure how she felt about that. It was sweet of him to care that she and Heidi were on the outs, but forcing a reconciliation wasn't going to work.

Still, that this mattered to him at all made her feel like she had when he'd brought her the sandwich the other day. Like he was paying attention and taking care of her.

So, she'd brought him a sandwich.

Now she felt a little foolish. Would he understand what the sandwich meant? Did she *want* him to understand that?

He turned to toss some shingles to the ground, and his eye caught her Jeep. The huge grin that spread over his face made her heart pound.

Yes, she did want him to understand that.

She got out of the Jeep.

She watched as he said something to the guys he was working with. They looked over and raised their hands in greeting as Jake made his way to the ladder propped against the side of the house. It was Max and Dillon. She waved back.

She had to admit, his taste in friends was another thing that made her think Jake was a good guy. Yes, they were his cousins, and they would have spent a lot of time together growing up regardless, but she knew the three men were close. Max Grady and Dillon Alexander were good guys. Really good guys. And they had a history together.

She envied that. She had never been close to girls her age. She'd gotten along with all of them in school, but she'd spent her free time at Jake's house with his mom.

It was pathetic now. Avery realized that as a teenager, she'd chosen a woman twenty-some years older than she was as a best friend and had preferred mani-pedi–and–milkshake nights over doing things with girls her age. Avery had learned at a young age that people who wanted her around, who liked her, especially those who *loved* her, were rare. So when Heidi—someone so sweet and kind and talented and smart and classy—had wanted her, Avery had clung to her.

It was why she'd do anything to protect the friendships she had with Bree and Kit and Liza. They didn't have a long, deep history like Jake and the guys, but the girls had worked at having a relationship with Avery, and that meant everything to her.

Whether it was gossip or a girls' trip out of town for the weekend, Avery was, for the first time in forever, part of a relationship that wasn't going to end in heartbreak.

But speaking of heartbreak . . .

Jake crossed the street, wiping his face with a bandanna he'd pulled from his back pocket.

"Hey," he greeted as he got close.

His smile said he truly was glad to see her, and her stomach flipped.

"Hi." She tried to keep her face and voice from seeming that she was *too* excited to see him.

"What's up?"

"I just wanted to . . . stop by." *Why* had she stopped by? Because she wanted to see him. She wasn't sure she was quite ready to admit that.

Now that he was up close, she was having a hard time keeping her concentration anyway. All that skin and those muscles were even more devastating up close. The glistening on his chest had combined into a few drops that were snaking their way from his pecs to his abs, and she couldn't have kept her gaze from following for all the money in the world.

"A?"

His voice was rough, and when she looked up, she saw his gaze was even hotter than his sun-kissed skin.

"Yeah?" She sounded funny even to her own ears.

"You know I'm willing and able to throw you over my shoulder. If you keep looking at me like that, it's going to happen again."

She wanted him to do it. So much.

"You're working," she said, because she felt like she should.

"I can take a break."

"Well . . ." Another drop of sweat ran past his left nipple, and she had to stop and swallow to keep from following it with her tongue.

"You're killing me." He said it softly as he stepped forward, backing her up against the side of the Jeep.

The hot metal of her vehicle was no match for the heat pouring off his hard body.

She looked up into his face. God, she wanted him. And she was sure he knew it.

"Come to my place. I'll shower and we can . . . do a bunch of stuff that will require another shower." He grinned down at her.

He wasn't touching her, but she felt as if he was. Her whole body was humming.

A shower. Things that would require another shower. His place.

His place.

She frowned. *His* place was in Kansas City. He was staying at his parents' house.

She couldn't have sex in Heidi and Wes's house.

"I brought you a sandwich." She remembered it suddenly and stuck it up between them, almost hitting him in the chin.

His gaze was knowing as he took it from her. "Thanks."

"Speaking of your *parents' house*." She wished he'd step back so she could think more clearly. "I got a voice message from your mom saying dinner Friday night was at six."

Jake pulled the sandwich from the plastic bag. "Good. I was wondering."

"About dinner," she clarified.

"The time."

"*Tomorrow* is Friday night."

"Right." He took a huge bite of the sandwich, then grimaced. But he covered it quickly and started chewing.

Avery narrowed her eyes. "You don't like ham salad."

He swallowed and took another bite.

"Jake."

"It's not my favorite," he said after he'd swallowed again. "But it's fine."

"You gave me ham salad the other day."

"I did," he said with a smile. "One of the ladies at the church was passing out sandwiches. I grabbed two because you hadn't eaten; I realized one was ham salad and one was turkey, so I kept the turkey." Jake was watching her closely as he ate. "That sandwich the other day got me some points, didn't it?"

What was the point in denying it? She wanted him to understand why she'd brought him one today. She nodded. "I kissed you because of that sandwich."

He leaned in. "What will you give me if I give you the other half of this one right now?"

She shook her head. "I don't especially care for ham salad, either. I thought you made the sandwich for me, and I thought that was sweet."

He moved in even closer, practically on top of her now. "I make the best fucking peanut butter-and-banana sandwich in the world. I'll even let you *watch* me do it. Think of how hot that will get you."

If her current state was anything to go by, the answer would be *very*.

"But that would also require us going to your *parents'* house. When were you going to tell me about dinner?"

"Mom was going to call you." Jake finished off the sandwich. He looked behind Avery, then leaned in.

She worked on not gasping—or moaning—as his upper body brushed hers. She prepared herself for the kiss she was sure was coming.

But she frowned when he leaned back a moment later. With the water bottle from her cup holder in hand.

"Hey." But she didn't get beyond that as Jake tipped the water back and drank. She was fascinated by the muscles of his throat working as he swallowed, the streak of dirt on his right shoulder, and the sheer *Oh, man, I want him* that washed over her as she watched him.

"Thanks for the sandwich," he said after he'd swallowed. He was looking at her closely.

She nodded. "Sure. I know the one you gave me the other day was just what I needed."

She almost grimaced at how awkward that sounded. But there was truth to it. She'd been hungry, and having Jake take care of her, even in that small way, had mattered.

He gave her a smile that seemed to heat her from the bottoms of her feet to the top of her head. "Yeah, this was exactly what I needed right now."

Something about that seemed like he meant more than the sandwich. Seeing her? Seeing her practically drooling over him? Whatever he meant, the whole exchange definitely made her feel lighter. Happier.

They stood smiling at each other for a moment in a dopey and confusing way she liked a lot.

Until a dog barked, grabbing Jake's attention. He swiveled his neck to locate the animal. It was a big black Lab that lived across the road.

"Damn," he muttered.

"You're still looking for the dog?" Of course he was. Mrs. Johnson had mentioned it to Avery that very morning.

"Yeah. Dammit. I don't know where else to look." Jake ran his bandanna over the back of his neck. "I put food and water out at the house, but nothing's been touched."

"At the house?" Avery repeated. "The dog's house?"

"Yeah."

Avery studied Jake's face. He looked right back at her.

"Have you dug through the house?" She'd seen the Huberts' house. There wasn't much left.

"We were there when we pulled Kayley out."

"And you started putting food and water out."

"Right."

"But . . ." She trailed off, hoping he'd follow her train of thought.

He frowned. "What?"

Nope, not following her train.

"I think you need to go back to the house. It's possible Cooper *is* there, you know," she said gently.

Jake looked at her for several heartbeats. Then he shook his head. "I promised her I'd find him."

Avery took a deep breath before opening her driver's-side door. "Then let's go find him."

Jake looked from the Jeep to Avery and back. "You'll come with me?"

She nodded. "Sure." Even if she didn't want to help him find the dog, which she really did, she didn't want him climbing around that house by himself. The Huberts' home was one of the most unstable structures in town. She was trained in search-and-rescue, just like he was. If nothing else, she could help keep him safe while he was going above and beyond in the heroic department for a dog.

He paused again and sighed. "Let me grab my shirt and stuff."

He jogged over to the pile of belongings on the tailgate of Max's truck and yelled up to the guys that he'd be back later.

They both grinned and Max yelled, "I won't wait up."

Jake came around to the passenger side of the Jeep and climbed in.

He looked solemn. She hated that look on him. Jake was supposed to look mischievous and happy.

They drove to the Huberts' house without talking. Avery didn't want to find Cooper in the house. She didn't want to see Jake upset about not keeping his promise to Kayley. She didn't want to see Kayley heartbroken. But the search with no results was starting to weigh on Jake, and Kayley and her family would be coming home soon.

They got out of the Jeep, and Avery grabbed two hard hats out of the backseat, handing one to Jake. She also grabbed work gloves, noticing Jake had picked his up when he'd retrieved his shirt and cell phone from Max's truck. They were both otherwise dressed for work, with boots and long pants on. Jake had, unfortunately, even put his shirt back on. They approached the rubble together, still without speaking.

Avery saw the dishes of food and water, and her heart melted a little.

"Fuck."

She turned to Jake.

"Do you think he's here?"

She shrugged. "I don't know. He's not very old. It's possible he ran off and couldn't get home."

Jake took a deep breath and shook his head. "I know I'm overreacting."

"You want to find a little girl's dog. There's nothing wrong with that."

"I just . . . She lost her house, probably a bunch of books and toys. Losing her dog, too, wouldn't be fair."

Avery felt her heart turn over in her chest. Damn. His caring about this little girl was hot. How could that make Avery want to take her clothes off?

She blew out a breath. "Tornadoes are anything but fair," Avery said softly.

He nodded. "That's why I work so damned hard to make as much of it okay as I can."

God. How was she supposed to resist this guy?

He looked so dejected that Avery would have done anything to ensure Cooper was alive. But without supernatural powers, all she could do was hold her hand out to Jake.

He took it and they climbed onto the first pile of debris.

At the back of the house, they split up. They both knew how to search, what to watch out for, how to deal with the hanging wires and unstable footing. They searched and dug without any sound other than that of throwing stuff out of their way. Avery prayed the entire time she would be the one to find the dog if he was, indeed, still in his house.

Her prayer was answered fifteen minutes later. She was in the area that had been the kitchen. The heavy appliances still stood, but the ceiling and walls had crumbled around them. She lifted a cabinet door and saw a tail.

She stopped, her eyes filling.

Dammit. It was the dog. She loved animals, but better the dog than the little girl who lived there. That was her general feeling. But this was going to hurt Jake.

She thought fast. Could she pretend she *hadn't* found Cooper and then come back later and take him out and bury him? The idea had merit.

She pulled on the cabinet door, and it shifted but wouldn't come fully loose. She jerked and yanked for a few minutes, but it was clear the door was still attached to something.

Crap.

She straightened, and stretched the kinks out of her back and neck. This sucked.

"Hey, Jake?"

She heard his footsteps coming closer. "You found something?"

"In the . . . kitchen." She supposed it was still technically the kitchen.

He came around the corner from the living room. "Is it him?"

She nodded slowly.

He took in a deep, shaky breath. "Dammit."

"I'm sorry."

He nodded. "I know. Me, too."

Avery realized that Jake had known, somewhere deep down, that the dog was here all along. He just hadn't wanted to believe it. And he'd kept working to keep Kayley's hopes up while she dealt with what else the storm had taken from her.

He made his way to Avery, having to duck under the crooked door frame and climb over what had been the wall separating the kitchen from the dining room.

"I was going to get him out myself, but he's under something that's not moving."

"Do we need tools?"

"I think we can do it together."

They did. Lifting together, they moved the entire cabinet up and over. Avery went to her Jeep for a blanket, and they wrapped Cooper up and carried him out to the front lawn.

Jake pulled out his phone and dialed a number.

"Hey, Dad, okay with you if I take that old wooden box that's in the garage?" He listened to his dad's reply and said, "Thanks. See you tonight," then disconnected and focused on Avery. "Can you take me home?"

She swallowed hard. He looked so sad. She wanted to hug him. When he referred to his parents' house—or anywhere in Chance—as home, her chest got tight.

Part of her loved that he thought of it that way. But it was also a sharp reminder that it was his home only in the sense that it was where he was from. He'd moved on, and she needed to keep that in mind. She needed to be unselfish and happy. For him, because he was living out his dream, and for all the people he was helping. She couldn't compete with the big, wide world out there that needed saving.

They drove to Wes and Heidi's, and Jake dragged the wooden box from the garage, dumping pieces and parts to old soapbox cars onto the driveway. They laid Cooper in the box, still wrapped in the blanket, and put the lid on.

They stood looking down at the box for a couple of minutes. Finally, Avery simply took Jake's hand.

A sigh went through him, and he squeezed her hand. The idea she might have given a tiny bit of comfort made her want to snuggle up and see how good she could really make him feel. And it was only slightly sexual.

He pulled his phone from his pocket again and dialed, still hanging on to her. A moment later he said, "Hi, Tim. It's Jake."

Avery squeezed his hand harder.

"Hey, we were over at the house, and we found Cooper."

There was a pause as Tim said something.

"No, I'm sorry."

Another pause.

"Yes, we're at my dad's house."

Another pause.

"See you then."

He hung up and pocketed his phone.

"They're on their way back to town. They're going to stop over and get him."

Oh. She didn't know what else to say to that. "Oh."

"Yeah."

They stood quietly. Finally, she tugged him toward the big wooden bench under the maple tree. She'd read the Little House on the Prairie books on that bench. The memory threatened to cut off her air for a moment, but she pulled Jake down onto the bench beside her. It was a good memory, and it comforted her. She wished she could give some of that to Jake.

He sighed and slumped against the back wooden slats.

She turned, tucking a foot up underneath her, and looked at him. "You did everything you could to find him. That's what matters. And it's what makes you so special. You know the truth, you see the destruction, you realize it's going to take hard work, and you understand it's not all pretty, but you have *hope* and optimism. You actually believe things can always get better."

She knew she was staring at him, but she'd finally put to words the ambiguous *thing* that drew her to him.

Jake sat up and turned to face her with a frown. "Things always *can* get better."

She nodded and bit her bottom lip. She wasn't sure she should say the rest of this or not.

Oh, what the hell.

"But *you* don't always have to be the one making it better."

She couldn't have described the look on his face. There was maybe a hint of surprise, as if he were surprised she noticed or said this to him, but there was also a collection of other things like anger and realization and . . . pleasure. That was the strangest of all.

"You're starting to understand me."

That seemed to be what he was pleased about.

"I think I might be. You do always think you have to be the one making things better?"

He shrugged. "I don't think I *have* to be. I've known a lot of great men—my dad, my grandfather, Max, Dillon, just to name a few—who can do everything I can. Maybe better than I can."

She wasn't sure she completely agreed that anyone was better than he was. "But?" she prompted.

"But I *want* to be the one making things better. I want to be the hero. I want to fix everything."

She looked at him closely. "So you want to be Superman?"

He gave a soft chuckle. "Of course."

"It's why you went into the Guard?" she guessed.

"Definitely. I remember my grandfather always being this big hero, and my dad, too. If there was a house fire, my grandfather helped save one family. If there's an assault or a robbery, my dad helps those people. But what if I could help even *more* people?" He gave her a wry smile.

Avery couldn't smile back. She'd known this about him. But hearing him say it made her feel sad while also feeling admiration and, if she was honest, even more drawn to him.

"Chance was never enough for you."

His expression went serious in an instant. "Chance was . . . is . . . my foundation. Chance is . . ."

"Not big enough," she filled in when he trailed off.

"Chance is hard on my heart," he said.

She looked into his eyes. "What's that mean?"

"It started when Abigail was killed our senior year," he said.

Avery nodded. Abigail and Dillon had dated all through high school. They were inseparable. They were a true love story.

"I was looking ahead to after graduation and considering what I wanted to do next. I was considering Chance and what I could do here. I was leaning toward the fire department." He gave her a little smile.

She tried to return it, but her entire body felt too tense.

"I knew I wanted to be in the business of saving people," he went on. "But, damn. Seeing Dillon, being there for him as he dealt with Abi's death, trying to get him through that . . ." Jake took a deep breath. "I knew it couldn't be that personal for me every day. I wanted to help people, but I knew it wouldn't always work out, I wouldn't always be *able* to save everyone, and I could not deal with that being friends and neighbors and family."

Avery nodded. She understood. She really did. And she fell a little more for him. How could she not? He cared enough that he would put his heart on the line every day with the people here.

"The job sure sucks sometimes," Jake said.

"It sure does."

They sat quietly for a few seconds; then Jake said, "There was a family in a tornado in Oklahoma."

Avery leaned in, making sure he knew she was listening. This more vulnerable, unsure side of Jake was interesting. And appealing. As if she needed more of *that*.

"The tornado hit their house. It was completely unstable, and we knew it was coming down. We got everyone out but the grandmother and her grandson. She wouldn't leave without him. He was about eight, a quadriplegic, in a wheelchair, and couldn't get himself out, and he was blocked in so that she couldn't get to him. She was the closest, the easiest to remove, so I picked her up and carried her out, kicking and screaming all the way." He was looking at their entwined hands rather than directly at Avery. "To get her to stay outside, I promised I'd go back in and bring the boy out. But . . ."

Avery felt a pang in her chest. "Jake."

"The house collapsed before I could get back in. We dug down and found him, but he was gone."

She reached up and rubbed his shoulder. "That wasn't your fault."

"The grandmother was screaming. She came up to me and pounded on my chest, told me it shouldn't have been my decision. That she would have gladly given up *her* life for his. That she'd lived a long life, but his was just beginning."

The woman had been grieving, in shock, blaming the easiest person to blame. But it was Jake, and he would take that all to heart and carry it around with him forever after.

Avery gave in to the temptation that had been nagging her ever since she'd shown up with the sandwich. She went up on her knees on the bench between them and wrapped her arms around Jake's neck.

There wasn't a second's hesitation. He wrapped his arms around her, too, and pulled her into his lap and against his chest.

They just held each other like that, breathing deeply, not saying a word until a car pulled into the driveway.

Avery leaned back and looked into Jake's eyes.

Again, there was a host of emotions difficult to name.

"Thanks," he said simply.

"No problem."

He smiled the smile she loved, and it even reached his eyes.

"By the way, the next time you're up against me like this—it won't be so sweet."

She gave him a smile, too, and wiggled her butt against his crotch. "Feels pretty sweet to me."

"A—"

"Jake!" Tim Hubert and his family had climbed from their car.

Avery pushed herself off Jake's lap, but he gave her butt a quick pinch before rising and extending a hand to Tim.

"Thanks for looking for Cooper," Tim said quietly.

"I promised Kayley."

Tim nodded.

Kayley and her mom and brothers joined them. Kayley looked somber.

Jake crouched in front of her. "Hey."

"Hi."

"How was your grandma's house?"

She lifted a shoulder. "Fine."

Then a tear slipped down her cheek.

Avery felt her own eyes sting, and she wished she could grab Jake's hand again. For his sake or hers, she wasn't sure. Maybe both.

"You found Cooper, huh?" Kayley asked.

Jake nodded and cleared his throat. "Told you I'd keep looking."

"And I was right. He was still at the house," Kayley said.

"Yep, you were right."

The little girl shot a scowl at her brothers.

"Daddy says we're gonna have a funeral," Kayley told Jake.

"I think that's nice." Jake cleared his throat again. "Kayley, I'm sorry. I really wanted to have him be okay."

She nodded. "I know. Mr. Landers told me you tried hard to find him."

Mr. Landers was the Huberts' next-door neighbor.

"I did," Jake told her.

"He said you put food and water out."

"Yes. I did."

Kayley stepped forward and put her hand on Jake's shoulder, looking at him intently. "Thank you. That was really nice. It's not your fault he got knocked down by the tornado."

Avery couldn't see Jake's face, but she had to wipe at her eyes.

He cleared his throat, then coughed and finally nodded. "Thanks. That makes me feel a little better."

"Let's get Cooper back home so we can give him a nice funeral," Tim said, his voice sounding a little scratchy, too.

They all turned and headed back for the driveway and the wooden box waiting for them.

Kayley hung back for a moment. When everyone else was out of earshot, she moved in close to Jake and said in a loud whisper, "Thanks for not telling me I was silly to think Cooper was still alive. You thought so, too, huh?"

Avery moved so she could see Jake's reaction. She was about to start blubbering herself.

Jake's face was tight with emotion, but she could see that one of those emotions was relief.

"There are plenty of people to think the worst," Jake told her sincerely. "I hope you'll always be on my side hoping for the best."

Kayley nodded and patted his shoulder. "I will."

Then she headed after her family.

The Huberts loaded the box and then all climbed into the car and, with a little honk, were gone.

Avery turned slowly to Jake. "I don't care what you say. What you said to that little girl was heroic."

He shrugged.

"And what she said to you was heroic."

"Yeah."

"That was amaz—"

He grabbed her by her upper arms, hauled her up against his body, and kissed her.

Avery didn't know what was going on, but she wasn't going to complain. She wrapped her arms around his neck and arched close.

Jake's hands splayed between her shoulder blades and on the curve of her lower back as he brought her up on tiptoe to fit belly button to belly button.

The kiss was hot but also sweet. It felt different again. Damn, was she ever going to feel like she knew what to expect with this guy?

Jake lifted his head, but only long enough to change his angle and come down again. He licked along her lower lip, then stroked firm and possessive against her tongue.

It felt like he was trying to absorb her, drink her in, and Avery let him. She gave herself over completely to the kiss, to the way he held her, to the moment—content to be there for him, whatever he needed from her.

Finally, minutes later, he dragged his mouth away. Breathing heavily, he rested his forehead against hers.

"For the record, *you* thinking I'm a hero makes me hot."

She felt her eyes widen. "That's what that was all about?"

He loosened his hold on her slightly, and she found her feet flat on the ground again. "Yep."

She didn't loosen her hold on him much. "Why?"

"Because you're you—you're hard to impress. Knowing I did makes me feel . . ."

She felt her mouth curving as she waited for him to fill in that blank.

"Hot," he finally said with a self-deprecating grin.

She laughed and started to step back, but with one arm still around her waist, he brought her up against his hard body again.

"Come inside with me," he said gruffly.

Her gaze skittered to the house, then back to his face. There were beds only a few yards away. Many times she'd imagined what she could do with—*to*—Jake on a nice sturdy bed.

But she shook her head. "I am not fooling around with you at your mom and dad's house."

"They're not here."

"They will be."

"I'll be fast." That damned grin was back in place.

She put her hands flat on his chest and pushed slightly, chuckling. "I've had your fast."

"That was my eighteen-year-old fast. My twenty-eight-year-old fast is a lot better."

She gave him a cheeky grin and pushed him back farther. "You were twenty-eight in the shed."

He groaned as if she'd wounded him, but she knew better.

"I need you, A."

The words, the nickname that she was *supposed to* hate, the husky tone of his voice, all made it nearly impossible to shake her head. But the problem wasn't that this was his parents' house.

It was that she'd just realized she was mostly in love with him.

Sex with Jake had always been great. Sex with Jake when she was mostly in love with him might be beyond great. How was she supposed to live her life after he left, having had beyond-great sex and knowing she'd probably never have it again? Or at least not with anyone else? Could she live the rest of her life having sex only four times a year when Jake visited?

Better to not know for sure what she was missing.

Or something.

The heat in Jake's eyes, the emotions of their afternoon—okay, of all the days since he'd stepped back into Chance—the nearly impossible *need* she felt simply looking at his mouth, all combined into a swirling ball of panic.

She needed to go back to work.

She needed to get ready for dinner. Here. With his parents. She had twenty-four-and-some-odd hours. She was going to need every one of them.

"I need to go back to work," she said, taking a big step backward, away from temptation. She started for her Jeep before she could change her mind. "I'll see you tomorrow morning at the strategy meeting."

"This isn't over, Avery."

She didn't respond. She kind of hoped that was true.

But she was going to keep pretending everything was normal, and that she was in total control, and that she wasn't on course for the biggest heartbreak of her life.

CHAPTER TEN

Jake walked into the Friday-morning strategy meeting with purpose.

The past two mornings, the meetings had been short and sweet. Everyone gave their reports, and then everyone got out, back to the tasks and people who needed them.

Things were going very well considering their timeline. Cleanup was ahead of schedule; rebuilding at the school was slightly behind, but only because some supplies had been held up in shipping. A problem that had taken Jake three phone calls to solve—two more than he liked to have to make. Still, the bricks and lumber and drywall paste were now in Chance and being put to use.

The reports wouldn't take long, and Jake was prepared to use the rest of the meeting time to fill everyone in on his brilliant new idea.

The thought had been niggling in the back of his mind for a long time. But at the meeting the first day in Frank's office, when everyone had come together, things had started to jell. Shelby had said something that had turned on a lightbulb. She'd said everyone in that room was important to the cleanup, that they were all a part of keeping the town together and getting it back on its feet.

Jake had felt a thrill shoot through him. He was used to being a part of teams, used to bringing people together, used to tapping into experts to get things done, but there had been something about *that* group in that room at that moment.

Then yesterday . . . between the roof and Dillon and Max talking about coming home and then, well, Avery. All of Avery—everything about her—from the way she'd checked him out when his shirt had been off, to the way she'd gone with him to look for Cooper and the way she'd hugged him on the bench, and the way she'd looked up at him, her eyes full of desire and vulnerability and fear and temptation . . . yeah, everything about Avery was behind this announcement.

Jake stepped into Frank's office. Everyone was already there just as he'd planned. The vibe in the room was noticeably different from the first day when everyone had been standing, a little tense, exhausted from the night before. Now everyone seemed much more relaxed. Kit and Bree were sitting in the chairs in front of Frank's desk; Max leaned against one wall; and Dillon, who flat-out didn't relax well, stood in the middle of the room. But his hands were in his pockets, and he was smiling.

And then there was Avery. She was also smiling, chatting with Shelby, in her white button-down shirt and khakis, her hair up, her glasses on. Hot and in charge. Happy.

The sight of her made him ache.

Then she turned and saw him. Her smile grew, and he knew he wanted her lighting up because of him forever.

"Morning, everyone." He strode to the middle of the room.

"Morning, Sunshine," Max said, giving him a funny look.

Jake was feeling almost giddy. Not a manly adjective, but accurate. Things were good—great, even.

"How are things around town?" Jake asked Avery, handing her a folder first.

"Um, great," she said. "But you know that."

"How's the mental health of our fair city, Doc?" Jake asked Kit.

She looked at Avery, then back to Jake. "Fine. For the most part."

"Great, good job." He handed Dillon a folder. "And the physical health?"

"Improving," Dillon said, taking the folder with an eyebrow up.

"How about the public safety?" Jake asked Bree.

"Everyone's safe and sound, Sergeant Major," Bree said with a salute.

He gave her a grin and handed her a folder.

"Mr. Mayor, our fearless leader." Jake handed Frank a folder. "How are things looking from your perspective?"

"Couldn't be better, Jake." Frank clapped Jake on the shoulder. "You've all done a hell of a job so far."

Jake moved over in front of Shelby. "And my beautiful, sweet, caring, impetuous cousin. Are you happy?"

She looked suspicious. "You're acting weird. What's going on?"

"I'm here to tell Frank that the idea he and I were kicking around the other day is going to go."

"The idea?" Shelby echoed, looking at her husband.

Frank glanced up from the folder. "Really?"

Jake grinned at him and nodded. "I've been thinking about it a lot, and I think we should do it."

"When was this?" Shelby asked.

"We were talking about it Tuesday morning," Frank said. "I was with the reporters, answering a million questions about how it felt to get hit for the third time in a row, what I thought about this area getting hit ten times total, all those stupid-ass questions, when one of the reporters asked me what advice I would give to other communities."

"It occurred to us that our tornado epidemic has made us the experts in preparing and recovering from them," Jake said.

"A training center?" Max and Dillon asked at the same time.

They'd obviously read the first page in the folders.

Jake nodded. "Right here in Chance."

He glanced at Avery. She was also looking at the folder. Staring at it, actually. As if she were stunned. He frowned. That wasn't exactly the reaction he'd been going for.

"It's perfect timing," Frank said to Max and Dillon. "We can get your input on everything."

"What do you mean?" Dillon asked.

"Everything from our warning systems to our posttrauma care has been tested over and over," Frank explained. "And, if I do say so myself, we're damned good at all of it. We can use our knowledge and experience to train other communities. Take the negativity of our repeated hits and turn it all into something good."

In his peripheral vision, Jake could see Max nodding. Bree and Kit had their folders open, but their attention was on Frank. Avery was still staring at the folder in her hands.

"Small communities like Chance, and ones smaller, don't have the resources bigger cities do. And preparation and recovery in a rural area is different from a metropolitan area, anyway. Small towns are, as you all know, dependent on volunteers mostly. This resource-and-training center will focus on those areas and people. We'll give them specific hands-on training they can take home and implement immediately," Jake went on.

"Obviously, you guys have a lot to offer us in regard to trainings and such," Frank added. "Honestly, having your stamp of approval on it would mean a lot. Especially when it comes time to fund it."

Jake did catch Avery's eyes roll at that.

"I told Frank on Tuesday that I'd be happy to endorse it," Jake said to the group. "I'm able to help secure some state and federal funds. I'm also happy to come and teach some sessions from time to time."

Frank's grin was enormous. "Jake, that's great! Having you directly involved will be huge. We couldn't ask for a better endorsement, and having you teaching here—wow."

Avery still hadn't said anything.

Jake looked over at her, but her gaze was on Frank now. Jake stared at her, willing her to look at him. She had to feel the weight of his gaze. But she remained stubbornly concentrated on Frank.

Frank was not that interesting. Ever.

Still watching her, Jake said, "We want the city departments involved. It's one thing to go in as an outsider to a community that's been affected; it's another to be *from* the community. You can all offer a fantastic perspective on what it takes to rebuild from the inside and work as a team. Typically, we pull in specialists from all over to lead a summit or training session. This will be unique in that people will be learning from a team that works together all the time. Our students would be coming here. They will see up close and in person what it's like in a community that's been rebuilt, how the town prepares, the immediate action plan, the long-term efforts, everything."

"Yes, yes, we'll want all of you involved," Frank agreed.

"We're going to share everything we know," Jake said. "From the off-season education and preparations to what happens on the day of a storm to what's happening the next day, the next week, the next month. And we won't need a specific building. We can set up the headquarters here at city hall and use the conference rooms. But we'll take our students all over town—to the police station and the fire station to witness some reenactments of what the day of a storm might look like, to some of the businesses and even homes that have been hit and rebuilt. The whole town will be like a living, working resource center."

"Avery and Bree, we would want you to walk other departments through the various stages of preparing and recovery," Frank said. His enthusiasm was apparent. "You can cover what your departments need to know, your roles before, during, and after the storm. All of that. Jake will be happy to help you, I'm sure."

Avery frowned at that. "We've done this before, without Jake."

They had. Jake would like to think it had been better with him around, but she seemed annoyed, and he wasn't sure pointing that out would be a good thing at the moment.

He did frown at her, though. What was she annoyed about? After their afternoon together yesterday, he'd thought maybe she'd be happier about having him around more.

"I'm sure Avery and Bree will do a great job," he said. "Though if you'd like some input, all you have to do is ask." He wasn't going to step on her toes and offer assistance unless he was sure it was wanted.

"I'd be happy to consult on emergency medical preparedness," Dillon offered. "We could run some drills. Maybe have some past injury victims talk about their experiences."

"Good idea." Frank nodded. "That would be good for those survivors, too, to focus on the positives."

Kit nodded. "I like that idea."

"This is so great," Shelby suddenly gushed.

Jake looked at his cousin. She was practically wiggling with happiness.

"All of this is part of the overall message we want to send—to the people outside of Chance and to the people who live here," Shelby said. "We want everyone who lives here to stay and feel safe, and we want people to not be afraid to visit or consider moving here. So we'll focus on expecting the unexpected."

"Expecting the unexpected?" Bree asked.

Shelby nodded. "Tornadoes aren't unexpected here. Neither is the damage or the cleanup needed afterward. That's our message. We know the storms will come, but that doesn't change our happiness. We live our lives fully in spite of knowing the rain will come again. We plant flowers in spite of the certainty of hail. We rebuild our churches and schools even though we know they could get knocked down. We appreciate the sunny, warm days more because we know not every day is like that."

No one spoke or moved for several moments after her little speech. That all sounded . . . very nice.

"We pull together," Shelby went on. "The storms remind us what's important and *who* is important." She gave them each a beatific smile.

Not for the first time, Jake wondered if Shelby wasn't planning to maybe make her own run for mayor when Frank's term was up.

"Nicely said." Jake finally broke the silence.

"And June will be our big month. We'll train all year, but we can invite people to Chance in June to see us in action," Frank said.

"Wait. You're going to invite people to Chance *during* the peak tornado season?" Avery asked.

"Sure. Even if we're not hit, we can show them how we prepare, stock supplies, watch the weather, run drills," Frank said. "And if we're lucky, they'll be here to see how we handle a hit."

Avery's eyes went wide. "If we're *lucky*? You're *hoping* for a hit?"

"Not really," Frank said. "I'm just saying if it happened, it wouldn't be *all* bad. They could see us in action then. Like . . . visiting a dude ranch. They'd get the true, real-life experience."

"This is crazy." Avery looked around the room for agreement.

"It's a wonderful opportunity," Shelby said brightly. "Inviting people to town in June shows we're not afraid, and they shouldn't be, either."

"We can't invite people to Chance during tornado season," Avery said firmly. "It's like we're a magnet for EF4s!"

"Which is why we should be the hub of all things tornado related," Jake said.

"We?" Avery repeated, looking up at him.

Yes, *we*. He was a part of all this. His heart had always been in Chance, but this past week, this recent tornado and recovery, had shown him he wanted more. Even if he were in DC with FEMA, he could find a way to get back to Chance more often. If there was another hit, or if there were training sessions going on, he could find a way to be here.

He intended to bring it up during his first meeting in DC, in fact. He wanted to be knee-deep in the mud here and picking up the pieces here and looking for lost dogs here. He wanted to put those pieces back together and give little girls words of comfort and join in the celebrations. Yes, it was tougher here when things went bad. But it also felt better here when things were good.

"Yes, we." He also wanted Avery to know she was a part of all this for him, what he wanted, what he needed. But that was a conversation for later, when they had some privacy.

"So," he went on, addressing the room, "we use the publicity surrounding our third hit in a row to promote Chance as the place to come to learn all about tornadoes and how to stay safe. We can put a little museum in city hall chronicling the hits and our recovery; we can have citizens talk about what it's like, what they wish they'd known, how they rebuilt."

"We can put in a gift shop with tornado-themed trinkets," Shelby added. "Mugs, necklaces, postcards, that kind of stuff."

Avery looked from Shelby to Frank to Jake and back. "This is ridiculous," Avery said. "You all know that, right?"

"It's *perfect*," Shelby gushed. "This is our opportunity to put a positive spin on everything. Pun intended."

"Hey, we could do a camp for the kids," Max said. "The kids could spend time learning about meteorology and storm tracking, how tornadoes form—"

"They could make their own tornado in a bottle," Shelby said, cutting in. "Have you seen that? It's, like, a science experiment where you have water and food coloring and you tape the two plastic bottles together."

Jake chuckled. He appreciated the enthusiasm. "We could go over tornado drills and stuff with them, too," he said. "Each kid could leave at the end of the week with a supply kit and safety plan for his or her family."

Avery opened her mouth—probably to tell him that bringing kids to Chance when there was almost sure to be a tornado was asinine—but she met his gaze and hesitated. Then closed her mouth without a word.

That was interesting.

"Avery?" Jake asked. They didn't have to agree on everything. He wanted her input, good and bad.

She pressed her lips together and swallowed hard.

"You know all the debris we've been gathering," she finally said. "I was thinking we could . . ." She took a deep breath. "We could use the debris to design a skateboarding park. Or a sledding hill. Or both."

Jake stared at her. She'd just offered an idea that went along with this plan.

"How would that work?" Shelby asked.

"We use the debris and rubble as landfill."

"I don't understand," Shelby said.

"We pile it up and pave over it," Jake said. "Or pile it up and cover it in dirt and use it for sledding in the winter."

Avery was still looking at him. She gave him a smile. "Right."

He liked that they could intelligently and passionately disagree on things, but damn, he loved it when they were on the same page. He winked at her. "Great idea."

Shelby clapped. "Perfect. I love it. The camp and the training center and the sledding hill! Everyone's going to agree that tornadoes rock!"

Well, that might be pushing it. But he'd said it once and he'd say it again: as far as natural disasters went, this tornado was turning out to be his favorite.

"Are you ready for tonight?" Kit asked Avery.

She, Kit, and Bree were sitting at their regular table at A Bar. This time Avery decided she was starting with dessert.

Was she ready for dinner with Jake and his parents? Avery shook her head. "Uh, no. Definitely not."

"You don't have to go," Bree said. "Just because Jake wants you to do it doesn't mean you have to."

She would love not to go. It was going to be awkward anyway, and now, after the meeting in Frank's office, her head was spinning and her heart was pounding, and she was sure that tonight was going to make everything worse.

Ten years ago, she'd spun a big happily ever after out of prom and graduation-night sex.

Now she had big feelings for Jake, she was going to have dinner and possibly reconcile with his parents, and he was talking about staying.

She had needed to keep a tight hold on her imagination ever since hearing Jake's idea for turning Chance into a tornado resource-and-training center. She could *not* let this turn into another big, naive fantasy in her mind.

Jake *wasn't* talking about staying, Avery reminded herself harshly. He had never once said he was moving back to Chance.

But the way he'd lit up about the project . . .

Her stupid heart had started to hope. Avery felt her eyes stinging, and she sniffed.

That sniff was like a fire alarm for her friends.

Kit looked up quickly and Bree gave a little gasp.

"Oh my God." Bree scooted her chair closer to Avery. "Talk. What's going on with you and Jake?"

Immediately, Avery's throat tightened and she felt the tears well up.

"Holy shit," Bree breathed.

"Give her a tissue," Kit said, handing Avery a glass of water.

"You give her a tissue; I'm getting her a shot." Bree waved her arm in the air for the waitress.

Crying was also something Avery didn't do.

Kit dug in her purse, and the waitress arrived with three shots of cinnamon schnapps—Bree's go-to.

"I can't have a shot," Kit said. "I have appointments this afternoon."

"I know." Bree took two of the shot glasses and pushed one toward Avery.

Avery did, in fact, tip the shot back. One wouldn't hurt, and if it would help, she was all for it. The cinnamon liqueur burned its way down her throat, and she dabbed at her eyes.

"Do you want to talk about it?" Kit asked after Avery had pulled in a deep breath.

"Don't *ask* her," Bree said. "Tell her to talk. She needs to talk."

"I don't *tell* people they have to talk," Kit said.

"You tell *me* I have to talk," Bree pointed out.

"You're different."

Bree rolled her eyes and turned back to Avery. "What's going on?"

Avery swallowed hard. She'd wanted to get better at girl talk. Here was her chance.

Kit and Bree loved her. They were the first people to give her unconditional love in her life.

She clung to that as she said, "I think I'm falling for Jake."

They both just sat looking at her.

After a moment she said, "That's it. That's what I need to talk about."

Bree and Kit exchanged a look.

"What?" Avery asked.

"Honey, we knew you were falling for Jake," Bree said.

Avery frowned and looked at Kit. Kit nodded.

"Not a crush. Not sex," Avery said. "Like, maybe really love."

Again, they didn't react at first.

Finally, Bree nodded. "Yeah. Really love. That's what we figured."

"You're supposed to be telling me it's not real," Avery said to Kit, her tone accusatory. "You're the psychiatrist. You're supposed to point out that it's my pattern to build up these fantasies and it only ends up hurting me. You need to tell me how to fix it."

Their food arrived, but they all ignored it. For Bree to ignore a bacon cheeseburger really said something about her feelings and concern for Avery.

Avery dabbed at her eyes again and wished for another shot.

Kit took one of Avery's hands. "What's your pattern? Tell me about that and these fantasies you're building up."

Avery took a breath. She was overreacting. She knew it. But she couldn't stop. "It's because of the meeting this morning," she said. "Jake was in there talking about all of these big, amazing plans. He was so excited, so into that whole training idea."

Kit nodded. "They all seemed into it."

"That got me thinking about how great it would be for him to put that together and make it happen and . . . that he would have to stay then. And my mind ran with it. I always do this."

"Do what?" Kit encouraged. "Your pattern?"

Avery nodded. These girls didn't know everything about her mom, but they did know about Jake and the river. "It started after we went to prom, and then when he kissed me on graduation night it blew up. One kiss and I thought all of my dreams were coming true. I thought we'd get married and have this amazing life and . . . it's ridiculous. I'm not a naive eighteen-year-old anymore. What's wrong with me?"

Kit shook her head. "Nothing is *wrong* with you, Avery. But I think this goes deeper than graduation night."

It did. Graduation night had been just one more fantasy that came from a mind that had been building happily ever afters her whole life. Make-believe happily ever afters.

Avery nodded. "It's what I always did with my mom."

She sniffed and Bree slid closer, taking Avery's other hand.

"Tell us about your mom," Kit said gently. "I know she was in and out of your life a lot when you were younger."

Avery nodded. She wanted to talk about this. That shocked her. She usually didn't even like *thinking* about it.

"My mom came to visit two or three times a year. She'd stay for a few days, and while she was here we had such a great time. But she never stayed in one place very long. She said there was a great big world out there and exciting places to go and people to meet."

Avery stopped, needing another breath. Until she'd said that all out loud she hadn't realized how much . . .

"That sounds like Jake," Bree said.

Yeah, that.

Kit was biting her bottom lip, something Avery knew meant she was thinking hard.

"Go on," she said.

Avery took another breath. She hated thinking about her mom and how every damned time Avery got sucked into the fantasy of Brooke staying in Chance and being a real mom—sitting in the front row at the spelling bee and beaming proudly, or taking Avery shopping and holding her hand, showing everyone they belonged together.

"The last time she ever visited was two days before my twelfth birthday," Avery said, hating how her voice wobbled. "She promised she was staying for my birthday, and we even planned a party. She was going to make me a cake."

"She *left* without doing the cake or having the party?" Bree demanded, clearly outraged.

Avery nodded, her heart a little lighter simply because Bree looked pissed enough for both of them. "Left the morning of the party. When I asked my grandmother why she'd gone, Ruth said, 'Got what she came for.' When I cried about it, Ruth told me that's what I got for thinking I was something special." Avery wished she was mature and wise enough to not let the replay of those words bother her all these years later, but she wasn't quite.

Kit squeezed her hand. "That's how you feel about Jake? That once he gets what he came for, he'll leave because you're not important enough for him to stay?"

It was precisely how she felt about Jake. She nodded.

"And you think the training center is like the birthday party," Kit said. "That he's making promises in the moment, but when something else comes along, he'll be gone."

Avery nodded again, feeling like someone was squeezing her heart in a vise.

"My God, I wish your grandma were still alive!" Bree exclaimed, sitting back in her chair, nearly vibrating with anger. "I would love to give that old bitch a piece of my mind."

Avery couldn't believe it, but she smiled. It was good Ruth was gone, because Bree would, no doubt, storm over to the trailer park to have a talk with her . . . and maybe end up looking out through the bars she was supposed to put other people behind. Avery's heart tried to expand inside the tight fist of emotions and memories that had a hold on it.

It was amazing what a little love could do.

"I've told myself over and over that there will always be something more important to Jake, that he's here short term. I was kind of okay with it. I didn't like having feelings for a guy who's always going to leave, but I was dealing," she said. "Then this whole tornado thing happened, and the Bronsons are coming to town so he stayed for the cleanup, and now he's talking about this training center. He's getting all caught up in things, and when I listen to it I find myself getting wrapped up, too, and thinking maybe this time is different."

"Maybe it is," Bree said. "People change. Their priorities can change."

That might be true. For some people.

"But it would have to be something more important than his current priorities."

"Something like *you*," Bree said loyally.

Avery gave her a smile. She would love for that to be true. She would love to think she was special to Jake, important enough for him to want to change his life.

"I'm just a girl," she said. "There are millions like me in the world. He's one of a kind, and what he does is extraordinary."

Kit looked both sad and concerned when Avery met her gaze.

"You matter, Avery. You're important to this town; you're important to Bree and me."

That was exactly why Avery was happy and content in Chance. She was the fire chief, and she was damned good at it. And now she was someone's friend. She was working hard at being damned good at that, too.

"Thanks. I l-love you guys."

God, that *L* word was a tough one.

Kit and Bree knew, and didn't even blink at her stuttering over the sentiment. Kit leaned in and hugged her; Bree squeezed her hand and then signaled the waitress again.

Kit sat back and looked at Avery with a touch of sadness but also a lot of affection. "I think I'm in on this round, after all."

"That's my girl," Bree said. "On her tab," she told the waitress, pointing at Kit.

Avery laughed.

Yes, it really was amazing what a little love could do.

CHAPTER ELEVEN

Jake was ticked the tension between his mother and Avery had not only ruined the bonfire, but was now ruining lasagna.

He loved lasagna. He loved sitting at his mother's dining room table to eat lasagna. He *should have* loved having the woman he was so enamored with he could hardly remember his middle name sitting at that dining room table eating lasagna.

Instead, he was ticked.

He watched Avery push a piece of pasta to the edge of her plate, and barely resisted the urge to point out she'd pushed that same piece to the other side of her plate a minute ago.

He chewed, staring at her, willing her to look up.

The tension wasn't helped by the fact they hadn't had a chance to talk privately since the meeting that morning in Frank's office. Jake wanted—no, *needed*—to know what was going through Avery's head about the training center. And, more specifically, about him staying.

His mother was blessed with the gift of gab and a hatred for awkward silences. At the moment, she was going on about Laura Grimes having to have a second surgery on her broken leg.

Jake felt bad about that, but he couldn't look away from Avery.

He felt like his nerve endings were crackling. He'd felt the zinging sensations ever since he'd looked over from that roof to see her sitting in her Jeep at the curb.

She'd come to him.

That revelation amped up the electricity.

Then she'd taken his hand at the Huberts' house and helped him look for Cooper. Then she'd listened to his story about the little boy in Oklahoma. Then she'd hugged him. Then she'd told him he was a hero.

Then she'd acted irritated throughout his presentation about the training center that could keep him in Chance for good.

What the hell was that?

He needed to talk to her. He needed more than that. Keeping his hands to himself was over. This woman liked him. She respected him. She thought he was a hero. Irritated or not, she was going to be naked the minute they were alone.

But first they had to get through this dinner.

And if he had to hear about how many plates and screws they'd put into Laura's leg for one more minute, he was going to snap.

Jake caught his father's eye, frowned, then gave a little nod toward Heidi.

Wes rolled his eyes, but he did interrupt.

"Avery, have you heard back on that grant you wrote?"

Jake perked up and turned his attention to Avery.

She looked startled that Wes had addressed her directly. "Um, no, I haven't. I'd planned to follow up with the mayor on Monday but then . . ." She trailed off. Obviously everyone had more important things to deal with on Monday.

"What's the grant asking for?" Jake asked, genuinely interested.

Avery shook her head. "A little idea I had. Not a big deal."

"I wouldn't say that at all," Wes interjected. "She's asking for funds to put together a new fire-education program for the kids in Chance."

"New, how?" Jake asked. He'd seen a variety of fire-safety and pre-vention programs across the country, and community education was a passion of his.

Avery's face was bright red, but she met his gaze across the table. "It's not anything all that innovative."

"Tell me about it."

Avery took a deep breath. "I think sometimes we focus so much on making kids aware of how dangerous fire and storms and things can be that we make them afraid, instead of careful. I think understanding something is the best way to respect it, and if they respect fire and wind and water and lightning, then they'll be cautious but not *afraid*. I want to teach them about how fire is created and the good things it can do, along with how to use it appropriately and how to calmly and correctly deal with problems when it's out of control."

She stopped talking, pressing her lips together.

Jake knew he was staring, but damn, that was sexy. A woman who got worked up about public safety and who was creative and passion-ate and willing to get her hands dirty for her community . . . yeah, he needed her naked soon. Very soon.

"I think that's awesome. Why didn't you bring it up when we were talking about the training center? That would fit right in."

She frowned. "It's about fire."

"I'd like to see the training center expand beyond tornadoes. Fire, flooding, mass casualties. All of that."

She shook her head. "I think this program should go out to schools."

"That's great, too, but bringing people to a central location would enable us to do a lot more hands-on training for crisis situations."

"I don't want to focus on the crisis part of it," she said, leaning in and putting her fork down. "That's the point. I don't want every discussion about fire and storms to be negative. I don't want to use words like *crisis*."

"Right. I understand." Jake also set his fork down. "I can work on the program with you," he offered. "I have a lot of resources. I'm happy to help you with this. Maybe we can take it out of the hands of the city. The state should get involved. I can call the governor's office. Or we could take it higher. Maybe take it into—"

"No. Dammit, Jake, you don't have to always make everything bigger and better."

"I'm not trying to step on your toes."

"Then sit this one out. I've got this. If I need your help, I'll ask."

He snorted. "Sure, right, because you do *that* so well."

"What's that supposed to mean?"

"It means that you're not so good about letting people get close."

"That's not true. Maybe I don't let *you* get as close as you think you should be, but that doesn't mean I don't know how to have relationships."

"Really? What about my mom? You've barely spoken to her in years—"

"Excuse me."

Jake stopped talking at his father's firm interruption, but he couldn't stop staring at Avery. Fuck. He'd stepped *way* over that line. But dammit. He hated the way she kept everyone at arm's length. She needed to be loved, and the current room was full of people who could, and wanted to, do it.

In that moment, he realized he was in huge trouble.

Because *he* was in love with her.

And she was staring at him like she'd very much like to throw her fork at him.

Jake slowly turned to face his father.

Wes's eyebrows were up, his eyes wide. "Yes, we're still here."

Jake looked from his dad to his mom. She looked less shocked than sad.

Fuck.

Once again, he and Avery had gotten so wrapped up in each other that they'd forgotten there were other people around.

He cleared his throat. "Sorry."

"Yes, I'm sorry, too," Avery said tightly.

"Jake." Heidi set her napkin to the side of her plate. "Wes." She pushed her chair back and rose. "You need to go to the store for ice cream. Both of you. Now."

Jake was confused. "Ice cream?"

Heidi was looking at Avery, who was not meeting her gaze. Avery was gritting her teeth and glaring at Jake.

Getting out of the house for any reason at all was suddenly very tempting.

But he couldn't leave Avery here. Could he? "Avery?"

"Don't you dare come back here without rocky road and a Snickers bar to cut up and mix into it."

Which he took to mean she was okay with him leaving, and that she'd still be here when he got back.

Yep, he was in love.

"Right. Got it. Of course."

"I'll drive." Wes shoved his chair back and headed for the garage.

Jake was right on his heels.

Avery took a deep breath, took her time folding her napkin and setting it beside her plate as Heidi had done, and then pushed her chair back and stood. Finally, she met the other woman's gaze.

"I'm sorry. Sometimes Jake and I . . ." But what was she going to say? That she constantly wanted to kiss him and smack him at the same time? She couldn't tell his mother that.

"You're the only person who can get him so worked up that he loses track of everything else." She gave Avery a little smile. "I like seeing him a little off his game."

"You do?"

"He's always so in control, so driven, so sure of himself," Heidi said. "Sometimes I worry he goes on autopilot, that he sets his eyes on the goal down the road and doesn't think about how he *feels* about things in the moment. But when you're around, it's clear that he's feeling a lot."

Avery felt her cheeks heat.

"Grab those dishes," Heidi said, indicating Jake's and Wes's dinner plates. "And tell me what's going on with you and my son."

As they cleared the table and filled the dishwasher, Avery told Heidi about their directive to get along and work together to get things done in time for the Bronson family visit and to show everyone that they were all coming together to make sure Chance had a secure future.

"It's to boost morale and make everyone stay optimistic and on task," Avery finished.

Heidi finished wiping down the countertop and turned to face Avery. "So you're only getting along because Shelby told you to?"

Avery cleared her throat. "No. Jake and I definitely have a mutual respect and a lot of shared professional knowledge and interest. Working together has showed us that we are . . . friends." That was not the right word for what she and Jake were, but she didn't have a better one.

"So you're not just pretending to like him?"

Avery shook her head. "No." She was most definitely not pretending about her feelings for Jake.

"Good. And I don't want to pretend about my feelings for you, either."

Avery felt her stomach tighten. Heidi sounded serious. Avery took a deep breath, then blew it out. "Okay."

"I hate pretending that we're only acquaintances when we see each other in town. I hate pretending that you're just a girl I once knew, or a classmate of my son's. I hate pretending that all I know about you is that you're the fire chief."

Avery couldn't swallow. "Okay," she said hoarsely.

"Sending you away the day after you graduated was one of the hardest things I've ever done. I loved you, Avery. I wanted every good thing for you. But I handled that horribly, and I've regretted it ever since. I'm very sorry."

Avery felt her mouth drop open.

Heidi continued. "I knew it hurt you, but I had hoped you would go out and see the world and do something amazing and eventually thank me for pushing you out of the nest."

Avery's eyes stung and she blinked quickly. "I did do something amazing." She was proud of her job, dammit.

Heidi nodded. "You did." She also blinked several times in a row. "I'm incredibly proud of you."

Avery stared at the woman she'd considered her best friend and mother figure for most of her life. "You're proud of me? You wanted me to go away . . . far away. You wanted me to stay away."

Heidi shook her head. "I didn't. I wanted you right here with me. But that wasn't fair to you. You needed the chance to do whatever you wanted. You never had choices before. That's what I wanted to give you. Even if it hurt. Both of us."

"Why didn't you tell me that?" Avery asked quietly.

"That day, I couldn't. You wouldn't have heard me. I don't even know that I could have made myself say it. That's why I wrote you the letter."

Avery frowned. "The letter?"

"The letter I sent that fall. You'd been gone a couple of months, and I knew—hoped, even—that you wouldn't be home to visit for a long time. So I asked Ruth for your address."

Avery started shaking her head slowly. "Ruth didn't know where I was. And I never got a letter."

Heidi frowned as well, clearly surprised. "What?"

"I had no contact with her after I left."

"Thank God for that," Heidi said. She shook her head. "I should have realized that. I certainly hoped that you wouldn't keep taking her abuse. I'm glad to know you didn't. But I can't believe she gave me a false address. God, all these years I've been thinking that you just couldn't get past what had happened to accept my apology."

Avery gripped the edge of the countertop behind her for stability, but she lifted her chin. "When I left Chance, I left it all here. All of my disappointment and sadness and insecurity. I decided that if no one wanted me, then I didn't want them."

Heidi's eyes filled, but she was smiling when she said, "You're an amazing woman, Avery Sparks."

Avery felt the words hit her directly in the chest, and then the warmth of their meaning spread through her.

"So many people would have ended up bitter," Heidi said. "So many would have used it all as an excuse to feel sorry for themselves and to not do anything worthwhile. But you went the other way. You stood on your own two feet and worked hard and made your dreams come true, and it all still led you into serving and taking care of others." Heidi wiped the wetness from under her eyes. "I admire you a great deal."

Avery felt her own tears threatening. This was all . . . exactly what she'd wanted to hear for so long.

Avery pulled in a shaky breath, letting that sink in. "I hated you."

"I know."

"But if you had called me and asked me to come back, I would have. I hated myself for that. That you could hurt me so much and I would still do anything you asked."

Heidi swallowed hard. "I know. That's part of why I didn't say anything that morning. I wanted you to stay, and I knew you would. But you deserved to make your own choices based on what *you* wanted. When you came back to Chance, after all, I cried. I was so happy."

"Even though we didn't talk?"

"It hurt," Heidi admitted. "But I was happy because you were so obviously happy. That's what a mother really wants."

Avery felt a sob catch at the back of her throat. She had to clear her throat before she could speak again. "I considered myself part of your family for so long, but then graduation hit and . . . everything seemed to be ending and changing, and I didn't want anything to be different. I wanted everything to go on exactly as it always had. I, um . . ." She blew out another quick breath. "I wanted to be a part of your family so much that I had hoped things with Jake would turn into more."

"Things with Jake?" Heidi asked carefully.

"Prom, the time right after, graduation night." Avery felt her cheeks heat.

"Did something happen graduation night?" Heidi asked.

"We . . . um . . ." Avery stopped and coughed lightly.

"Ah, I see," Heidi said. "Well, I can see why you would think that meant something more."

Avery nodded.

"You didn't know he was leaving the next morning, either, did you?"

Avery shook her head.

They were quiet for a moment, each replaying all the words, letting them sink in.

"And this time?" Heidi asked. "You're just working together? There's nothing more there?"

Oh, boy. Avery pressed her lips together. How much could she— should she—tell Heidi?

"I can't say that there's *nothing* more. But Jake . . . drives me nuts, but . . . I . . ." Avery trailed off, frustrated with the lack of ability to really describe what was going on. Even to herself.

"You love him."

Avery's head came up quickly. *That* almost knocked her on her butt. She started to shake her head. "I . . ."

But Heidi pinned her with a look Avery had seen more than once in her life. It said, *Don't you dare lie to me.*

Avery's shoulders sagged. "Okay. I do. But he doesn't know," she said quickly.

"You're not going to tell him?"

Avery shook her head. "I can't. I can't . . . ask him to stay, to give up everything."

"What if he wanted to stay? To come home?"

"Then he needs to do it on his own," Avery said. "He can't do it because of me. I can't put that on him. If he decides to come back to Chance, I'd be thrilled. But if not . . . his being happy will still make me happy."

Heidi's eyes filled. "Now I know for sure you love him. Because you're doing for him what I did for you. I wanted you to find out who and where you wanted to be." She came forward with her arms outstretched and pulled Avery into a hug. "I'm so, so glad you came back, though," Heidi whispered against her hair.

Tears flooded Avery's eyes, too, and she hugged the other woman tightly.

Her feelings for Jake seemed to open Avery up. She felt like all the walls she'd put up around her mind and heart, to keep out the things she didn't trust, had fallen. It didn't make sense that she was in love with a man who needed more than she could give him, who needed a bigger, more exciting life. But she was. In love enough to let him go.

Because of that, she believed Heidi really had loved her. It had hurt, being nudged in the other direction, but she understood how Heidi felt. What was best for Jake was for him to be in Kansas City . . . and beyond.

As always, Heidi's hug made it all feel better. It had been too long.

Jake had given this all back to her. If it weren't for him, she wouldn't be standing in the kitchen that felt more familiar and comforting than any other place in the world. If it weren't for him, she wouldn't have Heidi back.

"I made no-bake cookies." Heidi stepped back and dashed the tears from her cheeks.

Avery wiped her cheeks, too. "I made no-bake cookies every other weekend the first year I was away from Chance."

They'd always made no-bake cookies when one of them had a bad day. Heidi always said that when things were rough, there wasn't any time to spare for baking.

"The boys should be back soon with the ice cream."

Avery nodded. "I'm going to go freshen up. I'll be back down in a minute."

She climbed the staircase to the guest bathroom at the top of the steps, but the door four doors down on the left caught her eye. Jake's old bedroom. The last time she'd been inside had been graduation night when she'd come up to change her clothes and Jake had walked in and ended up inviting her to the party at the river.

She couldn't resist a chance to peek inside. And he had an attached bathroom she could use.

She was blotting the cool water from her face when the door swung open.

Jake stood in the doorway. "You made my mom *cry?*"

Avery stared at him in the mirror and sniffed. "Yes. But it was—"

"And *you're* crying?" He stepped into the bathroom and pushed the door shut. "Dammit, what the hell happened?"

She shrugged. "We talked."

"What about?"

"The morning after graduation. When she told me to leave."

Jake's jaw tightened and she could see he was angry. She turned to face him.

"I thought she was asking me to leave so I didn't say anything else stupid," Jake said. "I thought she was cutting off the conversation before it went any further. I didn't know you were going to rehash all those painful times."

"We needed to talk it out if we wanted to get past it."

"I wasn't aware you wanted to get past it."

She frowned. "I don't like the way things have been. It's been cold and awkward and . . . hurts whenever I see her. Of course I wanted to get past that."

"You wanted to talk about all of that stuff and dredge it all up again?"

"Yes. I guess so."

"Then why the silent treatment over the past few years? Dad said they've tried to talk to you."

"I guess I was punishing her. Or something."

"And suddenly you didn't want to punish her anymore?"

"I realized there was someone else getting hurt."

"My dad?" Jake asked with a frown.

"*You*, Jake."

They stood staring at each other. Avery felt her heart pounding. Oh, boy. That was close to an admission of how much he meant to her.

"You did it to make me happy?" he asked.

"I did it because . . ." She realized yes, that was definitely part of it. It mattered to Jake that she and his mom reconcile. She hadn't come to dinner tonight because it would look good to the town. She hadn't come for herself or for Heidi. She'd done it because Jake wanted it.

She cleared her throat. "It seemed important to you. I didn't know it would turn into all of this, and if you'd asked me ahead of time if I wanted that, I would have said no. But I'm glad it happened. I don't want to punish her, and I don't want anyone to be hurt by this anymore. Thank you for insisting on tonight."

"You're happy?" he asked, stepping closer, his voice lower.

"I'm happy."

"Because of something I did."

She felt her smile curl up. "Because of something you did."

"And you realize there are people who care about you? A lot."

He moved closer again, and she had to tip her head back to look up at him. He lifted a hand and wiped at a wet spot on her cheek with the pad of his thumb.

"I do realize that." She knew he was one of them. He cared about her. This had been important to him not just because of his mom, but because of Avery, too. That thought made her heart squeeze. She couldn't get her hopes up here. Jake belonged in Kansas City.

But maybe this time it would be harder for him to leave.

"Now you can have the family you always wanted. You can have weekly dinners and shopping trips, and my dad will be here if you ever need your car worked on, and my mom will make you soup when you're sick."

Avery blinked up at him.

Or maybe not. Maybe this wasn't about Avery and his feelings for her at all. He cared about her. But he cared about the whole freaking world.

He wanted to be the big-shot hero again. He'd seen someone in need—her—and figured out a way to fix it.

Dammit.

She pushed him back. "I'm not a charity case, Jake."

He reached for her. "That's not what I'm saying."

"But it is. I'm this poor, needy little girl who's sad about her dog missing."

He frowned and shook his head. "That's a bad comparison."

"Is it? I lost my family. I've been sad and lonely. Then you show up with the power to get us back together. You're the only one with enough influence to get us together to make up. Now it happened, and you can feel good about it and can tell yourself you're the big hero. And you need that. Like most people need water."

"Why is it that something that makes other people admire me is something that makes you so nuts?" he asked, advancing another step and backing her up against the bathroom counter. "Everyone else thinks my willingness to help and my heroic efforts are awesome."

"Then why do you need *me* to think you're awesome?" she asked, pushing against him again.

But he wasn't budging this time.

He stared down at her for a long moment. Then he said softly, "I don't know."

Her breath caught in her throat at the look of confusion and need on his face.

"But I do," he said. "I really do."

She swallowed hard. "It's because I'm a challenge," she said, her voice breathless anyway.

He lifted his hand and cupped her face. "That's what I thought, too. But . . ."

He leaned in and brushed his lips over hers. It was a fairly chaste touch, especially considering all the other touching they'd done, but it rocked Avery to her core.

Jake lifted his head.

But he didn't say anything. He didn't finish his sentence, either.

She needed to hear the rest of that sentence.

She frowned. "But what?"

"Huh?"

"You said you've been telling yourself that I'm a challenge, but—"

"But I don't think that's it."

She stood, watching him, waiting. When nothing more was forth-coming, she pinched him on the arm.

"Hey."

"You're making me squirm on purpose."

"I really like it when you squirm," he said sincerely.

"Let me put it this way," she told *him* sincerely. "If you don't tell me what is going through your head right now, I'm never squirming for you again."

He laughed, and before she knew what was happening, he'd picked her up and deposited her on the bathroom countertop. He leaned in and kissed the side of her neck.

She was already squirming. But she wasn't going to show it.

"Tell me what you were going to say."

He licked a sweet path from the edge of her jaw to her ear, then sucked gently on a spot behind her ear that definitely made her squirm.

"I did not keep coming back to see you . . . and to kiss you . . . because you were a challenge," he said.

He kissed down her neck to her collarbone. She felt the first button on the front of her blouse open, and her shirt gaped, allowing him access to more skin. Avery tipped her head to the side and sighed, unable to control her reaction to him.

"I did not think about you all the time in Kansas City because you were a challenge."

Two more buttons opened, and the front of her shirt separated to reveal the front closure of her bra.

Jake kissed across the upper curve of one breast, his other hand cupping the opposite one.

"I did not go out to the shed with you the night of the tornado because you were a challenge."

Avery unbuttoned the rest of her shirt on her own, pulling it open and slipping it off.

Jake groaned his approval, opening the front of her bra and peeling it back.

"Where are your mom and dad?"

"Out for ice cream."

"I thought you brought ice cream home."

"We did."

"But—"

He leaned in, his lips touching hers. "They are very intelligent people."

She pulled back, looking into his eyes. Could she have sex with Jake in his parents' house with them *knowing* she was having sex with Jake in their house?

He brushed his thumb over her nipple and kissed her deeply, and all she could think was, *Oh, yeah.*

She pulled back only far enough to slip his shirt up his torso. He leaned back and stripped it off. He started to move back in, but she stopped him with a hand on that gorgeous chest.

"Let me look."

"You've seen it before," he said with a grin, but he stopped and let her ogle him for a moment.

"I have. But the lighting in here is excellent."

The ten brilliant bulbs above the mirror did make it deliciously bright in the room. She could see every ripple, every ridge, every scar. Just looking at him made her ache down deep, beyond the physical, beyond where she could describe it—except to say she *needed* him.

"Is that right?" He gave her a wicked grin.

"It's an improvement over the river at night or the shed during a tornado," she told him, her gaze still tracking over every inch from his collarbones to the low-riding waistband of his jeans.

"Let's see."

Before she could process the words, Jake went to his knees in front of her.

Oh, God.

"Trust me." She reached for him, intending to pull him back to his feet.

"This is really something I need to see for myself." He looked up at her with eyes dark with desire, yet twinkling with humor and mischief at the same time.

She sat staring at him, her heart pounding. She knew exactly what he was thinking, and she was having a hard time swallowing.

There was being intimate with a guy . . . and there was being *intimate* with a guy.

But as she studied Jake's face, the face that made her hot and crazy—in many ways, for so long—and the broad shoulders that carried so much weight, actual and otherwise, she knew she'd never say no to him about anything.

Which should scare the crap out of her.

But in that moment, it didn't.

"Avery," he said gruffly, "take your clothes off."

Her gaze glued to his, she kicked off first one sandal, then the other. She undid the button and zipper on her shorts, hooked the top of the shorts and her panties with her thumbs, and wiggled them off, letting them drop to the floor in front of where he knelt.

Jake's hands went to her knees and spread them apart.

Avery held her breath.

She felt heat wash over her from her scalp to her toes as he ran his palms up her thighs.

"Dammit, you're gorgeous," he rasped.

"Told you the lighting was good."

"I can see every single shiny pink inch."

She gasped in surprise. "Jake!" But damn if his words didn't make her want to spread her knees farther for him.

He gave her a grin that made her even hotter. "I wonder if good lighting makes things taste better, too?"

Her heart pounded, and she resisted the urge to scoot to the edge of the counter and say something *really* naughty.

"You've never—" She broke off as he ran a hand up the inside of her thigh, his fingers dangerously close to her center. Her whole body seemed to be straining toward him, and she was on the verge of being completely shameless.

Not that she thought Jake would mind.

"Oh, but I have," he drawled. "In the shed. I licked every drop of that sweetness off my fingers after I—"

"Jake!" Avery felt her mouth drop open, and she tried to close her legs.

"No way." He applied gentle but firm pressure on her thighs. "This is happening."

"Can we do it with a little less narrative?" she snapped.

He looked up. "No, actually, we can't. I intend to tell you everything I want to do to you and how you make me feel for the next hour or so. In detail. Possibly loudly."

"It won't take your parents an hour to get ice cream." But she gave up trying to close her legs.

"Remember, very intelligent people."

He stroked his hand up and down her inner thigh again, but this time, his fingers brushed over the sweet spot between her legs.

Though it was far too light of a touch.

She gritted her teeth.

"As I was saying. You taste like a combination of whipped cream and honey."

At that she snorted.

He looked up with a grin. "What?"

She couldn't help the smile he evoked. "That's cheesy and not true."

"That's what comes to mind," he said with a little shrug. "But maybe I need to be sure."

Before she could prepare herself, he reached around, took her butt in his hands, and pulled her forward to his tongue.

He licked and she gasped. Her legs seemed to naturally settle over his big shoulders, and she leaned back, staying upright only by bracing a hand on the marble countertop behind her.

Hot electricity. That's what it felt like zipping along her nerve endings.

Jake didn't let her take a deep breath, didn't let her adjust, didn't give her a second to think. He licked and sucked; he added a finger, then a second, all the while murmuring words like *sweet* and *hot* and *more*.

Her eyes slid shut, and she absorbed all the other sensations. The feel of her head pressing against the mirror, the silkiness of his hair between her fingers, the delicious stretch of her inner muscles, the pounding of blood through her veins. And the sound of his voice, telling her she was beautiful and how much he wanted her and how he'd never get enough.

It was the never-get-enough part that finally wound her orgasm tight within her and then let it go.

Pleasure crashed through her and she cried out, Jake's name bouncing off the tile walls and floor of the room, the acoustics perfect for him to hear exactly what he did to her.

"Fuck, Avery." Jake kissed his way up her body. He licked at a nipple, stroked his hand over her hip, dug his fingers into her hair, and tipped her head back for a deep, hot, slow kiss.

She tasted herself on his tongue—not whipped cream and honey, but darkly delicious all the same.

"This time it's on a bed, and I want to feel you clamping down on me just like that."

The talking. It was going to kill her.

"The bed's too far." She bit gently on his bottom lip. "Here, now," she whispered.

"The bed," he said firmly.

She reached between them and slid her hand into the front of his jeans, stroking along the steely shaft she needed like she needed her next breath.

"I can't make it that far." It was true. Her legs were still shaking.

"Good thing I have all these big muscles, then." He scooped her up with his hands under her butt.

She had no choice but to wrap her arms around his neck and her legs around his waist as he turned and started for the bed.

The denim covering his erection rubbed against her now incredibly sensitive spots as they walked, and she was squirming again by the time his knees bumped the mattress and he dropped her onto the duvet.

He quickly undressed the rest of the way, and Avery was thankful for the equally good lighting in the bedroom. Jake's body was a masterpiece. The scars, the bump on his right collarbone left over from a healed break, the uneven tan lines that spoke of work in the sun in various types of shirts, all added to the picture of the strong, courageous hero. The man who wanted to save the world. The man she wanted with her body and her heart.

"Lie back," he told her, climbing onto the bed and kneeling between her knees.

"Maybe I want to be on top this time."

She wasn't sure where the words had come from, but the way they affected Jake made her glad they'd spilled out. He froze, his eyes darkened, and a half smile curled his lips.

"Second-sweetest words I've ever heard," he said sincerely.

He braced a hand on the mattress on either side of her head and leaned in for a long, slow kiss. Avery wrapped her arms around his neck, arching her body up closer to his.

Hell, she didn't care what position they were in. As long as he was against her, she was good.

And he was *against* her. Jake wrapped an arm around her, plastering them together from chest to knees. Then he rolled to his back, taking her with him.

She propped herself up, her forearms on his chest. "What are the sweetest words you've ever heard?" she asked. "If those are the second sweetest?"

"*Oh, God, Jake, yes.* Though they don't have to be in that order. *Oh, yes, God, Jake* works, as does, *Yes, Jake, oh, God.*"

She narrowed her eyes. The things she wanted to do to him. He was so cocky, so sure she'd never had better, so . . . right. He was the best kissing, the best flirting, the best sex she'd ever had. He was also the best time she'd ever had. That made her very nervous.

But instead of dwelling, she decided to make the most of the moment they were in.

She wouldn't mind hearing an *Oh, yes* or two out of him.

Her eyes still on his, she slid down his body. She licked over his pecs, circled a nipple, traced the bumps of his ribs with her tongue. She ran her hands up and down his sides and over the silky trail of hair bisecting his abs.

Then lower.

She knew the moment he realized what she intended. But unlike her on the bathroom counter, he didn't protest at all. In fact, he widened his legs slightly and ran his fingers through her hair.

As she kissed his hip bone and wrapped her hand around his shaft, Jake groaned, and she saw the hand on the bed tighten into the duvet as she felt the hand in her hair curl into her scalp.

She stroked up and down his length a few times, watching his breathing speed up. When she licked her lips, his lips fell open, and when she shifted and her gaze moved to his cock, his buttocks tightened.

Then she licked him.

The word *fuck* came from him as more of a groan and encouraged her to do it again. And again. Looking up his long body, she could see he was struggling to stay in control, and that was from the simple application of her tongue.

She wondered what the effect would be if she applied her whole mouth.

A moment later, she knew. She found herself flipped onto her back, her legs spread wide.

"What about—" she started, her body responding to the dominant display with an enthusiasm that shocked her.

"Next time," he growled. He reached between them, somehow managing to roll on a condom, then arched his hips, thrusting into her.

Yep, there were definitely going to be more *Oh, Jake*s coming right up.

"Avery, Avery," he whispered as he moved inside her. "It's never like this."

She linked her ankles behind him, drawing him closer and deeper. "Good."

He chuckled, then groaned as she contracted her inner muscles around him.

"I don't want to come because I want to stay right here," he told her gruffly.

"Then stay right here." *In Chance. With me,* she added silently.

"Can't," he panted. "You feel too fucking good. You're too hot, too sweet, too tight."

"Then—" She gasped as he stroked deep. "I guess we'll have to do it again later."

"Damn right."

He picked up the pace, stroking deep and long and fast. The friction sent sensations rushing through her body, and she felt everything winding tighter and tighter until suddenly Jake hit *the* spot, the perfect angle, the perfect pressure, the perfect stroke, to make it all burst free.

"*Yes*, Avery. Fuck, yes," he growled in her ear, thrusting hard and fast as she came around him.

Then he went over the edge, too, calling out her name, their bodies pressed as deep and tight as they could get, shuddering and shattering together.

It was almost an hour later when Jake heard the front door of his parents' house open and shut. He stretched and looked down at the woman in his arms.

She'd been asleep for about twenty minutes, and Jake had let himself drift into a light doze.

Having Avery in his arms, pressed against his side, her legs tangled with his, was the most comfortable place he'd been. Ever.

It felt right. The warmth of her body, the silkiness of her skin, the scent of her hair, the tickle of her breath against his chest.

He could do this every day for the rest of his life.

He was a smart guy. He'd seen a lot of destruction, a lot of loss, a lot of sadness. He knew when something was good, when something was right. And knew that he should hold on to it, appreciate it, revel in it.

This—Avery, his bed, Chance—was right.

Now he just had to figure out how to tell *her*.

He heard his parents' voices in the kitchen below his room. He knew it should feel awkward with them in the house while he lay naked with Avery in his childhood bedroom. But he also knew that his parents had seen what he'd only now discovered.

He was in love. With a woman they already considered a daughter.

It was very likely that Heidi and Wes were celebrating all this.

But Avery was going to kill him when she found out he'd let her sleep until they got home.

"A," he said softly, nudging her, "wake up, babe."

She snuggled down deeper into the duvet he'd pulled over them.

He snuggled down with her. "I'm good with you staying." He wrapped his arms around her and pulled her closer. "But, so you know, my mom and dad are downstairs."

She sat up so quickly she almost broke his nose.

"Jake!" She scrambled off the bed and ran for the bathroom.

"Holy crap, Avery, calm down." He'd never seen anyone wake up so fast.

"They're back? They're downstairs *now*?" she asked from the doorway where she was already jerking on her shorts and pulling on her bra.

"Yes. But—"

"You'll have to distract them while I slip out. Tell them I left. Like an hour ago."

"No way," he said, getting out of bed and pulling on his jeans. "If they think you left, they'll think I did or said something to piss you off."

"So?" She pulled her shirt over her bra.

"I don't want them to think that."

She propped her hands on her hips. "Why not?"

"Because I *like* people knowing I—" Was she ready to hear that he loved her? Was he ready to say it?

She raised an eyebrow. "You like people knowing you got me into bed?"

He didn't *mind* people thinking that, of course, but there was more to it now.

"I want my *parents* to know you're still here."

"That's creepy," she told him. "Even if we are adults, we don't need to be obvious about doing it in their house."

He blew out a breath. He wasn't doing this right. "What I mean is, I want my parents to know how I feel about you. How we feel about each other."

At least, he hoped like hell she had some of the same feelings.

It seemed he'd spent ten years thinking about how Avery felt about him. In the beginning, he'd loved that she'd chosen him to be her first, the boy she'd trusted and liked enough to give her virginity to. Then he'd spent years driven nuts by the idea she didn't feel *more* for him, that she'd let her feelings for his family influence her feelings for him.

Now . . . he'd never been in love before. Not really. And it didn't surprise him in the least that he'd fallen for Avery.

Nor did it surprise him that he was still hoping and wondering about *her* feelings.

Avery pulled herself up straight and focused on his left earlobe instead of his eyes. "What do you mean? Your parents think, know, we're . . . doing this . . . for the town during the cleanup."

"Avery," he said quietly, crossing the room to where she stood, "I told you, my parents are very intelligent people." He took her hand. "Look at me."

She did, slowly.

"You said you came over tonight because it mattered to me."

She swallowed and nodded.

"Why do you care if it was important to me?"

"Because you need this. You need to make everything better for people around you. You need to fix things."

He tugged on her hand, bringing her close. "I need *you* to be happy. And I need to be part of that." He looked into her eyes. "I'm in love with you, Avery."

She pulled in a deep breath, then blew it out slowly.

"And," he continued when she didn't say anything, "you like me a lot, too." His tone was light.

She pressed her lips together and nodded.

"And I want the world to know."

"That I like you?" she asked.

"Yes. Getting on your good side has taken me a long damned time." He smiled and brushed his thumb over her cheek.

He was in love. For the first time in his life. With Avery Sparks. It felt like something needed to happen to commemorate that.

Avery deserved that. She hadn't had nearly enough love—and demonstrations of it—in her life. He knew she was reeling from his confession of his feelings for her. He knew it would take time for it to sink in so she could believe it. But he could be very convincing when he put his mind to something. His mind was most definitely on Avery.

He'd spent his early life barely noticing her. The riverbank had been one night and had been between the two of them—well, and Max and Dillon, but they didn't count. The times Jake had kissed her in Chance had been semipublic in that everyone knew about them, but there hadn't been anything more. The past week of the town seeing them together had been more speculation than actual fact.

Now he wanted it to all be a fact. A solid, irrefutable, widely known fact.

He grinned as he thought about how fun it would be to show Avery that he wanted the world to know how he felt about her. "I'm in the mood for ice cream."

She groaned. "Come on. That's a little embarrassing."

"The whisker burns aren't anywhere they'll be able to see them," he said with a grin.

She blushed.

Dark pink.

He loved it.

"You don't look all innocent, either," she said.

He ran his hand through his hair. "Well, *I'm* not the one who's embarrassed. You want to take a quick shower?"

"Sure, that won't be obvious." She similarly ran her fingers through her hair, took a deep breath, and said, "Fine. Let's go."

Grinning like an idiot and feeling like a kid who just got his dream bike for his birthday, Jake took Avery's hand and headed for the kitchen.

CHAPTER TWELVE

"This might not have been my best idea after all," Jake said huskily, his eyes on her mouth.

Avery licked her tongue along her bottom lip and tasted the chocolate that had smeared on her mouth from her s'more.

Even more than the chocolate, she very much enjoyed the way Jake growled softly in the back of his throat.

"Who knew s'mores were something we should do in private?" he asked softly.

She glanced around. They were in the town square, sitting on plastic crates under some trees. The moon was up and bright, other than the clouds that scuttled by from time to time. The humidity had been cut dramatically, but the cold front moving in stirred the air with a cool breeze.

Most of the town had gathered in the square, as they had for the past three nights. Tonight they were having s'mores and watching their friends and neighbors sing karaoke on the makeshift stage Max and Jake had thrown together. She and Jake were alone enough that they could have a private conversation, but, yeah, they were not alone enough for the things they were both thinking.

Avery was keeping her eyes on the charcoal grills they were using for the s'mores, especially with the increased wind tonight, but for the most part she was having a great time relaxing.

"I don't know. I think this is a great idea. You and the guys are amazing." She looked back at Jake, her heart filling. He was definitely amazing. And he was in love with her.

She was still processing that. It had been seven days since he'd said it. She'd seen him consistently since then—around town as they cleaned up and rebuilt, and at the strategy and update meetings. They'd even worked on helping brick up the opening at the church side by side for seven hours, two days ago. Every time she'd seen him, he'd given her smiles that made her stomach flip, whispered words that made her hot and happy at the same time, and kissed her in a way that made her toes curl. He'd sent two humongous bouquets of flowers to the station. He'd brought her lunch each day—though no ham salad, thank God. They'd had dinner at his parents' house again last night, along with four other couples, including Jake's grandma and grandpa. But they hadn't really talked, and they hadn't had any real alone time together.

The town had to be their focus, of course, and they—along with everyone else—had been putting in long hours of physically and mentally exhausting work. They were all working hard and fast, and it was wearing on everyone.

Thankfully, they were almost done.

Her crew had burned the majority of the remaining debris last night, all the windows on Main Street that had been hardest hit had been replaced, and four trees at the park had been taken down that afternoon. The bakery, the hardware store, and the post office were repainted; the wall of the school was back up; and the steel building that replaced the one that had been destroyed at Montgomery Farms was finished.

The Bronsons would arrive tomorrow for their first visit, and each night the feeling of merriment—fueled by relief and the need to let off some steam—had grown. In no small part thanks to Jake, Max, and Dillon. In fact, Dillon was leading the way with a lot of the festivities, and it was uncharacteristic enough that Avery had to wonder if some of it was Kit's influence.

But if she hadn't had time to spend with Jake, she certainly hadn't found a chance for any more girl talk. She didn't know the details of what was going on with Bree and Max or Kit and Dillon, and she was as curious as the rest of the town.

No matter whose idea it all was, though, the little parties in the town square were saving everyone's sanity.

The first night's gathering had started because of the three Boy Scout troops and various other people who had come to Chance to help with the cleanup. They'd made a campground out of the town square, and Jake, Max, and Dillon had gone door-to-door to collect hot dogs and burgers and had grilled them for the visitors as a thank-you.

The next night they'd gathered popcorn and set up a projector in the square to show a movie on the side of city hall. The next they'd taken root beer and ice cream and had asked a couple of local teens to act as DJs, playing music and setting up a crazy charades tournament. Each night, along with the visitors, more and more of Chance's citizens had shown up for the festivities.

It was all great. It was. Avery was happy as she looked around the square and thought about all they'd gotten done.

But then she looked back at Jake, and not only her body ached, but her heart did, too. They worked all day and then relaxed at night with the rest of the town, which meant they weren't alone together. At all. Jake was incredibly sweet and demonstrative. He always had his hands on her—an arm around her shoulders, holding her hand, or a big palm on the back of her neck. They'd been together constantly during the town-square events. He'd even coaxed her into dancing with him the night before. It had been wonderful. But it hadn't been *enough*.

She wanted just five minutes alone with him.

She looked at Jake's mouth as he studied hers.

Okay, more than five minutes.

"Did I get it?" she asked, licking her lip again.

He leaned in. "Actually, you missed a bit of marshmallow over here." He took her chin between his finger and thumb and licked his tongue along her lip.

Her heart pounded, and heat and desire pooled low and deep and fast. She cupped the back of his head, curling her fingers into his hair, gripping gently, not wanting to let him go.

With a groan, he possessed her mouth. His grasp on her chin tightened, and he tipped her head so he could get deeper.

Avery wasn't sure if he pulled her to him or if she stood up first, but a second later the crate she'd been sitting on was on its side, and she was in his lap. His hand gripped her hip, grinding her down against his erection. She moaned and ripped her mouth from his. "Let's go. Please."

At that moment his phone rang in his pocket. He didn't even pull it out. He reached in between them and silenced it. "Where?"

"Anywhere."

He grinned. "People will notice."

"I don't care." She meant it. Everyone thought she was in love with him and . . . she *was* in love with him. Everyone also considered her relatively bright. If both of those things were true, why wouldn't she take him to the first private place she could find and strip him down?

Jake took her face in his hands and stared into her eyes. "Say that again."

"I don't care if everyone in the world knows I'm doing hot, naughty, naked things with you."

Something flickered in his eyes. They heated up, as usual, but there was something else. *Satisfaction*, if she had to put a word to it.

She started to get up. They could go to her place. She could have him the rest of the night. Neither of them needed sleep. The next day would just be more painting and meetings and—

"I want to stay."

"So we'll—" Then his words sank in. She turned to face him. "Stay?" She frowned. "What do you mean?"

He took her hand, tugging her back into his lap. "I want to stay. I think it's important."

She looked around, confused. "Are you on graham-cracker duty or something?"

He ran his hand up and down her back. "A, I want—Hell, I want to throw you over my shoulder, take you home, and not let you out of bed for the next week and a half."

She pulled in a long breath. "Yes, let's do that."

He pulled her closer, but it was more of a hug than a sensual embrace. "But I love being here, in public, able to touch you and just *be*. The feeling we're in this together. Knowing everyone knows we're involved."

She tried to turn in his lap, but he clamped his arm tighter around her waist.

"Don't wiggle," he said through gritted teeth.

"Jake." She wiggled again but he was stronger. She slumped against him. "Everyone knows we're together. In fact, leaving would prove we're together."

She felt his nose in her hair and heard the big breath he took. "Don't tempt me."

"I *want* to tempt you." She wiggled again and managed to turn to face him. "What's going on? What's so magical about being here in the square?"

"I want *everyone* to know how I feel about you."

She looked into his eyes. "But—"

"You. I want you to know." He puffed out a breath. "I want you to know that I want to shout it to the world."

She glanced around again. It wasn't exactly the world, but all the people who were important to her were here tonight.

"I think they know."

"You," he repeated, firmer now. "I want *you* to know."

"You don't think ripping off my clothes in *private* would help reiterate that point?"

His eyes narrowed and he shifted her on his lap. She grinned.

"Look, I've been thinking about this. Staying here every night and just holding your hand has been killing me. But I'm more than willing to do it. You need this. You need to know that I don't just want you, I love you. I'm proud of you, proud to be with you. That I want these moments, too. Not just the naked ones. Over the past year I've kissed you a lot, and then there was the riverbank and the shed—but there were never moments where we watched a movie or danced or ate s'mores."

Avery felt her chest tighten. He was so earnest about this. And what he said was true—their moments up until these past two weeks had been few and far between, and they'd been filled with a strange combination of desire and antagonism.

This past week had been sweet. Simple in a way she needed. Even when they weren't working side by side, they'd been focused on the same goal. When they were done with the work, they sat enjoying the people they both loved in the town square that meant home to both of them.

This had been good in a way she hadn't even realized.

That he had been working to give it to her made tears sting her eyes. Trust was tough for her. But with Jake, she wanted to learn.

Almost as if he read her mind, he pulled her in to rest her head on his chest, his hand on her hair. It was a posture someone might use with a child, but it made Avery feel warm and cared for.

"Your mom and grandma never made you feel wanted or good about yourself. My mom was great, but it was always in our home. You didn't go out together. You didn't have a lot of friends." He took a deep breath. "No one has ever . . . shown off how they feel. They've never . . . claimed you."

Avery felt her eyebrows shoot up. She heard him. Every word, and her heart felt full as she realized what Jake was trying to give her.

But the whole claiming thing—yeah, that was kind of hot.

She leaned back, put a hand on each of his shoulders, and looked into his face. "You want to claim me, Jake?"

She felt his hands on her hips and saw him swallow hard. "I do. In so many ways."

She felt a surge of power and heat and . . . love. "Then I think—"

The fire alarm at the station went off at the same moment her pager began beeping.

They stared at each other.

"Dammit," she breathed. For the first time in her career, her thoughts didn't immediately jump to the fire and getting ready.

It took him another few seconds, but he pulled air in through his nose, then blew it out and nodded. "Yeah."

She leaned in and kissed him hard on the mouth. "I will see you later."

He stood up, his hands still on her hips. "I'll come see if there's anything I can do."

His cell phone rang as they started toward the station at a run. Fortunately, all of the fire crew was in the square, and the station was only about two hundred yards away.

"It's Max," Jake told her. "What?" He answered the phone.

She glanced at him as they jogged together. He frowned and looked up at the sky. She followed his gaze. It was too dark to see anything, but the moon was now covered, and she noted the wind had picked up. Crap. Fire and wind didn't go well together.

"Be safe." Jake disconnected. "Max and Bree are out checking the weather. There's a storm coming in."

Of course there was. "I haven't looked at the radar since this morning."

"Max has been watching."

They arrived at the station. Everyone was already in motion. The alarms were still sounding, and the crew was pulling on their gear and getting the trucks loaded up.

"I'll see you later," Avery told him.

Jake looked from her to the activity behind her. "I . . ." He clearly didn't want to leave but didn't know what to do. He wasn't trained as a firefighter. She almost laughed. There was actually one thing in the world that Jake Mitchell couldn't do.

"Go get everyone into shelter. We have a town square full of campers."

His eyes flickered to the truck behind her and back to her face. "Right. Yeah."

Still he hesitated.

"Jake, I've got to go."

"I know, I just . . . haven't seen you going into a fire."

That was true. In the week and a half he'd been here, she'd been working as fire chief, but she hadn't been a firefighter. The two jobs could be pretty different.

"I'll see you later," she repeated.

Jake hesitated, then he grabbed her upper arms and pulled her onto her tiptoes for a kiss. A long, hard, deep, sweet, hot kiss she drank in greedily.

He set her back on her feet a moment later and turned on his heel and stalked out of the station, already pulling out his phone.

Avery pulled in a deep breath, feeling a strange sense of satisfaction wash over her. She was here with her crew. Max and Bree were out watching the storm, Jake would organize things in the square, Dillon and Kit were there for medical and emotional emergencies—everything was covered. Everything was going to be fine. The team was in place.

The skies opened up fifteen minutes later. Jake was shouting and trying to direct people while taking calls from Frank and Max.

"We're under a tornado watch, too!" Max shouted in his ear.

Well, that was no surprise. "Watch your asses," Jake told him.

"Always."

"Is everyone going to city hall?" Frank asked a minute later when Jake flipped over to his call.

That was the plan. They could get the campers into the basement level of the big building to ride out the storm. They'd be dry, and if things did kick up into something more serious, they'd be in one of the safest places in town. But the party atmosphere was hindering the efforts.

"As soon as we can convince them that inside is better than outside," Jake said.

Most of the crowd was scattering in several directions, shrieking and laughing. Some were attempting to hold protection over their heads, but the downpour had already soaked everything. Others were still in the middle of the square, finishing off the s'mores and trying to pack up camping equipment.

Lightning flashed in the clouds to the west, and Jake sighed. This was going to be a long night. Even without the knowledge that the woman he loved was somewhere fighting a fire at the same time that strong winds, hail, and another possible tornado threatened.

Jesus. Jake thrust his hand through his hair. Feeling helpless was like his own personal hell, and that was how he felt at the moment.

Lightning cracked overhead, and Jake felt like his nerve endings were jumping with the same anxious energy looking for an outlet.

His phone rang again. He jerked it out and looked at the display. Then hit "Ignore." He could not deal with that call at the moment. He'd silenced the same call four times today and was likely in deep shit with his boss, but he couldn't handle the governor of Iowa and his problems right now.

"Hey."

Jake turned to find his father striding toward him. "Get these people inside," Jake said, indicating the still-partying crowd.

"Where are you going?"

"The fire."

Wes gave him a look. "You're not a firefighter, Jake."

"No. But Avery is."

"You have to let her do her job."

"Yeah. But I can be there while she does it." He couldn't stay here. At least not without losing his mind and decking a few people who thought they could screw around with lightning overhead and sixty-mile-per-hour winds coming.

"You can't go every time she's called out." Wes put a restraining hand on Jake's shoulder. "If you come home, if you're with her, this is going to happen again and again."

Jake forced himself to breathe. It shouldn't surprise him that his father was reading the situation so accurately. Rain fell over them in sheets, but Jake had no desire to be anywhere safe and dry—not as long as Avery was out there battling everything.

He knew his dad was right. This was going to happen. Of course it was.

Avery was a firefighter. Sometimes she'd be called out at three a.m. Sometimes it would be ten below zero. She would be at risk each time.

And there wasn't a damned thing he could do about it.

It really hadn't hit Jake before this. He'd been home for almost two weeks now, and since the tornado, in which he'd been able to hold her and ensure she was as sheltered as she could be, the greatest risk to Avery had been fatigue and dehydration. He'd been plying her with water and trying to be sure she rested whenever he could—for one, by not crawling into her bedroom window at night and keeping her up until dawn with more physical activity.

He'd told himself he was trying to show her he cared. But was that truly all this was? Maybe he couldn't let her be at risk. Maybe *he* couldn't handle that.

Fuck.

"I need to go. This time," he told Wes.

Jake knew he had to stand outside that burning building, knowing Avery was inside, and see if he could do it. If he could leave her alone to do her job. See how it felt.

It didn't get any more personal than this. Not only was the woman he loved in a burning structure, but there wasn't a thing he could do to help her. Firefighting was one of the few things involved in disasters that he was not trained in. He knew he would be more of a liability than help.

This was Avery's specialty. Could he stand back, literally, and watch her do it, knowing that if something went wrong, if it turned bad, he could do nothing?

Not wanting to come back to Chance and possibly fail someone he knew and cared about had kept him away all these years. But being here for the good stuff these past days had shown him that he could take the bad with the good, because there was a lot of good. He was willing to take the risk now.

Especially because the past week had shown him something else— he'd been waiting until he could have Avery. He couldn't have imagined living in Chance, seeing her, working alongside her, and not having her in his life—at his mother's dinner table, his friends' barbecues, in his bed, and in his heart. Now he had her, now that she would be a part of his life in Chance, he was ready. He hadn't fully been aware he'd been waiting for her, but now . . . it was as clear as anything had ever been.

But in this moment, this moment of helplessness and worry, he was also very aware that he liked having control. He liked knowing he could keep her safe.

"She's good," Wes said in all seriousness. "She knows what she's doing."

For some stupid reason, that made Jake's breath hitch, too. Avery knew what she was doing, she wasn't on her own, she had her crew, but she was the leader. She was in charge there. He'd be nothing but an onlooker.

"The fire is at Fourteenth and Oak," Wes said. "House fire."

"Thanks."

"Don't do anything stupid." His dad moved his hand.

"Who, me?"

Wes frowned at his son's attempt at flippant. "I'm serious, Jake. I want to know she's safe."

Jake swallowed hard. "Do you mean at the fire? Or something else?"

"Everything."

That also caught Jake in the chest. His parents loved Avery. He had to take care of her for them, too.

Jake nodded, and Wes turned his attention to herding the remaining revelers into city hall. Jake started for his truck. He calmly inserted the key in the door, calmly got inside, calmly started the ignition, calmly eased the truck out onto the street.

All the while his heart was threatening to beat out of his chest.

Avery had been exhausted when they'd started, and now, an hour later, she was . . . she didn't know a word for "beyond exhausted."

"Second floor clear?" she asked. The fire had spread quickly, and she and a lot of the crew had been working on the first floor, trying to contain things to the east side of the structure.

It sounded crazy that they'd been battling to put out a fire in the rain, but when the fire was in the walls, it didn't matter much what was going on outside. In fact, the rain had complicated things immensely by impairing the firefighters' vision and making the surfaces they needed to cross, including the ladders, slippery.

Tom and Dean both nodded.

"We got it out. But it's a loss," Dean said.

Dammit.

This was one of the houses with only minor damage from the tornado. Now the fire had finished off what the storm had started.

"Okay." Avery sighed. She hated to give this news.

She pulled off her gloves and tossed her helmet to the side as the crew began packing up their equipment. She welcomed the cool rain against her hot skin as she headed for the family that was huddled on the porch across the street.

The little girl, Sami, came running toward her, ignoring the rain. "Did you get my pillow?"

Avery squatted in front of her. "I'm sorry, Sami. We couldn't get anything out of your bedroom."

The little girl's eyes filled with tears. "My gramma gave me that pillow."

Avery put her hand on the girl's head. "I know. I'm sorry, sweetie. But you did the right thing leaving it behind. We can get you a new pillow, but we can't get another Sami."

Sami's bottom lip was still protruding.

"I mean it, Sami." Avery said it firmly, holding the girl's gaze. "That was the right thing to do. Every time. I know you'll miss your pillow, but if this ever happens again, you have to do the same thing."

It turned Avery's stomach to think that having lost her prized possession, Sami might put herself at risk next time there was a threat to one of her belongings.

"Sami, promise me."

Finally, the girl nodded. "Okay."

"Thank you."

Avery looked up to see Sami's mom, Rachel, running toward her. "Sami, you're soaked!"

Now her mother was, too.

Thunder boomed overhead and Avery glanced up. "Do you have somewhere to stay tonight?"

Rachel looked at their house, her expression heartbreaking. She nodded.

"Let me know if you need anything," Avery said. "We've got resources. Don't be shy."

Lightning ripped through the sky, and Avery felt the angry rumble of the thunder vibrate through her.

"Now inside, ladies," Avery ordered.

Lightning flashed overhead again, and then a sharp streak arched toward the ground.

Avery heard the crack a split second before she reacted. She lunged forward, hit Rachel in the back with her palms, and sent her to the grass just as the tree branch hit the ground where she'd been standing. The branch clipped Avery's shoulder as it went down, knocking her to her knees. Avery caught herself with her outstretched arm.

Pain knifed into her shoulder, and she rolled to her side, her arm failing to hold her up.

She grabbed her shoulder and tried to catch her breath.

"Avery!" she heard Rachel shout, but she'd closed her eyes against the pain and the pouring rain.

"Get inside!" The harsh order came from a very familiar deep voice.

Avery gasped and rolled to her noninjured side, looking for Jake.

"Jesus, A, lie still." Then he was over her, glowering down at her.

"My shoulder."

"I know." He crouched and scooped her up in his arms. "Dammit, girl."

"Are they—" She craned her neck, trying to locate Rachel and Sami.

"They're inside. Dean's got them."

She sagged in his arms, resting her head against his chest. The pain in her shoulder was radiating out like claws sinking into her skin and pulling more and more of her flesh toward the wound. She felt a little sick and was suddenly really, really tired. Shock, she knew, but knowing what it was didn't keep it from threatening to take her over.

"Why are you here?" she mumbled, feeling lightheaded.

"I've been here the entire time."

She tried to blink her eyes open to look up at him. She didn't know if it was the injury or what, but that didn't make any sense. She'd told him not to come.

Jake took a deep, shuddering breath she could feel through her whole body. "I've got her," he said, and it took a second for her to realize he was talking to someone else. "I'm taking her up to city hall. Dillon's there."

Then they were at his truck. "I've got to put you down for a sec," he said gently, swinging her legs to the ground.

Her own arm bumped her injured one, and she sucked in a breath as pain seemed to stab from her shoulder through her heart.

"Dammit," he muttered, fumbling with the slick door. Finally, he got it open and helped her up onto the seat.

"I've still got my gear on."

"I'm not going to be yanking that coat off you until we're somewhere Dillon can look at you." Jake slammed the door and headed to the driver's side.

He sounded pissed, and she frowned as he climbed up behind the wheel.

"What's your problem?" It was *her* damned arm that felt like it was on fire.

"Nothing." He threw the truck into drive, and the tires squealed as they tried to grip the wet pavement.

Avery supported her injured arm with her other hand under the elbow and worked to keep her eyes open. They were definitely open for the stop sign Jake tore through.

"Hey! What the hell, Jake?" She wasn't out of it enough to not notice him breaking every traffic law in the book.

"What the hell?" he asked. "What the hell? I'll tell you what the hell! For more than an hour I stood there behaving, staying out of the way, almost going out of my mind but letting you do your job, just watching. I did good. I didn't ask anyone how things were or where you were. I didn't go stomping into the building. I did *nothing*. Do you know how fucking hard that is for me?"

He gave her a scowl, and Avery tried to make her mouth work. But honestly, it was impossible. She did, actually, know how hard it was for Jake to do nothing. She was trying to wrap her mind around the fact that Jake had been only a bystander when there was a crisis going on.

"You just stood by?"

"Yes. Then you came walking out, and you took off your helmet, and I knew you were fine. I *handled it*. I was there and didn't do a damned thing. I was *proud* of myself."

She had to admit she was proud of him, too. Not doing a damned thing for Jake was like . . . Well, she was blanking on a perfect example, but it was amazing. Jake couldn't even do nothing when there were Boy Scouts camping in the town square. Even then he had to jump in and get involved. He couldn't just be sure they had sandwiches and water. No, he turned the whole thing into a party with music, dancing, and s'mores.

"Wow, Jake, that's—"

"Then you get hit by a tree branch. A fucking tree branch. You made it out of a tornado and a fire, but then a tree branch comes down and you just have to be the one standing under it, don't you?"

She started to respond but he wasn't done.

"Do you know the statistical probability of you being underneath a tree when it gets struck by lightning?"

She shook her head, her eyes wide. "No. Do you?" Was there a statistic for that in one of his manuals?

"A gazillion to one!" he roared.

One look at his face told her that pointing out that those numbers were not an exact statistic would be a very, very bad idea.

They pulled up in front of city hall, and Jake slammed the truck into park. Avery gasped against the pain the jerking of the truck caused.

Jake must have heard the gasp, because he looked over at her and his scowl intensified. He shoved a hand through his hair. "Jesus, Avery, my heart almost stopped when I saw that branch fall on you."

"I'm fine," she insisted. Her shoulder hurt like a mother, and she was probably on light duty now for a while, but she was alive and, more important, Sami, Rachel, and the rest of their family were, too.

"You're hurt."

"I'll live." She managed a smile.

"I might not," he muttered.

Wes was at her door a minute later, swinging it open and pulling her from the seat, as if he'd been waiting for them. "You okay?"

Avery rubbed her arm. "Nothing a bag of ice and some ibuprofen won't fix."

His gaze followed her hand. "You're hurt."

"I'll be okay."

Wes's big arm went around her. "I've got you. Lean on me," he said in the deep, firm, but gentle voice she'd always associated with him. It wasn't unlike Jake's commanding voice. Though Jake tended to get louder.

Avery did as she was told. And it felt wonderful. Wes was solid and strong, and she knew he'd take care of her. She felt her throat tighten and concentrated on walking toward city hall and not blubbering all over him.

It was her shoulder. She didn't need help to walk. But she'd take it.

Somehow she sensed that meant a lot to both of the men with her.

◆ ◆ ◆

They made it only as far as inside the front doors.

"I've got this, Dad." Jake bent and swung Avery up into his arms again, careful not to bump her shoulder.

There was no way he was *not* going to touch her at this point. As he'd told her, he'd behaved, he'd watched for an *hour* as she and the crew battled the fire. He'd controlled himself while she'd taken care of the scene with calm and poise. He'd been *able* to watch her take that risk and not charge in there to protect her. He'd convinced himself that it was all okay, that it was proof that he didn't always have to be taking care of her. That she could be all right even if she was in the middle of it all and he was on the sidelines.

Then a fucking tree branch had knocked her down.

"You're overreacting," she said, but it was a weak protest.

Of course he was. She was hurt.

It wasn't anything life threatening, but he felt like his blood pressure would never be normal again.

"Let me," he told her gruffly.

She snuggled in. "Okay."

And he thought his heart might burst.

She was letting him take care of her. Finally.

Avery Sparks, the tough, independent, wounded woman who didn't let people take care of her anymore was letting him carry her. Literally.

She had come around. She'd let him close.

And now he was realizing that having her trust meant even more pressure to not let her down, and loving her meant even more risk to *his* heart.

He carried her into the mayor's office, where Frank, Shelby, Dillon, and others had gathered to review what was going on.

Not because he wanted to be in there. He wanted to take her straight into an empty room—with a lock—and check her over from head to toe.

But Dillon was in Frank's office, and she needed Dillon's attention more than Jake's right now.

One more time when he was going to have to be nothing more than a spectator.

He was not good at being a bystander. Especially when he was in love. Apparently.

Having never been in love before, this was all new to him. But he probably wasn't going to handle this well.

The minute he stepped through the doorway with her in his arms, everyone got to their feet. Dillon was the first across the room. "What happened?"

"Tree branch knocked her over. It's her shoulder."

Jake knew he should put her down on the couch, but instead he sank onto the cushions with her still in his arms.

Dillon gave him a look, but when Jake scowled at him, Dillon didn't say a word and crouched in front of both of them.

"You got hit by a tree branch?" Dillon said as he checked her pupils.

Jake worked on relaxing his hold so he didn't crack one of her ribs.

"It was hit by lightning," she told him.

Dillon looked from her shoulder to her face. "Seriously?"

Avery nodded. "I saw the flash and heard the crack."

"Do you know what the odds are of you being under a tree when it's hit by lightning?"

"A gazillion to one, I've been told," Avery said drily.

She's able to be sassy, Jake thought with an eye roll. That had to be a good sign.

"I can't lift my arm. It feels like it's on fire."

Dillon nodded. He and Jake helped her out of her big, heavy fire coat first. Jake had to grit his teeth through the entire process as Avery tried to cover her soft gasps and grimaces of pain. They got her boots and pants off, then settled her back on Jake's lap. Jake knew Dillon was going to give him a hard time about that later, but he didn't care. He wasn't letting her out of his sight for the foreseeable future.

Dillon poked and prodded the shoulder joint, her shoulder blade, collarbone, neck, and upper arm. Then he tried to lift it for her.

She sucked in a hard breath. So did Jake.

"Ow."

"I know," Dillon said. "Sorry."

"No, Jake's squeezing me."

Everyone chuckled, and Jake tried to relax his hold.

"You've dislocated it," Dillon said grimly. "There's also likely a soft tissue strain at best, a tear at worst. Without an X-ray and MRI, I'm going to say nothing's broken. I need to reduce the dislocation. Without pain meds it's going to hurt like a mother."

Avery nodded, but Jake jumped in. "Can it wait until you have the meds?"

Dillon shook his head. "The dislocation could be impinging nerves or blood vessels. We need it back in alignment." He frowned at Jake. "Maybe you should step out for this."

"Step out?"

"Leave."

"You think I'm going to *leave*?" Jake asked him.

"You're not handling this very well," Dillon said with an eyebrow up.

Yeah, well, he'd called that.

"Just fucking do it if you're going to do it."

Dillon sighed and focused on Avery. "You're small enough that I can probably do this pretty easily."

"Probably?" Jake asked.

Dillon gave him a frown. "Reductions can be tough."

"So you could hurt her and it might still not work?"

A muscle in Dillon's jaw ticked, but he nodded.

"Then we're not doing it."

"Jake," Dillon said tightly, "you need to go in the other room."

"Unless you can *guarantee* that she's going to be all right, you're not doing anything," Jake said, his head and chest aching.

"There are no guarantees that she'll always be perfectly fine," Dillon said, giving Jake a look that said he knew things were more complicated for Jake than Avery's shoulder injury. And that Jake needed to chill out.

But Dillon's words hit harder than anything else.

There were no guarantees that Avery would always be fine.

Jake wasn't sure he could deal with that.

He knew he was being unreasonable. He knew he was overreacting. He hated it. But he couldn't stop. And he, Avery, Dillon, and everyone else were going to have to get used to it because he didn't see it changing anytime soon.

Dammit.

He hated being out of control—of a situation, of an outcome, of his own emotions.

But he was tonight. For sure.

Just when he'd fixed things for Avery, just when the town was getting back on its feet and she was back together with Heidi and she'd been happy again, safe and secure, confident and strong, a freaking bolt of lightning had shot from the sky and reminded him that he couldn't control everything, and he couldn't protect her every minute.

Of course, cognitively, he knew that. But when he wasn't here, when he was in Kansas City or Washington, DC, he didn't have to face it.

Now he *was* here. Right in the middle of it all. And he was going to have to decide if he could stay front-row center and watch Avery sometimes struggle and hurt. He was also going to have to decide if he could stand by while others took care of her. Tonight, she'd put her life in the hands of her crew. Right now, Dillon was the only one who could take care of her arm.

There would be many more nights like this.

Jake pulled in a breath. Fuck. He wasn't a firefighter, he wasn't a doctor, he wasn't even that good at fixing cars. There were lots of things that Avery would need that he couldn't do. There were things she was going to have to do for herself. And there were things no one could fix. That was life.

And if he wanted to be a part of hers, he needed to deal with all those things.

He felt Avery's good hand tighten on his arm. "Jake, you have to let Dillon try to fix this."

"Fine, do it," he told Dillon. "But I'm not letting go."

"Good. I need you to hold on to her anyway." Dillon focused on Avery. "I'm going to hold your arm here and here." He put his hands on her. "Then I'm going to—"

"No!" Jake interrupted. "I changed my mind. Are you sure we can't wait?"

"No," Dillon said firmly. "We can't wait."

Avery shifted on Jake's lap so she could look at him. "Stop. It's fine. This is Dillon. You trust him with your life."

"Yes. *My* life," Jake said, looking into those big green eyes that had been his downfall for so long. "Not yours."

"This isn't my *life*, Jake. It's my shoulder. I'm not going to die from this."

"Doesn't matter. It's going to hurt. And the pain might be for nothing."

"You're being melodramatic," Avery said.

"I'm being *concerned* and *protective*," he insisted. "I realize you don't have a lot of experience with it, but this is how someone acts when he loves you and you're in pain."

"Crazy?" she asked, but her expression was gentle.

"Yes, crazy. It was crazy for me to make love to you while a tornado was coming, and it was crazy for me to stand outside while you went into a burning building. You make me crazy. But I want—"

"Ahhh!"

Avery yelled out as Dillon popped her shoulder back into place.

She grabbed her arm with her other hand. "Fuck, Dillon," she said, tears in her eyes.

"Sorry. But it was best to do it while you were distracted. Made it a lot easier. On both of us." Dillon looked up at Jake. "You can breathe now. She's fine."

Jake blew out the breath he'd sucked in when Avery screamed.

"I guess our ability to forget anyone else was around helped that time," Avery said with a tiny smile.

Jake stared at her.

She was fine.

His heart, on the other hand, felt like it was about to explode.

He honestly wasn't sure if he was going to survive loving her.

"You're going to need some ice and some painkillers. I want an MRI as soon as possible," Dillon said.

"Yes to everything but the painkillers," Avery told him.

Dillon stretched to his feet. "No?"

"Ibuprofen or something, but I can't be foggy."

Dillon nodded. "If you change your mind, let me know."

The room was still full of people, but they all moved away from the couch—as away as they could get and still be in the same office—but Jake didn't let go of Avery. He couldn't.

"You okay?" she asked, tipping her head to look up at him.

He chuckled in spite of the fact that every inch of him was tight and tense—and not in the usual way it was tight and tense when Avery was this close to him. "I'm fine."

"You don't seem fine."

No, he didn't. "Just give me a minute."

She did. She relaxed against him and didn't say a word.

Which was nice. And strange.

They sat like that for several minutes. Holding her felt good. Knowing that she was letting him do what he could, little as it might be, felt even better.

They were both still soaking wet—Avery less so having been protected by her gear—but he had no desire to move, and she didn't seem inclined to change their positions, either.

If only they could stay like this, right here, forever. Here she was safe, and here he could *do* something for her. Kind of. He could hold her, he could comfort her, he could get her ice . . .

Who was he kidding?

He wasn't doing anything to make her feel better right now. It was all to make *him* feel better. And it wasn't really working anyway.

He had to fix things. That's who he was. He *especially* had to fix things for the woman he loved. Could he really handle being a bystander to parts of Avery's life? He couldn't even handle being a bystander at a disaster site in a faraway town full of strangers.

Frank was checking various sites on the computer, Shelby and a couple of women were talking about what to do about feeding everyone who was now sleeping inside, and Dillon and two other men were watching the television and flipping to various news channels.

From where he was sitting, Jake could see all the information, and it looked like the storm cell was moving off to the east and there was nothing on the radar behind this storm. They'd be in the clear in another thirty minutes or so.

Avery sat up straight all of a sudden.

"What—"

"Shh!"

Her gaze was on the television in front of Dillon.

Jake focused on what the news was showing. He realized what it was the second before Avery turned on his lap.

"Are you supposed to be there?"

A small town in Iowa had been ravaged by a tornado earlier that afternoon.

"No," he finally said. "Not this time."

She pushed herself up off his lap, and he sighed. He hadn't told her about the job in DC. And right now, a part of him wanted to *run* to DC. Far from where Avery would be facing more possible storms—emotional and actual—more burning buildings, more possible injuries.

He could go to DC and know this time, for sure, that Heidi and Wes were in her life. No more assumptions. He would *know* that she was happy and successful and confident and surrounded by people who loved her. She had Kit and Bree. Once Max and Dillon moved back, she could lean on them as well. Jake didn't have to be the one here taking care of her. Tonight had shown him that. He could hide out across the country and not think about all the things he couldn't prevent or fix for her. And he wouldn't have to feel like he was having a heart attack every single time she got so much as a damned hangnail.

Yep, DC was tempting.

"You have to go. They need you," Avery said.

The town that had been hit was a small, rural farming town much like Chance. It sat in the northwest corner of Iowa near the South Dakota border. Of the three hundred homes there, two hundred had been damaged, and 130 were completely gone. Their main street had been destroyed. Half of all their businesses had been wiped out.

It was devastating. It was a major disaster.

Those scenes usually fueled him. As he'd listen to reports, the ideas would begin to form—the plans, supplies, and personnel would come together in his mind like the pieces of a puzzle—and he'd be hopping to get on scene and get things going.

Not this time.

Not because he had anything against people in northwest Iowa. Not because he didn't feel terrible for what had happened. Not because he couldn't help them.

But it was someone else's responsibility now, and, strangely, he was fine with that.

Unlike having someone else fix Avery.

"My replacement is probably already en route. David will do a great job."

"Who's David?"

"The guy taking my position in Kansas City."

She stared at him for a moment. "You *quit*?"

"No. I took a promotion. In Washington, DC. With FEMA," he told her.

Her eyes widened. "You're going to work for FEMA?"

Jake tried to read her expression. Was she happy? Upset? "I *was* going to work for FEMA."

"What's the job?"

"A deputy administrator's position," he told her, watching her carefully.

She swallowed and nodded. "That's . . . great. Wow. That's a dream job for you." She turned toward the TV. "And you might end up in Iowa anyway. That's a bad one."

It was. And she was right—FEMA would very likely be on-site as well.

He'd be great there. He'd do a hell of a job. He was perfect for it.

"FEMA will have to send someone else, too," he told her.

"Someone else?" Avery looked confused. "But *you're* the one who goes."

He nodded. "Usually. But you're hurt and—"

"It's my *shoulder*, Jake. It's not . . . important. Not as important as Iowa."

"Avery—"

"Jake, I need some people to head out with me and check things over," Frank interrupted, striding toward them.

"This isn't a great time, Frank," Jake said, gritting his teeth, his eyes on Avery.

"Yeah, well, I'm sorry I didn't plan this storm around your schedule," Frank snapped. "But we need to see where we're at. The Bronsons will be here *tomorrow*. These fucking storms!" he exclaimed. "If the cleanup is set back now, I swear to God, I'm going to start looking into the ancient burial-ground nonsense."

In spite of everything, Jake and Avery shared a smile at that. It was apparently Frank's new mantra.

"I'll take Avery with me to the hospital," Dillon said, joining them. "We can get that MRI done."

"I'd really rather . . ." Jack started, then trailed off.

Fuck, he'd really rather concentrate fully on Avery. But he wasn't what she needed right now. Chance did need him, though. The Bronsons would be there the next day. If this storm had caused any new damage or ruined anything they'd done, it would be an all-night, all-hands-on-deck project to get it cleaned up and repaired.

He gave Avery a long look. "We're not done talking about DC."

She gave a little laugh that definitely sounded forced. "Sure. I'm so happy for you, Jake."

"No, you don't—"

"Oh my God, Avery!" Heidi rushed into the room just then. "I heard you were hurt at the fire."

Avery was holding her sore arm with her good one as she turned to Heidi. Jake stepped protectively between them to keep Heidi from grabbing her.

"She dislocated her shoulder," Jake said.

Heidi's eyes flew to Avery. "Are you all right?"

Avery stepped around Jake and shot him an annoyed look. "I'll be fine. Dillon is taking me up for an MRI."

"No, we'll take you," Heidi said as Wes came in behind her. "I thought my heart was going to stop when I heard you were hurt."

"It wasn't the fire," Avery said as Wes and Heidi flanked her and both put a hand on her upper back, ushering her through the door.

No one even spared Jake another look.

"She's in good hands," Dillon said, slapping him on the shoulder. "I'll head up and finish the exam. You go keep Frank from having a stroke."

Jake felt his whole body tense as the situation spun completely out of his control.

But Dillon was right. Avery was being taken care of.

He glanced at the TV and the coverage of the Iowa tornado.

He could get in his truck and start driving west. He'd be there in about five hours. He'd be smack in the middle of a situation where he could take charge and make real progress, impact hundreds of lives, and then walk away when the job was over, knowing he'd done some good and not worrying about what was next for them. What was next wasn't his responsibility. He only needed to fix the big, obvious, immediate things. What came next was on someone else.

Avery would be okay. She was with Heidi and Wes and Dillon. She was happy and loved. He'd fixed the big things. He wouldn't have to worry about what was next for her, either.

He pulled out his phone and dialed one of the many Washington, DC, numbers that had been calling him over the past two weeks.

His new boss answered on the second ring.

"Hey, Ryan, it's Jake Mitchell."

The MRI showed no major soft-tissue damage. Dillon told her she'd be sore for a few days, he wanted her in the arm sling for a while, and he wanted her to talk to a physical therapist about some stability exercises, but she was going to make a full recovery.

Avery wondered if he had any suggestions for her broken heart.

She was so conflicted. She was happy for Jake. And of course he'd gotten the job with FEMA. He'd be perfect for that job. Thousands of people were going to be better off because Jake Mitchell was moving to Washington, DC.

But the selfish part of her heart hurt.

She wanted him here, with her. Forever.

Avery let Heidi and Wes fuss over her and tuck her into the backseat of their car and even buy her ice cream.

She knew it made them feel better to be doing those things for her—their son came by his need to serve others naturally. And she didn't have the energy for doing anything for herself that she didn't have to do. She had to admit it felt good to be fussed over. She couldn't remember the last time someone had wanted to take care of her.

Other than Jake.

But if it couldn't be him, maybe his mom and dad were a good substitute.

Even as she thought it, though, she almost laughed. Ten years ago she'd thought she'd made up her feelings for Jake because in actuality she'd wanted his family. This time she was under no such delusions. Her feelings for Jake were all about Jake. Even some of her feelings for Heidi and Wes were about Jake.

Sleepy from the pain meds Dillon had insisted she needed for at least one night, and from the sheer emotion and adrenaline of the evening, Avery simply sat back in the seat and let her mind wander.

"Are there any direct flights from Omaha to Washington, DC?" Avery asked after a few minutes.

"Washington, DC?" Wes asked. "Why do you ask?"

"I might go visit Jake," she said. "Or I could move there."

Heidi turned in her seat. "Move there?"

Oh, had she said that part out loud? But she nodded. She felt like her thoughts were coming a little slow, thanks to the meds, but they were clear. She wanted to be where Jake was. "I can be a firefighter anywhere. Jake can only be . . . Jake . . . in DC."

"And you want to be with Jake?" Heidi asked with a smile.

"Yes. For sure. If he wants me to be with him," she added with a frown. Jake hadn't asked her to go with him. But that didn't matter, did it?

"He wants you to be with him, sweetie," Heidi told her.

"I don't know," Avery said, shaking her head and feeling a little dizzy from the motion. "He didn't say that."

"Well," Heidi said, glancing at her husband, "Jake is more of a doer in a lot of ways."

Avery wasn't sure what Heidi meant by that. Then she got distracted as she realized that Wes wasn't driving toward her house. He was headed out of town.

"Where are we going?"

"We have to show you something." Heidi looked back at her. "Two somethings, actually."

Oh, no. "Is the farm a mess again?" They were headed that way, and Avery prayed everything was still intact and ready for the Bronsons' visit.

"The farm is fine, actually," Wes reported. "Some leaves and branches down. Already cleaned up."

Thank God. "Then what?"

Her phone buzzed in her pocket before they could answer.

Maybe it was Jake. She pulled it out quickly.

The text wasn't from Jake.

It was from Bree.

Is Jake leaving?

Avery felt her heart squeeze. Oh, she was so not ready for this. **Why do you ask?** she texted back.

But the next message was from Kit. **Did I see Jake head out of town with his truck packed up?**

Avery felt a little dizzy again, and this time she hadn't moved her head. No. No, Jake couldn't be leaving. Not *tonight*. Not like this. Not without saying good-bye.

She felt tears stinging the backs of her eyes.

She blinked and looked up to see that they were, indeed, driving to Montgomery Farms. The farm looked better than it ever had. In preparation for the welcome party for the Bronsons, the trees around the main drive were wrapped in twinkle lights. There was a huge plastic banner across the main barn that read WELCOME HOME, and that was, amazingly, still intact in spite of the wind and rain. There were a dozen long tables on the lawn under the trees by the main house. Tomorrow night they would be draped in red-and-white gingham tablecloths and laden with plates and bowls and Crock-Pots of food.

But Wes kept going past the driveway.

"What's going on?" she asked.

"You'll see," Heidi told her.

Two miles later, Wes turned the car off the paved road onto a gravel road, but Avery barely noticed. She was texting Jake. And not getting answers.

Avery worked on not panicking. "Have you seen Jake?"

Heidi looked back. "Not since Frank's office."

"So you don't know where he is right now?" Avery asked.

"Well, actually . . ." Heidi pointed out the windshield.

They pulled up in front of a huge two-story house with a single light burning in one of the windows and a truck sitting in the drive.

Jake's truck.

Heidi turned in her seat to look back at Avery. "He was going to wait to bring you here until this weekend when he had it all inspected and cleaned up. But I think you need to see this tonight."

"Jake wanted to bring me *here*?"

What was going on?

The front door opened, and Avery's attention was pulled from Heidi to Jake as he stepped out onto the porch. He braced both hands on the railing that ran the length of the huge front porch and just watched them.

"Come on," Wes said.

He and Heidi got out of the car, and Avery had no choice but to follow.

"Mom, Dad," Jake greeted, "thought we had a plan."

"We did. But then Avery started talking about plane tickets to DC," Heidi said.

Jake's gaze swung to Avery, and she felt the force of it even across the twenty feet separating them.

"Is that right?"

Avery nodded.

He'd changed since she'd last seen him. He was dressed in faded blue jeans, an even more faded T-shirt, and work boots.

Okay, so obviously he'd packed up his truck with tools and supplies—not to head to Iowa or to Kansas City or DC or wherever his next stop was—but to come out here. Why?

"What did you think you were going to do in DC, Avery?" he finally asked, straightening away from the railing.

"I was going to see you."

"You looking for a personal tour guide for the national monuments or something?"

She took a deep breath. "Just you," she said simply. "I'd just be there for you."

She watched him swallow before he asked, "And how long were you thinking about staying?"

Avery felt her heart pounding so hard she could swear her body shook with each beat. "For as long as you'd let me."

Jake slid his hands into his front pockets. "Well, now, that would have been forever."

His words washed over her. She felt tears sting her eyes. "That sounds like the perfect amount of time."

He was quiet for a moment. Then he asked, "You would really say good-bye to my mom and dad, just when you're getting close again?"

They were pretty far apart to detect a note of gruffness in his voice, but she was sure she heard it.

Jake knew what Heidi and Wes meant to her, what family meant to her.

She nodded. "And Kit and Bree. And I'd give up my job as chief, and I'd sell the house that I've put so much time and money into."

"Your family, your house, your job . . . that's everything."

God, she really did love that he referred to them as her family. "But it's not." She took a step forward. "Those things are *part* of my happiness, yes. But my family will always be here, and there are other houses and jobs. *You* are the only you. And you, Jake Mitchell, in spite of it all, make me happy." She took another step forward.

He moved to the end of the railing but didn't say anything, just stared at her from the top of the steps.

"Believe me, you being the source of my greatest happiness is a bit of a shock to me, too," she said.

Finally, he pulled in a long breath and shook his head. "It's not a shock to me at all. Of course I'm the source of your greatest happiness."

There was the Jake she knew . . . and loved.

She was at the bottom of the steps now. She was taking a risk here—the realization flashed through her mind. He could shoot her down. He could say he was leaving and didn't want her to come. He could break her heart.

But right on the heels of that thought came another—a stronger one. It was time she trusted what Jake had been saying to her and *showing* her. It was time she trusted that she was important to him.

She took a breath and let it out slowly. Then she met his gaze. "This past week you've shown me that you're really good at loving me. And I'm ready for you to do that full-time, forever. So after you finish this house project, I'm ready to go. With you. Wherever you go."

She saw gratification and heat flash through his eyes. She knew he understood that she'd just given him the thing she'd held close, safe and protected from everyone, for years now—her heart.

But instead of making a big declaration of love or sweeping her up into his arms, he ran a hand nonchalantly through his hair and looked over his shoulder at the house. "Well, that's going to be a while. I want to finish the basement and add on a deck, for sure. And I'll need you to weigh in on how many bedrooms we want upstairs. Max doesn't think a hot tub will fit in the bathroom upstairs, but if we take out part of the closet, we can do it. I guess I need to know how many pairs of shoes you have."

She frowned. "*What?* Shoes?"

"And before you even ask, yes, I do plan to build us a shed out back," he said, coming down the steps. He stopped on the first step, just above her. "With a big, sturdy workbench."

Her mind was spinning, her heart was nearly bursting, and parts of her were apparently programmed to begin tingling at the word *workbench.*

"But what about DC and FEMA and all the disasters and everything?" she finally managed to ask.

"I called them just before leaving Frank's office and turned down the job."

Her whole body shook with that news. Still, she couldn't help but ask, "Jake, are you *sure?*"

"I would be *really* good at the job they want me to take. But other people can do that job just as well. I need to stay here because, while other people love you and can take care of you, *no one* can do *that* job as well as I can."

"Jake . . ." But she just shook her head. She had no idea how to express everything she was thinking and feeling.

"Loving you won't be easy," he said. "Not being able to fix every little thing every time will chip away at my heart, just like it did tonight." He came down the final step, practically on top of her. "But the good times, the happy times, the times I *can* be your hero, will put it back together. Just like being with you, even only every few months, has healed me of all the devastation and loss I've seen for the past ten years. So, I figure you're stuck with me for a while."

Avery couldn't breathe; she couldn't speak.

Which was evidently fine, because Jake wasn't done. "I will be behind you no matter what you do, and I will support you and pray for you and be there when you get home all of the times when that's all I can do. But Avery, if and when I am capable of helping you or making things better for you or flat-out saving you—I *am* going to do it."

No one had ever been so adamant about her happiness or about being a part of that happiness. She pressed her lips together and nodded. "Okay." She sniffed. "That's definitely okay."

He started to reply, but she went on quickly before he could.

"I love you."

That stopped him. The look in his eyes was so hungry, so hot, so possessive, she had to struggle to take a deep breath.

"You're trying to distract me," he said accusingly.

"I can't not say it any longer."

His expression grew more intense. "Say it again."

"I love you. So much. More than I ever knew anyone could love someone."

His voice was hoarse, almost pained, when he said, "I've wanted to hear that so badly, and it's even better than I imagined."

Happiness, warm and bright and all-consuming, swept through her.

He reached for her, but there was something more she needed to know. She held up her hand. Because once he touched her, it was all over. "But, be honest. You're not giving everything up, are you? You're fantastic at your job, and people need you."

"Well . . ."

She knew it, and she was relieved. Jake couldn't give up everything he loved professionally. That wouldn't be right. "Spill it. What's really going to happen?"

"I'm going to be active in the Guard again, so I'll be out at disasters when they get to that level, and I'm going to be doing some consulting on emergency-management and disaster planning. I'm going to run the training center here. And . . ."

"Oh boy, I know that look," Avery said.

The I'm-up-to-something gleam was in his eyes.

"That was the other thing I was going to show you."

Heidi came forward and handed Avery a piece of paper.

Correction—a flier. A campaign flier.

"You're running for city council?" She looked up at Jake.

He nodded. "I can't give up the stage entirely."

She wasn't even a little bit surprised. Jake would be an amazing city councilman.

"That's perfect."

"But," he went on, with a very satisfied look in his eyes, "during the long, boring weeks when nothing happens—which I'm *really* looking forward to, by the way—I'll be working with Max. And renovating our house."

Their house. In their town. With their family and friends.

Avery couldn't resist any longer. She put her good arm around his neck and pressed as close as she could with her injured arm between them. "You are absolutely my hero, Jake."

"So say yes."

She pulled back, her heart thumping. "Yes?"

He grinned down at her. "Lose the question mark. Avery Jane Sparks, will you marry me?"

She was surprised for only a second before the sense of absolute rightness swept through her. She nodded and sniffed. "Yes."

His answering grin was full of satisfaction and wicked intent. He grabbed her butt and lifted her up against him.

She wrapped her legs around him and hugged his neck.

"Welcome home," he said, his voice full of emotion.

The same emotions filled Avery's heart.

As he climbed the porch steps, he brought her mouth to his, kissing her deep and sweet. With promise.

But Heidi and Wes were . . .

She heard the car doors slam and the engine start.

She glanced over her shoulder from his—their—new front porch. "They're leaving?"

"They're very intelligent people." He kicked open the front door and carried her across the threshold of the house.

Their home. In Chance.

Oh, yeah, Jake Mitchell was most definitely back in town. And this time she knew it was to stay.

ACKNOWLEDGMENTS

Thank you to Rebecca Gegenheimer, Kristy Michels, Becky Kroft, and Shannon Bereza, who shared knowledge and experiences that helped me get the book right. You girls are the best! And Kim Brooks, Crystal Singer, and Rebecca Gegenheimer for reading, reassuring, and leading the cheerleading squad.

BONUS MATERIALS

DRINK RECIPES

Twisted Sister
In a blender, mix:

- Ice
- 1½ oz. lemon vodka
- 1 oz. orange curaçao liqueur
- 2 tbsp. frozen raspberries
- 6 oz. lemonade

Blend and serve.

Liquid Lightning
In a shaker, mix:

- 2 oz. Blue Kinky liqueur
- 1 oz. coconut rum
- ½ oz. tequila
- 4 oz. lemon-lime soda

Mix, and serve over ice.

ABOUT THE AUTHOR

 Erin Nicholas was fourteen when she first fell in love with love stories. Not long after that she started writing romances of her own, often spending family vacations in the backseat filling notebooks with stories. Now the *New York Times* and *USA Today* bestselling author of the Sapphire Falls series writes about women getting their happily ever after with humor, heart, and hope. From the fireworks of that first kiss to the thrill of passion, Nicholas strives to create novels that celebrate the magic of true love.